PRAISE FOR LAUREN BARATZ-LOGSTED

Crossing the Line

"A terrific read—a story that is dryly funny, brightly written and emotionally satisfying."
  —Peter Lefcourt, author of *Eleven Karens*

"A delight! Buckle up and hang on for a joyride with Jane, an admirably eccentric heroine. This fast-paced, fun-filled novel about babies and breaking the rules brims with laughter, love and a unique and buoyant wisdom."
  —Nancy Thayer, author of *The Hot Flash Club*

"Chick lit with a twist!"
  —Meg Cabot, author of *The Princess Diaries*

The Thin Pink Line

"Faking it—hilariously... Wonderfully funny debut with a fine sense of the absurd and a flair for comic characterization."
  —*Kirkus Reviews* (starred review)

"Baratz-Logsted's premise is hilarious and original."
  —*Publishers Weekly*

"Here written with humor and scathing honesty, is the diary of a (mad) pregnant woman chronicled with acid glee by Lauren Baratz-Logsted in a debut novel to share with every girlfriend you know before, during or after the baby comes. It's a winner!"
  —Adriana Trigiani, author of *Big Stone Gap*

"A sassy and beguiling comedy of reproduction that proves once and for all that a woman can indeed be half-pregnant. Bridget Jones is snorting with laughter and wondering why she didn't think of it."
  —Karen Karbo, author of *Motherhood Made a Man Out of Me*

A Little Change of Face

LAUREN BARATZ-LOGSTED

**RED
DRESS
INK**

™

First edition July 2005

A LITTLE CHANGE OF FACE

A Red Dress Ink novel

ISBN 0-373-89525-9

www.RedDressInk.com

Printed in U.S.A.

To my husband, Greg Logsted, for half a lifetime's worth
of love and patience above and beyond

Acknowledgments

Thanks, as always, to Margaret O'Neill Marbury, for being a joy of an editor to work with, and to the rest of the RDI team. Special thanks this time to Annelise Robey for being the kind of agent a girl can really love.

I'd also like to thank Sue Estabrook and Lynn Kanter for being great first readers and great friends. I don't know what I ever did to deserve such support and encouragement, but I'll take it.

Another special thank-you goes to librarians everywhere, since librarians form the inspiration for this book. In particular, I'd like to thank Danbury Public Library, my current hometown library, and Bethel Public Library, which figures prominently here: I hope you're all in your lovely new quarters by the time you read this.

Thank you to my family and friends for loving me and for not leaving me over my being the self-involved person I am.

Finally, thank you to Greg and Jackie for everything.

prologue

"Come here often?"

"God, what a line," seethed Pam, who happened to be my best friend as well as being a world-class seether. "Yes, she does," she added, summarily turning away Bachelor #1 from our table, "but not to meet people like you."

"Buy you a drink?" Bachelor #2 asked me, somewhat timidly I thought, but maybe he'd already seen #1 get shot down by Pam. Despite his timidity, he was steely in his determination not to make eye contact with her, keeping his gaze firmly fixed on me.

Pam tapped his elbow. "Can't you see she already has one?" Pam asked him with the kind of overly sweet tone of voice that was petrifying in its Stepford extreme.

That was all Bachelor #2 could take; off he slouched.

"Now, I *know* I don't know you from anywhere… *yet*…but I'd sure like—"

"Get OUT!" screeched Pam, finishing off Bachelor #3 before he could even finish off his first sentence.

"Gee," I said ruefully, sucking off the vodka from one of the ice cubes that had been clinking around in the bottom of my empty glass, "you could have at least let me accept a drink."

"Oh, right, and then sit here for yet *another* Saturday night, watching one man after another fall in love with you? No, thank you!"

"I'd ask you who pissed in your Wheaties, but somehow I'm getting the impression it was me."

"You know, Scarlett, it's not always that easy being your best friend." For a world-class seether, Pam was looking awfully deflated.

And, for the record: yes, my mother *did* have the balls to name me Scarlett.

"Scarlett O'Hara, the Scarlet Woman—okay, so maybe that only has one t, *but still—you're going to love it once you get older!"*

I'd heard this repeatedly for thirty-nine years—i.e., the entire length of time I'd been alive—all thirty-nine of which I'd spent hating my name.

"You're going to love it one day! I promise you!" my mother had promised.

As if.

With forty beginning to stare me in the face, along with what friends were warning me was going to be one hell of a midlife crisis—which I preferred to think of as an LRWS (Life Reassessment Way Station)—it seemed increasingly less likely that my mother would see her promise fulfilled. Of course, with forty beginning to stare me in the face, it was probably also a good time for me to begin thinking about giving up using the phrase *"as if,"* but I supposed I could always worry about that another day.

But back to our story.

I'd rather have a seething Pam than a deflated Pam any day of the week. *Her* deflation was deflating *me*.

"Why, Pam?" I asked, deflated, all seriousness now. "Why isn't it always easy being my best friend?"

"Because you're…you're…you're…*you*."

"That's not helpful."

"Fine," Pam seethed one last time, seething at me for once. "Did you ever wonder if you'd still get so much male attention if you weren't so goddamned pretty, if you weren't so goddamned thin, if you didn't have those two—" and here she gave voice to what I had secretly suspected most people thought of first when they looked at me, but hoped was not the case "—spectacular breasts?"

And that's basically how it all got started.

1

Actually, Pam was wrong about a couple of things.

I wasn't "so goddamned pretty," and I wasn't "so goddamned thin."

(Okay, so maybe I did have spectacular breasts, but still. Besides, that was a whole other issue, and one that even sometimes bothered me.)

Regard my face for a moment, if you would, please, a face that will henceforth be known as Exhibit A: Note the long dark hair, the root color of which currently needs assistance from the bottle it's been getting assistance from for over a decade, the assistance made necessary by the prematurely gray hair that, rather than being prematurely seductive, had caused coworkers to run shrieking from my path. Note (admittedly pretty) dark eyes beneath brows that have passed their expiration date for plucking. Note the slightly imperfect nose (erring on the side of largeness), the slightly imperfect chin (erring on the side of pointiness), the slightly imperfect chee—

No, actually, *that* would be a lie. My cheekbones kick butt.

Yes, I do know that this is coming perilously close to tipping into that odiously annoying territory that has been heretofore uniquely occupied by that hair-product commercial that used to run all the time years ago, the one in which the actress says "Don't hate me because I'm beautiful," making the viewer long for technology to be advanced enough so that the actress would be able to hear it when viewers everywhere shout back at their TVs: "We don't hate you because you're beautiful! We hate you because the you that you are in this commercial is *the single most annoying woman IN THE WORLD!*" I do know how close I am coming to that awful-awful place, but please bear with me.

Regard the body now for a second moment, please, the body to appropriately be called Exhibit B: Note the lack of significant height (a smidgen below five feet, but just enough to make claiming a full five feet qualify me as a breaker of one of the Ten Commandments), which, when combined with the genetic legacy of good skin, is what makes people always howl, "Omigod! You don't *look* that *old!*" whenever I say I'm thirty-nine. (That and "Omigod! You don't look that short!" and "Omigod! You don't look Jewish!" are the three phrases I've heard repeatedly all my life. And, yes, my full name is Scarlett Jane Stein; so sue me.) Note, also, the all-American flaw: the slight swell of lower belly that nothing short of lipo and a tuck would ever eradicate.

And, when I say all-American flaw, I really do mean that all American women have that flaw. I mean, come on: After you rule out those who've been sucked or sewed, and then you take away the actresses/models/overly wealthy who have had actual ribs removed, who do you have left? Oh, okay. So maybe you have the growing legion of anorexics and anorexic-wannabes; but after them, who do you have left? Answer: *the rest of us.* You're left with the rest of us and our, at minimum, slightly swelling lower bellies.

And, yes, I am aware that I have much to be thankful for in that I'm located at the minimum end of the spectrum of swelling.

True, back in high school, I'd had one of those freakish metabolisms that necessitated my going home after school and eating a banana split just so that I wouldn't get any thinner (Pam would have really hated me if she'd known me then…*and I was not bulimic!*), but those days were long gone and I had finally joined the female race. If I wanted to still fit into my size 6s, 4s and 2s (which one was always dependent upon mitigating factors like time of the month, emotional need for Ben & Jerry's, which jeans I was wearing, etc.), and I did, then I needed to walk regularly, press weights regularly and engage for the short term in whatever latest exercise fad came down the pike.

Overall, though, not bad: This was the body that Pilates had built for me.

I guess then that what had rankled so much wasn't Pam's implication that I had a reasonably good body, because I guess I did, so much as the undertone that had suggested it was some kind of an unearned perk. I'd done my sweating, I'd done my pumping and, as a result, gravity was yet to become my sworn enemy. Okay, so maybe I hadn't earned my face, but I'd earned my body.

Time to cut to the chase.

(Besides, we can talk about my breasts later.)

In short, then, while the only runways I'd ever been on

had all involved planes, no one on the beach had ever begged me to put more clothes on. Objectively speaking, on bad days, I was acceptable; on good days, I was substantially more than.

The basic building blocks for Exhibit A and Exhibit B, with the exception of the color-enhanced roots and the weights-at-the-gym flab-free upper arms, were what God had started me out with in life. Just like the spectacular breasts, I hadn't earned those building blocks; they were with me when I arrived. Exhibit A and Exhibit B had been with me my whole life so far.

Exhibit A and Exhibit B were what the world first saw whenever they saw me. (*Untrue,* that nasty little voice in my head, the one I heard upon occasion, niggled. *What the world sees first about you are your breasts. You remember, don't you? Exhibit C?*)

Exhibit A and Exhibit B were the face and body I took to work with me every single day.

2

If you ever feel the need to hide in plain sight, you can do it by becoming a librarian.

I swear to God, sometimes I feel as though I'm some sort of nonwoman forty hours a week. Which is a good thing, in a way, since it gives me a nice bumper of time not to contend with my breasts and how the world sees them. Oh, sure, I still see people registering them first thing when they walk up to the reference desk, but it's a passing registration, more fleeting than if, say, I were a nurse (people always check out nurses' breasts) or a go-go dancer (ditto) or a guest star on the *Baywatch* reunion movie (no parenthetical aside necessary). Since the public pretty much views librarians as some sort of asexual alien life force, and since the wearing to work of braless tanks is kind of frowned upon by the city that employs us, it's a pretty safe place for a spectacularly-breasted woman to hide.

Not that hiding my breasts was the original impetus for my career choice, a choice that had ultimately landed me at

Danbury Public Library. No, the real reason I had originally gone after my Master in Library Science was that I love books. Duh. And librarians make much more money than bookstore clerks. It just never occurred to me that instead of recommending great books to read, which was the chief joy in working in a bookstore, I'd spend my days called upon to answer questions ranging from, "Where can I find information on the economy of the Galapagos?" to "Why can I never find the books on the shelves where they're supposed to be?" to "Why *can't* I download porno from the Internet on your computers?"

But the pay was good, thepaywasgood, *thepaywasgood.* (If that sounds like a mantra, it's because it is, itis, *itis.*)

Plus, the way I figured it, someone had to be an underachiever so that all of those overachievers out there could feel superior about what they'd achieved. In a way, I was performing a social function here.

When I had originally declared my intention of becoming a librarian, I got this from my mother: *"A librarian?"* Like I wanted to be a welder or something. "I sent you to the best schools so you could become *a librarian?"*

"It's not like I'm going to be selling crack. I *will* get to use my mind there."

"I didn't name you Scarlett so that you could grow up to be *a librarian.*"

"Oh, yeah, right. And I'm sure if I became a lawyer named Scarlett, I'd just get a ton of respect."

"Maybe not." She'd shrugged. "But the pay is good."

Seven years into what was now my twelve-year stint at the library (four weeks vacation a year! The pay is good, thepayisgood, *thepayisgood!*), I'd run into an old high-school boyfriend at a party at Pam's.

"So what do you do?" He'd leered at me over the vodka punch.

"I'm a librarian."

"A librarian?" He'd gaped at me as if I'd just sprouted a bun or something.

"Why? What'd you think I'd grow up to be—a welder? a nurse? a stripper?"

"I don't know," he'd confessed, looking slightly sheepish. "It's just hard to picture you behind the reference desk." His gaze settled on my chest. "It just seems…I don't know… *wrong* somehow."

"Call me when you grow up," I'd said, walking away.

"He always was a dick," Pam had said when I found her in the kitchen.

"Yeah," I'd sighed, "but he was always such a good-looking dick. Too bad he's so narrow-minded."

Pam, of course, had never been narrow-minded about my career choice. No, in Pam's case—Pam, who really was a lawyer—it was downright hostility.

"You have a great brain, Scarlett. So what if your breasts get in the way a little bit? You could do what I do."

Duh.

(Sometimes, I can't believe I'm thirty-nine and still saying "duh.")

"Okay, so maybe you couldn't do exactly what I do— I mean, with those breasts, you could hardly be in litigation—but you could certainly be a tax attorney. Hell, if you became an entertainment lawyer, you'd probably clean up!"

I didn't even want to know what she meant by that.

"Really, Scarlett, I'm sure that if you just put your mind to it, you could become one of us." The "us" referring to

Pam herself and T.B. and Delta, the two other women that made up our quadrangular friendship.

"I suppose I could," I conceded, "except for one small fact."

"That being?"

"I'm not one of an 'us.' I'm one of a 'me.'"

"So you say. I just think it's a shame that you feel the need to waste this brain that God gave you."

I tried the same not-a-crack-dealer line I'd used on my mother, but Pam wasn't having any.

"It's a waste, Scarlett, I don't care what you say, it's a waste. Locking that mind of yours away in a library is like winning the lottery and then just putting it all in the bank for the rest of your life, it's like some kind of brain-cell chastity or something."

"Gee, thanks."

"Don't get defensive. But, I mean, come on. Wouldn't you like to find out what you could really become in life, if you weren't so downright weird about the career world taking you at breast-face value?" Then she'd given a heavy sigh. "You've always been so pretty, though, with everything handed to you because of it—why would you ever have to know what it's like to have to maintain the drive to go after something in life and earn it on sheer merit alone?"

You're probably wondering right around now just exactly why this woman, this woman who could be considerably more hostile than she's being here, was considered by me to be my best friend. Well, I did feel sorry for her a lot, and she did have some endearing qualities that are perhaps not so easy to see.

Plus, when I'd first met her and T.B. and Delta, Pam had made a point of—no other word for it—*courting* me. Like a second-string center on the football team with broken black glasses held together by masking tape, Pam had called and e-mailed me virtually every day, as though hoping to win a date for the prom. Finally, the will in me crushed under a deluge of daily questions along the lines of "So, what are you making for dinner tonight," I'd caved and, muttering "uncle" under my breath, conceded, "Okay. Fine. You can be my best friend."

Actually, though, Pam was my default best friend. But, like my breasts, that would take a lot of explaining, far too much explaining for right now.

So there I was, on a lovely Wednesday in July, hiding in plain sight behind the reference desk at the Danbury Public Library. I'd just dispensed with a patron who wanted books on pursuing a writing career, having led her to the 888s, and was hoping to sneak in a couple of reviews in the latest *Publishers Weekly,* which had just arrived. Besides, all working and no sneak-reading make Scarlett a very dull librarian. But this was not to be…

"Excuse me?"

"Hmm…?" I stashed the *PW* away. Damn! I was never going to learn what it had to say about the latest Anne Perry.

The excuser was a harried-looking woman, around my age, with a toddler in a stroller and a girl in tow. The girl looked to be about ten years old, her black hair cut in an old-fashioned pageboy that would have been more suitable on a woman sixty years ago than on a young girl today. Despite that handicap, you could tell she had pretty-potential, what with her warm brown eyes and wide smile, whenever she forgot to be self-conscious and just let one rip. More hampering than the hair was a mild case of premature acne. Poor thing. She was probably going to get breasts early, which would lead to much teasing at school from both the nonbreasted girls and the prepubescent boys, something I knew much about. Any day now, she'd have too much hair on her legs, her mother wouldn't let her shave yet, and the other kids would all start calling her Monkey. I was sure of it.

Harried Mom put her hand proprietarily on the girl's shoulder. "Sarah here needs to get some books from the summer reading list."

"That's great," I said. "Much better than waiting until the end of summer like so many of the kids and then having to cram it all in at the last minute. Just go upstairs to the Juvenile Library—"

"Oh, no." Harried Mom cut me off. "I want you to recommend specific titles from the list." She handed me the list. "I don't want her reading just anything."

"Yes, but upstairs—"

"Please?" she pressed, then she looked up at the sign over my head: Information Desk—Reference. "This is what you're here for, isn't it?"

Well, she kind of had me there. Although I still would have said that upstairs was where she should go for help.

I looked at the list. "Well," I said, "you can never go wrong with *A Separate Peace* or *The Great Gatsby*."

"She needs to read three," Harried Mom said.

"Well, then, how about the *Harry Potter*, too? Might as well, if they're going to put it on the list…."

"Thank you," Harried Mom enthused, as though I'd just done her a great favor.

Just then, the girl coughed.

"Cover your mouth, Sarah," Harried Mom admonished. Then she turned to me with an embarrassed smile. "Sarah's just getting over the chicken pox, but she just can't seem to shake that cough."

"The chicken pox?" I took an involuntary step backward.

"Oh," Harried Mom pooh-poohed as she headed off with her kids for the double doors that would lead her upstairs to the Juvenile Library, "she's not contagious anymore. And, besides, hasn't *everybody* had the chicken pox already?"

3

No. Not everybody.

About fourteen days after Sarah coughed in front of me, I developed a fever, along with an all-over achy feeling as though I'd spent the night in the ring with the WWF. At first, I thought it was the summer flu. Having not used any sick days yet that year, I called in three days straight at the library. That's when the spots began to appear.

I'd never been troubled with acne when I was younger. And, yes, I do know that that's another one of those statements that could make some people hate me. But it's true. All through junior high and high school, I could barely buy a zit to save my life. Except for the occasional one or two around my period, I was blemish free. How odd then to suddenly be seeing spots at nearly forty. *Could my period be due again so quickly?* I wondered, studying the spot on my cheek, the one on my forehead.

But then, as the hours went on, and one day turned into

the next, I developed more spots on my face…and a few on my neck…and then on my chest.

I called my doctor's office in a bit of a panic; don't ask me why, but I was certain I had the measles.

The receptionist at Dr. Berg's office was very accommodating when I told her I thought I had the measles, saying that he could see me that afternoon. Since it was usually necessary to call two to three months in advance to get a regular visit with the most popular doctor in the city, and even the average garden-variety emergency complaint still required at least a one-day wait to get seen, I recognized how seriously she was taking my spots. The appointment slot I was given was the first after the lunch break, presumably so I wouldn't infect a bunch of other patients in the waiting room.

Okay, am I the only woman out there who's a little in love with her doctor?

I'd been seeing Dr. Berg for about a dozen years, ever since my previous physician—whom I'll call Dr. X—had nearly killed me, which had seemed like a good reason to stop seeing him. Dr. X had been treating me for an infection that wouldn't go away, and when he started me on yet another round of medication, I began feeling weird. Repeated calls to his office to say just how weird I was feeling had merely yielded the usual "just another hypochondriac" tone from his nurse. Well, naturally, once my body broke out in tiny little red spots from head to toe—a nice indicator of anaphylactic shock—they told me to stop taking the medication. Immediately. That another dose might kill me. But when I tried to get them to admit their mistake, that they should have listened to me in the first place, they insisted that standard practice dictated they do exactly what they did and that they'd do it again tomorrow. That they'd never heard of anyone nearly dying from that particular drug, even though it had nearly killed me. I suspected they didn't want to admit culpability because they were terrified of a malpractice suit. Well, I wasn't interested in a malpractice suit, but I was interested in having a doctor who was a mensch, which clearly was not anyone in that office. And they'd nearly killed me.

Did I mention they'd nearly killed me?

Well, naturally, after that experience, I was leery of doctors.

And I was still leery of doctors when I'd first started seeing Dr. Berg, but he'd quickly won me over. He was just so nice, so reassuring, and he took so much time to just talk to his patients—and not just about their illnesses, answering all questions with extreme patience, but even about their lives or whatever was in the news. I always felt so much better just seeing him—that balding head, those steel-rimmed glasses—that I often found myself telling people, "Who cares if he knows anything about medicine? I still love him." Too bad he was married and a grandfather already.

"So, I understand you're not feeling so good today, Scarlett," said Dr. Berg, glancing at what the nurse had written on my chart as he entered the examination room, hand outstretched for a warm shake; Dr. Berg never looked scared that he might catch something from a patient. Dr. X, on the other hand, had always given a can't-you-people-keep-your-distance look at the audacity of patients coming to see him while sick. "What seems to be the trouble?"

"These spots." I indicated my face. "I think I have the measles."

"The measles?" He spoke in a soothing voice as he felt

my lymph nodes, examined this, looked at that. "What makes you think so?"

"I don't know," I said. "All these red spots—it just seemed to me like this is what the measles would look like."

"No," he said, sitting down on the stool next to the examining table, pen already flying across his page, "you don't have the measles. I'm pretty sure what you have is the chicken pox."

"The chicken pox?"

"Yes," he said, starting to write a prescription. "Have you been exposed to anyone recently that may have been infected?"

I told him about Sarah, the girl with the list in the library two weeks ago.

"Yup," he said, doing the math on the dates, "that's the incubation period."

That damned precocious little reader, I thought. Why couldn't she have waited until later in the season, just like the rest of the kids, to come in for her books? Or at least have waited until she *really* wasn't contagious. I suppose that's Harried Mom's fault….

"Here," he said, handing me the prescription he'd written. "Now, I want to warn you. This is going to get a lot worse before it gets better."

"You mean I'm going to feel even worse than I do now?"

"I'm afraid so. Chicken pox when you're a kid is pretty easy. But as an adult? The older you get, the harder it is. You're also going to be contagious for another seven to ten days, so no going out in public places until all the pocks scab over."

Great.

"Now, I want you to call the office every day to let me

know how you're doing." There was my reassuring Dr. Berg again. With all that talk of worse pain and the need to be quarantined, I'd wondered where he'd gone to. "This isn't going to be easy for you and I'm going to want to keep a close eye on you until you start feeling better."

"Thanks," I said, glancing up and catching sight of myself in the mirror on the wall. Damn! I already had more spots than I had when I'd first come in there. "Um…can I ask you a question?"

"Of course."

"Am I going to look like this forever? I feel like that animal in *Put Me in the Zoo.*"

"Put me in the zoo?" he asked, puzzled.

I sighed the sigh of the long-suffering librarian. It's amazing how often people don't get book references.

"Kids' book," I elaborated. "Animal keeps changing his spots. Big spots. Little spots. Red, blue, all the colors, really. Am I going to wind up like that?"

I felt strange, exposing myself that way. Over the years, we'd often talked about socio-cultural issues and he knew that I was big on saying that I didn't think that appearances were as important as people made them out to be, that most women would be a lot happier if they stopped worrying about the outer so much and just focused on the inner. And I'd even backed it up by being the kind of woman who usually dressed casually, almost never bothered with makeup. Would he think now that all that had just been a sham? Would he think me shallow for being so concerned?

But he laughed, that reassuring sound. "Of course not. Provided you don't scratch, before you know it, you'll be just as beautiful as you've always been. Even with the spots, you still look good, Scarlett."

It really was too bad about that wife and those grandchildren.

"Can I ask *you* a question now?" he said.

"Sure."

"Why didn't you get the chicken pox as a kid, just like everybody else?"

4

(And now for a little station break, as we talk about my breasts…)

It's really bothering you, isn't it? I mean, like, you're not going to let me go any further until I tell you about those breasts?

Am I right? Come on, I'm right, aren't I?

Fine. You asked for it. Don't say I didn't warn you.

It all started when I was ten years old….

Hard to believe that this silent war I've been having with a particular body part has been going on for nearly three-quarters of my life, *for twenty-nine years.* You'd think I'd be over it by now. God, I need to grow up.

But really, it all started when I was ten years old. Ten was when I went through puberty, got my first period, got my first hint of a pimple and when I heard the words for the first time, those immortal words that no girl or woman can ever hear enough of in her life—can you hear my sarcasm?—as spoken from the still prepubescent wise-guy mouth of Don Deeble, "*Man,* I'd like to grab a hold of those tits!"

Yeah, *my* life has been fun.

And it's only gotten better from there.

On the trampoline; out jogging, even with a humongously camouflaging sweatshirt on; walking by construction sites—there hasn't been one clichéd set of circumstances I've ever encountered in life where a member of the male population has failed to hold up his end of the cliché, has failed to make a loudly rude utterance something along the lines of the above citation from Don Deeble.

And they always preface it with that one italicized word: *man.*

"*Man,* those are great…!"

"*Man,* would you look at those…!"

"*Man, man, man…*tits!"

It got to the point, pretty early on in life, where it started to seem as though, based on the evidence of those sentences, my breasts could not exist in a man-less vacuum. The way I figure it, the fact that I'm heterosexual has as much to do with the fact that the male population has linguistically linked my breasts to their manhood for all time through the employment of a simple sentence structure as it does to any natural inclinations on my part.

Of course, none of the really fun stuff I've mentioned above gives any hint of the dark side of having spectacular breasts: the dates that turn ugly because mere possession of nicer-than-normal mammary glands is somehow interpreted as a law requiring willing sexual congress under risk of penalty for refusal; or the odd male relative who starts showing an unusual interest in your development, or worse; or the fact that some girls write you off without a chance, visibly resenting you, as though you had some kind of control over such a fate, as though you'd made an unholy alliance with the devil of pubescence.

But that's just yet more of the good stuff.

Did you ever notice how, in today's world, the most notoriously-breasted woman are all triple-namers? In the past, it was the alliterative that had it, the Marilyn Monroes. Nowadays, it's the Pamela Sue Andersons and the Anna Nicole Smiths. Which is really bizarre, because that triple-namer thing means there's still room left on-bimbo-board for…Scarlett Jane Stein?

Okay, now here's the *really* killer part:

I do not—repeat, do not—have notorious breasts, not like those other women do.

I have spectacular breasts, which is nowhere near the same as notorious breasts, but *is* the same as average breasts… which you'll soon see.

All of those triple-namers—who, by the way, are all blond, which I am not—have breasts that are creeping up on or have even tipped over to the other side of the forty-inch mark. Plus, they have cup sizes that all equal or surpass the enough-is-enough alphabetic place mark embodied by the fourth letter.

I, on the other hand, am a 36C, which is—collective gasp here!—average.

Yes, folks, that statistic is really true: the average American woman is a 36C.

So, why so much fuss about me? Why have all the men I've been naked with each uttered some version of the personalized phrase, "*Man,* Scarlett, but you've got great breasts!"? I've heard that phrase so often, it's been so universal in my life, that on more than one occasion I've been tempted to inquire of whichever man was humping above me, "Um…uh…excuse me? But this is really an honest question here: Do you say that to all the girls? I mean, is saying that, like, some kind of thing with men?" But I've never had the nerve. And, truth to tell, the guys, even though they *all* say the same thing and all *look* the same way when they say it, all somehow also have that "Eureka!" look on their face, like they've discovered hooter gold where previously they've only encountered hooter tin.

Oh, and, parenthetically speaking? Yes, I do know that a lot has been made over the years of the fact that men have a tendency to be—hmm…what's the most delicate way to put this here?—*penis-obsessed,* but we gals can be pretty breast-obsessed ourselves, this entire chapter standing as some kind of monumental proof of that fact. We just don't like to publicize it.

But back to my breasts. Which I still maintain are average.

Did you ever notice how the most spectacular thing that any American kid can aspire to is to be average? Being top of the class is nothing to boast about; being head cheerleader is an open invitation for people to wish obesity on you later in life; being too good at chess is like requesting to get your ass kicked. On the other hand, being stupid means people calling you that; being fat means people calling you that *and* stupid; being not good at even chess means there's not even a lowest rung for you to stand on.

The middle. Keeping to the middle ground in everything is the safe place to be as a kid in America.

And this middleness extends to adulthood as well. The wealthy are resented, the poor are blamed, and the message is clear: the safest place to be, even if it's getting harder to keep up with the housing payments, is middle class.

In the breast department, if in nothing else in this life, I represented the national average, which was interpreted as being a smashing success, breastwise.

So, basically, I was spectacular mostly by virtue of being so damned average.

Oh, and plus the fact that with a waspish waist on a short Jewish woman, my 36Cs really did look like they might be one of those triple-named women's 40+s.

There was that, too.

5

One of the things about being quarantined for seven to ten days: it gives you a lot of time to think.

Pam herself was not as much of a slouch as she liked to think she was, except for when she slouched, of course, which was often. This had been a big stumbling block in her attempts to build a bridge to the opposite sex; it's been my observation that, while some think meeting Mr. Right or Mr. Wrong or even Mr. *Anybody* has to do with the luck of the draw, it's really all about not being a slouch. A slouch says, "I'm worried about what you think of me, but I don't think much of me, so why should you?" The non-slouch, on the other hand, says, "Even if you're not interested in me, I'm having a pret-ty fucking good life here all on my own. So there." Or she might just say, "My annoying mother always elbowed me in the back when I slouched." Whatever. The real point is how the world interprets the non-slouch, and the world sees her as confident. Oh, I suppose there are times when the world sees her as arrogant…but who gives a fuck what the world thinks?

Slouchers, that's who. Slouchers give a great fuck about what the world thinks, which neatly leads us back to our physical description of Pam.

Pam, an attorney, mind you, looked like she made a daily conscious decision to distance herself as much as possible from the thankfully archetypal uber-skinny female lawyer usually portrayed on TV. Now, I'm not saying that Pam was fat. Rather, in an effort to make sure that every male she came in contact with would not even think of treating her like a Twinkie, she had made herself work-asexual. Never mind those micro-mini-skirted suits that the TV lawyers seemed to favor, Pam was determined to furnish her entire career wardrobe from the sales rack at the back of Casual Corner. Thus, Pam owned a lot of brown.

The perverse flipside of Pam's determined daytime devotion to a dour dress code was that whenever we went out on the town at night, she always went overboard. She tried too hard. Looking at her was like leapfrogging back in time twenty years to the heyday of all those shows about oil barons with wives who never had to work, instead spending their days beating one another up in the swimming pool. She was the epitome of big hair and shoulder pads and enough sequins to choke Liza Minnelli. She was the exact opposite of Daytime Pam, and it required sunglasses to look at her.

Oh, and scary makeup. Truly scary-scary makeup.

I couldn't tell her, of course. I mean, obviously she thought she was making wise decisions.

Underneath the neutered daytime version and the

vamped-up nighttime version, Pam was average: average height (5'4"), average weight (which, in America, currently equals a size 14), average coloring (neither albino nor African-American), average-average-average. Which wouldn't be a problem for most people, since, as pointed out previously, average is currently the most desirable thing for any American to be, except that in Pam's case she wanted to be below average in the daytime and above average in the nighttime and she was mostly a dismal failure at both.

Oh, and she did have average American breasts—36C—but, coupled with a size 14 waist, as opposed to my own 2/4/6, well, let's just say that she was of the belief that side-by-side was never a fair way for us to stand.

If she'd asked me, which she never did, I would have maintained that her failures were caused by being a slouch, both literally and psychologically, while I know she would have insisted that she'd just been cursed with faulty packaging and a low self-image.

"Take *you,* for instance, Scarlett," she'd said the Saturday night following the Saturday night when she'd first shot down Bachelors #1, #2 and #3 like duckpins at the carnival.

As I looked into yet another mai tai in yet another bar on yet another Saturday night, I thought to myself, *I hate it when we take me, for instance. Why can't we take someone else for a change?*

"If we have to take me," I said, "can't we at least take me somewhere exciting for a change?"

"No."

"Oh."

"I say 'no' so quickly, only because you've already had more than your fair share of unearned excitement in your life."

"Oh. Right. I had forgotten about that."

"Now, now. There's no need for you to do that 'oh' thing you do with me."

"Oh. Okay."

"You know, Scarlett, I don't know why you always feel the need to make having a conversation with you so diffi-cult."

"Isn't this the point where, if I were a lawyer like you, like you're always urging me to be, I'd say to you, 'Let's move on'?"

"Point taken."

I attempted a winning smile. "Redirect?"

"Are you asking for permission to question *yourself*?" She shook her head. "Honestly, Scarlett, you're not that good at being a lawyer."

"Oh."

"You're doing it again."

"Oh."

"So cut it out."

"Oh, okay."

"No. Really. I mean it—*cut it out.*"

"Fine. For some real fun, then, why don't we get back to your 'Take *you,* for instance, Scarlett.' I'm pretty sure that's a line of discussion I'll *really* enjoy."

"Be snippy, if you want to. But I meant what I said the other night."

"What other night? What thing you said?"

"When we were out last Saturday night, when all those men—one, two, three—kept hitting on you, when I asked you if you didn't maybe think the real reason behind all the male attention you receive had something to do with the unfair advantage you have in the looks department."

"Oh. That."

"Yes. *That.* Well, what do you think?"

"I think that I've decided to forgive you for bringing it up and for saying it in the first place."

"Forgive *me?*"

"Yes, you."

"Whatever for?"

"Well, just for starters, the implicit message in your assessment is that I have no merit as a woman in my own right, that no one's ever wanted to be with me simply because I'm—oh, I don't know—*fun* to be with."

"Now you're sounding touchy. I thought you said I was forgiven."

"You are. But just because I've forgiven you, it doesn't mean I've forgotten what you said. Or what you must have meant by it. I mean, God, Pam, are you actively *trying* to insult me? Are you *trying* to instill free-floating feelings of worthlessness in me?"

"Uh, *no.*"

"Then what?"

"I'm just *trying* to get you to acknowledge that you were born with an unfair advantage."

"How is it unfair, when I had nothing to do with the features I was *born* with? And I prefer to believe that I—oh, I don't know—*earned* whatever I have in life."

"How have you earned it? By going to the *gym* regularly?"

"*No.* That's just how I earned some specific body parts. And, anyway, have you ever noticed how whenever we get into a heated discussion with each other, we always feel the need to verbally italicize key words for emphasis? I mean, are we juvenile or what?"

"Uh, in answer to your first question, *no.* And in answer to your second, uh…*NO!*"

"OH!"

"Come on, stop being like this. I'm really trying to have a conversation with you here."

"What conversation? You're basically saying that men only like me because of how I look, that it has nothing to do with whether or not I'm fun, whether or not I'm nice. You don't think I'm *fun?* You don't think I'm *nice?*"

She ignored my questions. "Look, if I were to accept the fact that you receive more male attention than I do because of something other than your looks, then where does that leave me? Does that mean that I'm *not* fun? Does that mean that I'm *not* nice?"

I returned her earlier favor by not answering her questions, either. Truth to tell, her questions made me uncomfortable. I mean, she was my Default Best Friend, after all. So what could I tell her? Sure, she could be fun…sometimes. Sometimes, she could even be nice. But she could seldom pull off both at once, and, anyway, they weren't exactly qualities that radiated from her to such an extent that they could function as a man magnet.

Still, I thought about what she'd been saying, and not just tonight or the other night, but the message that had pretty much become an undercurrent of our about-the-opposite-sex conversations practically since we'd first met. Truthfully, I couldn't understand why guys never called her a second time. Okay, there was that slight fashion-sense problem she had, but clothes weren't everything. She really could be fun, sometimes; and she could even be nice, sometimes. Plus, she was a lawyer, for crying out loud, which meant that not only was there tangible evidence of intelligent life lurking within her, as witnessed by the J.D. initials (for Juris Doctor) that she brandished at the end of her name like a fishhook and a club, but also meant that she could uphold her end of any sizable mortgage in Fairfield County—no small feat for a woman in a two-income real estate world. I thought about all that, and I thought about the things that I had to bring to any relationship table—my looks and being fun, my looks and being reasonably nice, my looks and…and I began to wonder: Did Pam maybe possibly have something there? Had I been occupying an unearned seat on the gravy train all of my life?

I slumped back, sighed. "What exactly is it that you want, Pam?"

She leaned in closer to the table, eager. If I was deflated by the direction our conversation was taking, she was excited. "What I want is for the playing field to be leveled a bit. What I *want* is for you to have a little less of what you have, and for me to have a little more of what you have."

It was at this point—I know, I know, I *know*—that I should have stopped and asked myself, Did I really want this woman to continue in the role of my Default Best Friend? And, why had I ever chosen her in the first place?

But I never got the chance to ask myself that question—not then, at any rate—because it was then that that evening's Bachelor #1 chose to approach our table, insinuate himself between Pam and me with his back to her as if blocking out some kind of Martian sun, and utter the unfailingly catchy words: "Buy you a drink, pretty lady? I just hate to see a pretty lady sitting all by herself."

On any other night, that "sitting by herself" part would have been enough to topple Pam over into a seething frenzy, which would have, in turn, prompted her to hit the eject button on my Bachelor #1 before I even had the chance to avail myself of the free beverage on offer. But not on this night. Not on this night that was all of a sudden different from all other nights. No, on this night, instead of doing the usual, Pam craned her neck around the side of Bachelor #1, a smug smirk on her face revealing her satisfaction at having obtained proof of the inherent unfairness of the world, and mouthed the words at me, "See what I mean?"

And, for a moment there, I guess I kind of did.

6

Dr. Berg was right: my illness got worse.

Oh, did it get worse.

The hardest thing about living alone is being sick all by yourself.

Home for me was a condo three-quarters of the way up a high hill in Danbury. I'd purchased it the year after I got the job at the library, so I'd been living there for a long time, but you couldn't really call it a home. Maybe that's the thing about condos; even when you own one outright it still feels like temporary lodging, like the place you're living only until you get serious about what you're going to do in life. At any rate, that was certainly the case with my condo, which I'd only decorated in the most marginal sense. Sure, I'd hung things on the wall—framed photographs that Best Girlfriend, who had made a whole career out of being something of a camera buff, had taken. And of course there was furniture, mostly of the looks-like-Domain-but-bought-at-a-shop-cheaper-than-Domain variety. I'd even painted: yellow in the tiny kitchen, leaf in the bathroom, heather in the dining and living rooms, periwinkle in the master bedroom. Every now and then I bought a few plants; but, with my black thumb, none of them ever survived for very long. So, despite my meager efforts, it still all had the look of a way station, a place to provide temporary shelter until I found where I was really meant to be.

For a week I remained there, alone in my temporary shelter, contemplating my current pain and the past life I had lived.

There are really no words to describe the physical pain of chicken pox at thirty-nine. I'd certainly experienced my own fair share of pain in my life—the usual sprains and broken bones brought on by a life lived both athletically and carelessly. (Okay, I'm a klutz.) And I'd even had a fair amount of dental work done without benefit of Novocaine. (I hate needles.) But nothing had prepared me for this. (Nothing.)

I wondered, through my pain, if this was what it had been like for Sarah, the girl who'd given me the chicken pox. Had she been this miserable? A part of me, the part that was still irrationally mad at her for giving the disease to me—when really it was her mother I should be mad at, for letting her out of the house!—was glad in a vengeful way. But then I remembered what Dr. Berg had said about it being much harder the older you are and I was suddenly glad to realize Sarah hadn't suffered as much. After all, it wasn't her fault she'd been out and about, *it was her mother's.*

For the first three days, my fever raged at 103. And, as the pocks spread downward from my face and chest, eventually covering my entire body—even places that it would be indelicate of me to mention, but damn!—it became as though a thousand painful bonfires were roaring beneath my skin. When awake, I tried to obey Dr. Berg, tried not to scratch; but whenever I would actually fall asleep, I'd wake to find that I'd been involuntarily scratching while unconscious. I took the oatmeal baths as recommended—gross!—but they were just a stopgap measure, only serving to relieve the pain for the two twenty-minute periods a day I was submerged in the tub.

Of course, my mother offered to come over and take care of me.

"Scarlett, you shouldn't be alone!"

"Um, really, that's okay, Mom." Please don't come, please-dontcome, *pleasedontcome,* I fervently prayed. The last thing I needed was for her to walk in the door and, first thing, tell me how awful I looked.

As if I didn't already know.

Each morning, as the illness progressed, I rose, dragged myself to the bathroom, looked in the mirror. And then really-really wished I could avoid looking in the mirror. For, each day, I looked less and less like the me I'd always known. What had started out as a few pinkish-red spots had turned into an angry eruption, the spots multiplying and taking on the appearance of a plague until I no longer recognized myself. I didn't know this woman. This woman was ugly.

Again, I found myself wondering what it had been like for Sarah, encountering an ugly version of herself in the looking glass. True, Dr. Berg said kids didn't get it as bad, but I was sure he was referring to the pain and not the pocks. Surely, the quantity of pocks would still be great. Had Sarah felt as horrified at her image as I felt at mine now? Had she been scared, or at least reluctant, to have her friends see her?

Why, when I had first seen her, I'd been sure her problem was prepubescent acne and I'd pitied her.

I pitied me now.

What, I began to wonder, would life be like if I always looked like this? What if this was the face that the world saw all the time?

As Pam had pointed out, and as I well knew, I'd never had any problem attracting men, being that literature-defying rarest of birds: an attractive librarian with a good sex life. Okay, maybe I'd never managed to marry any of those men but I'd never had trouble attracting them. I'd always assumed, unlike what Pam implied, that men were attracted to me because, well, I was just so damned much fun to be with.

I was the girl that, never mind men needing excuses to justify playing poker, played poker with.

I was the girl at the ball game, always rooting for the right team.

I was the girl who was nice.

I was the girl who was fun.

You're probably wondering right now, "If she's so god-awful wonderful, so *nice,* then why hasn't anyone asked her to marry them yet?"

Actually, I had been asked, more than once, but that's not the point here. Because this isn't so much a "Why isn't she married yet?" story, as it is a "Why doesn't she seem to care that she isn't married yet?" story.

I guess I don't want things just because everyone else has them.

I guess I don't want to settle.

I guess I've just been—gasp!—waiting for the right man.

Best Girlfriend always maintained that not only am I too nice, but that I also scare men.

"*I* scare men?"

"Of course you scare them, Scarlett. Men are more terri-fied of a woman who seemingly *isn't* looking for something than they are of a woman who obviously *is.*"

"You mean they worry about what I might have up my sleeve?"

"Oh, who the hell knows why they think like they do? *They're men!*"

"So then why do they keep asking me out, if they're so scared?"

"Because they're men!"

"You're kind of working that angle both ways, aren't you?"

"Not really. They ask you out because you're bright and you're beautiful and you're funny and you're available. They may be men, but they're not totally stupid."

"But you think they're all scared of me?"

"Yup."

Nice and scary; scary and nice—what a combination.

But, I wondered now, how many men would ask me out if this face and body—this *Put-Me-in-the-Zoo* face and body—was always the first thing they saw upon meeting me?

Naturally, my local friends—Pam, T.B. and Delta—all of whom had been smart enough to have chicken pox when they were kids, offered to come over, to bring me things, to keep me company.

But I declined.

At first, I declined because the pain was too intense; it was all I could think about. But as the third day of confinement turned into the fourth, and the pain began to abate some-what—and even thoughts of Sarah, as both agent of and imagined companion in my misery, had receded—I realized that I just really did not want the world to see me this way. If it meant eating packets of ramen noodles three meals a day, which was pretty much all that was left in the house, so be it. I had on my giant T-shirt from my UCONN days— big enough that it barely touched any skin when I was standing—and I had my remote control for the TV. I ask you, what else did I need?

Of course, being a librarian, having spent my entire life in books really, I wasn't much for TV. But when you get that sick…and then you get that depressed…it's a whole new ball game.

Pam, T.B. and Delta always spent part of the time we were all together rehashing whatever the hot programs were on TV. For three attorneys, they sure watched a lot of what I thought of as junky TV. Didn't anyone else read anymore? And they particularly loved reality shows. They'd been following *Real World* ever since it was launched and were constantly mentioning shows with words like *temptation* and *fear* in the titles. Fear and desire seemed to be the great motivating factors of these programs; love and death lay behind everything.

I clicked through the channels, clicking past comedies (not funny enough), dramas (I didn't have the concentration) and political talk shows (who cared what was going on with the world? I was sick!).

Click, click, click.

I thought about looking for a legal show. I'd always liked legal shows, especially when I was younger. It seemed like, back then, the shows were reinventing the justice system so that things were as they *ought* to be, rather than how they were: common sense prevailed over racism and last-minute stays of execution were granted just in time. But lately I'd noticed TV had grown more cynical, and the legal shows, rather than restoring order to the universe, portrayed a hellishly topsy-turvy world in which the guilty always walked on a technicality and the innocent fried.

Click, click, click.

Then, all of a sudden, my screen was filled with...plastic surgery?

But I was fascinated. For a whole hour I watched as three people, none of whom I thought ugly but I was sure the world had called each just that at one point or another, were nipped, tucked, reconstructed, cut and dyed—you name it—until they'd each undergone an *Extreme Makeover,* intended to change their lives forever.

Well, they certainly looked better.

If not exactly swans now, they no longer had the residue of facial or body features that had no doubt earned them all kinds of insults as children and probably even as adults. At the end of the show, they were all dressed in great clothes—they'd received wardrobe makeovers, too—and were now ready to embark on their new lives.

I wondered, sitting there with my spots, which had finally stopped spreading and were finally starting to ease up a bit in terms of the anger of their appearance, if their lives would really be changed. I mean, they had to change, right? But would those changes all be good changes?

Reality shows hadn't been around for that long and I began to wonder if anyone had done any kind of follow-up studies on this sort of thing yet. *Were* people really happy afterward? I knew that they'd done many studies with lottery winners, all showing that, in general, becoming wealthy did not make people's lives better; in fact, it often made their lives worse.

Well, I sighed, clicking off the TV and praying for sleep, not to mention praying that I'd wake to a face more recognizable than the one I'd wakened to that morning, *being one of life's sort-of swans had not made my life better, not if the definition of better was some kind of lasting romantic love....*

7

As I said, one of the things about being home sick for an extended period of time is that it gives you the chance to ponder the little things in life, like, say, how I had come to be thirty-nine and was still seriously unattached. After all, even if I wasn't overly concerned with getting married, it still didn't mean I wanted to be alone forever.

Maybe, I was beginning to think, it had been my career choices?

If you want to meet good-looking men, don't expect to do it in a library or a bookstore. Trust me on this: it only happens in movies, that two cinematically perfect human beings fall in love over the dusty stacks while doing research on the mating rites of the South African tree frog or bump lattes at the local chain. Real life in a library looks more like this:

Regard Mr. Weinerman, if you will, please (I know you might not want to, but you kind of have to, since this is my story): Mr. Weinerman is your prototypical library patron. He is here every day. He sits at the same chair at the same table every day. He sits there and he reads all day long—newspapers, magazines, books—and he only moves to either (a) go outside to smoke a cigarette; (b) go to the bathroom for twenty minutes at a clip (you can hear him eating his lunch and snacks in there, among other things you can hear that you'd rather you couldn't [the acoustics in this building *suck*]); (c) read things on his favorite computer terminal (he intimidates other patrons into moving whenever he wants to sit there).

Mr. Weinerman is omnipresent in my library life. He is here waiting when we open in the morning, he is the last to leave before the staff at night, he has a complete nervous breakdown if we have to close because of a severe snowstorm or power outage. He is omnipresent and he is perhaps the single most physically hideous human being that I have ever set eyes on in my life.

Not that looks matter, mind you, but does he have to take every poor building block that he started out with in life and then make what looks like a *conscious effort* to exaggerate every hideous feature to its worst extreme?

He is just so…*rubbery* is really the only word for it. He is the kind of person that when asked a question that necessitates your taking a library material and passing it on to him, you dread that his hand might glance against yours and that you would actually be forced into social contact with that very antisocial-looking hand, that hand that looks like it only ever gets social with its owner, and in places I didn't like to think about.

Granted, every library patron didn't look like Mr. Weinerman, but the whole lot were a far cry from anything halfway good, and believe me: every library does have its Mr. Weinerman.

And bookstores are the same. I know that for a fact, because I worked in one before I got my MLS. The sighting of a decent-looking man in a bookstore is so rare that the few times one passed through, I was dumbstruck. Oh, sure, I saw plenty of great-looking men whenever I went to the bar or the beach or even Super Stop & Shop, but almost never in the bookstore. When it did happen, it made me feel like I was the lone gas station attendant at the only stop within a hundred-mile radius in Nebraska on a hot July day when there comes Brendan Fraser pulling up in a Jag, looking for a full tank of octane, a Vanilla Coke and a tube of Rolos. Really, it felt exactly like that.

Now, then: If you ask me why you never see good-looking guys in these places, what do you think I'll say—that hunks don't read? That they're too stupid? That they'd rather watch it on the video? That they're too busy getting fucked?

Nah.

I think the real reason is that they all have good-looking girlfriends, that they have these good-looking girlfriends fully trained in what their own tastes in reading material are (as well as exactly how they like their blow jobs, standing or sitting or on the hood of a Jag in the middle of the Nebraska desert while drinking a Vanilla Coke), and they send their girlfriend minions out to do their book-shopping for them, so that they don't have to undergo the bug-under-the-microscope discomfort of having the desperate women working in the libraries/bookstores across the land ogle them.

Just so you know: You do see an awful lot of good-looking women in libraries/bookstores.

Too bad I'd never been interested in women *in that way*.

Over the years, when people asked me why I was a librarian, they always said I should be a writer instead—not because I had any talent that anyone knew of, but because I loved books so much. And I'd tried. In secret. Oh, how I'd tried. But I was just no good at it. Like a music lover with no ear, I was doomed to listen and never play.

8

Now for the eternal question, the one that has been tormenting humans down through the ages:

How is a woman like a green M&M?

(I'll bet you can tell I was starting to feel better.)

I'd always claimed that the green M&M's were the best in the bag—the precise order, before they started adding new colors, going green, yellow, orange, brown, blue, red—a claim for which I'd encountered many detractors.

My mother: "It's just different-colored dye, you can't taste dye."

Best Girlfriend: "Okay, I can see where there might be a discernible difference between green and red, since they really are so far apart. But green, yellow and orange? Uh-uh. Too close to call. In a blind taste test you'd never do more than equal the statistical probability of naming them by chance." (She was right, but it was fun, since we were very drunk.)

Pam: "They all taste exactly alike, for chrissakes—just eat the damn things!"

Despite the reluctance on the part of the world to adopt my candy-theorizing, I'd felt heartened when, in a getting-to-know-you campaign by Mars, Inc., little pieces of informative cardboard began accompanying officially licensed products, in this case a giant plush toy (don't ask). My favorite, of course, was the one that read, "*Read About Green:* Green is quick-witted and intelligent; she says it like it is. She knows she's attractive, so she's flirty, but not in a tacky way. While feminine, she keeps up with the boys; finds the rest of the gang a bit childish. She knows how to handle trouble. She will get what she wants."

That, in a candy-coated shell, was me.

I was all of those things and—except on days when I was PMS-ing and was therefore less—more. Okay, except for maybe the very last sentence, but I was hoping that, in the fullness of time, that might prove true, too.

Just like Cathy once proclaimed, "I *am* Heathcliff, and he is me," I *am* a green M&M. Further, as far as I'm concerned, the fact that I'm a green M&M has pretty much well explained for me the reason why getting dates has never been a problem.

Pam, on the other hand, has always viewed the matter quite differently.

9

Okay. Okay *okay* OKAY! I know you're not going to let me go any further without first explaining how Pam came to be my best friend and just what exactly a "default best friend" is.

Straight out of college, my best friend—my *real* best friend—known as Best Girlfriend, the woman who thinks men find me scary, embarked on a series of geographical moves purposely designed to keep her out of Connecticut. The distance has only grown farther as the years have gone on. Having started out in New York, six moves later has seen her temporarily settled on the Oregon coast. It's my private belief, one of the few beliefs I have never shared with her for fear of giving her an idea that she hasn't had yet, that she's just one last move away from Alaska. After that, I'm sure I'll lose her to Russia—she'll probably walk across to it one day when the ocean is frozen really good—and then the world.

I know we're supposed to be a mobile society, but mobility is just not something that people in my family *do*. And it's not that I mind Best Girlfriend's independence, her freedom, her sense of adventure. On the contrary, it's one of the many things I admire about her. I just wish the distance between us didn't make it so hard for us to sit on Irwin Lerner's face together.

Perhaps I need to explain that last remark.

While we were at UCONN together—me in Liberal Arts, she in Fine Arts—we fell into a set of fairly regular habits, the kind of habits that helped normalize a life lived during an uncertain time when the drinking age was just beginning its incremental progress from eighteen to twenty-one (hence, we were all doing the constant-slow-IV-drip kind of drinking as opposed to the binge drinking that occurs in the much safer college atmospheres we have now) and AIDS was just thinking of poking its head over the American horizon (meaning that most of us were getting laid, fairly regularly, sometimes by people we barely knew, and none of us were using rubbers). Some of our life-raft habits included practical things, like always letting the other know approximately where we'd be when we went out ("A party, I think over in South Campus") and approximately when we'd return ("Tomorrow morning? Tomorrow afternoon? Definitely sometime in there"). All right, so maybe we never were so exact with the information that any efficient sort of police report could ever be filed, should such a thing prove necessary, but it was just barely enough to technically pass the telling-the-truth test whenever I told my mother, "Not to worry: Best Girlfriend is keeping tabs on me." Did it really matter how close those tabs on me were?

Other life-raft habits included: eating breakfast together

(8:15 to 9:45 a.m.), but only if we were still up from the night before, because otherwise we'd never be up by then; lunch together (10:15 a.m. to 12:45 p.m.); and dinner together (4:15 to 6:45 p.m.); oh, and milk shakes at the snack bar set up in the cafeteria after dinner (8:00 p.m. to whenever). So maybe we didn't make it to a lot of our classes, and maybe that does sound like a lot of time devoted to eating (which might also finally explain the notorious weight problem known as the Freshman 15), but I swear to God we did not spend all of that time eating. It was just that we always seemed to have a lot of stuff that we needed to talk about, and food was always in the immediate vicinity whenever we did so.

And then there were those vast forty-eight-hour wastelands of time at that suitcase college that were more commonly referred to as the weekend; weekends where the dorm cafeteria was closed and we often resorted to the Student Union for our hungover-Saturday and Sunday eating-lunch-for-breakfast meals: tuna melts and milk shakes, grilled cheese sandwiches and Funny Bones, lots of diet soda and lots of cigarettes. Eateateat, talktalktalk.

But the most important Student Union meals of all were the rare ones that occurred late on Sunday afternoons at the tail end of rare weekends when one of us had stayed on campus alone while—gasp!—the other had gone home alone. This meant that, not only did we have a pressing need to discuss the usual pressing-need stuff—guys we were interested in, parties, other girls who annoyed us, diets, whether we'd pass any of the classes we never seemed to be going to, the inherent impossibility (slurp!) of sticking to any milk-shake-free diet while going to a school with its own agricultural college, the fact that she was indeed now a smoker since she had passed the pack-a-day mark and should therefore probably contribute to our daily nic tab, the fact that I could be petty from time to time—but we also had all of the pressing-need stuff that we'd been acquiring *independently* while (gasp!) *apart*.

These extra-special talks, during which we each felt as though we were talking to a whole new other person, given our protracted separation, required foodstuffs that went beyond the usual Nutrasweet/Funny Bones double-whammy. It required something beyond smoking while eating. It required something extra-special to recement us as the friends we'd always been and always would be, reconfirming the fact that it would always be okay for us to grow while apart just so long as we never grew apart. And, leave it to Best Girlfriend to come up with the perfect reconnection ritual climax: miniature peppermint patties consumed while sitting on a bronze plaque commemorating some man we never knew anything about.

"It's gotta be his face," Best Girlfriend had said, taking a teensy bite from the patty in order to make it last longer.

"Ya think?" I'd asked, taking my own first nip. "How can you possibly know such a thing? How come not the feet? In graveyards, aren't headstones at the head and plaques at the feet?"

"But this isn't a graveyard. I mean, what're you talking about?" It was amazing how, for two girls who'd grown up entirely within the state of Connecticut, in most of our discussions during our college years, we both sounded remarkably like Joe Pesci. "If there were a real person underneath us here, buried on the lawn outside of the Student Union, right around the area where we usually sit for movies sometimes, that would just be way too gross for words. It's just a commemorative plaque."

"So, wait a second, then. The reason you said we're sitting on Irwin Lerner's face is because…?"

"It's because I said so."

"Ah."

And Best Girlfriend was just enough months older than me that she always had the edge in any heated debate.

But then she moved away after college, and there was no more sitting on Irwin Lerner's face together for us.

Our friendship was like being married to someone who gets sentenced to a really-really long prison term. On the one hand, you've sworn to wait for him and maybe you even intend to, and maybe you'll even be able to. But in the case of a best friend that moves far away, even though she remains your official best friend, you still need to hook up with someone close by, someone you can go shopping with so that you can reject whatever the current fashion trend is together, someone with whom to attend chick flicks, someone to talk to on a daily basis, sharing each other's soap opera.

Hold on. So maybe it's not like being married to someone who gets sentenced to a really-really long term in prison so much as it is like being the husband who is in fact sentenced: you might start having sex with some beefy bruiser named Bart, but he's not really who you want and everyone knows it.

Pam was my Bart while Best Girlfriend was the real deal.

This might not sound like such a great deal from Pam's perspective, but Pam had known what she was getting herself into—being the Default Best Friend of someone who already had a real Best Girlfriend (and, yes, I do realize how immature I sound right around now)—and had in fact campaigned for the position, beating out Delta and T.B. (more on them later). As for me, I'd needed someone to go with me to see the latest Jennifer Aniston movie (you can go alone to dramas, but never comedies, because the laughing part just never works the same, which I suppose says something profound about the fact that people can suffer alone, but to celebrate the joys of living—laughter, success, popcorn, new shoes, finding out that Jamie Lee Curtis doesn't have a better body than you after all, the comical/ironical/blissful sides of love—you mostly need someone to celebrate with. It's like getting a Ben & Jerry jones on: when you share a pint with a friend, it's like, "Hey, I've got a friend," while if you eat that same pint alone, it's like, "Wow, I'm pathetic," (and not just because you will have eaten twice as much).

As I said, I needed a pal to go to the movies, and Delta had to work late and T.B. had a first date, so—tag!—Pam was it. She called me that one extra time, I said "uncle" and the rest was Default Best Girlfriend history. It was that simple. The two other friends in our foursome were busy and thus Pam became my Default Best Friend.

But, just like sex with beefy Bart, it just wasn't the same. Pam could laugh with me in a crowded theater, and agree that hip-huggers sucked and that most of the people who wear them shouldn't without it sounding like sour grapes, but she could never be someone who saw me for everything I was and hoped to be, and everything I wasn't while loving me just the same, with the clarity of a god, nor, I suppose, could I see her in that way.

Best Girlfriend was the only woman who'd ever been able to actually see me; Best Girlfriend was the only woman I could honestly say I knew.

Did it suck for Pam? Probably. I don't know; she never said. And besides, we did have fun most times. But it also sucked for me and it sucked for Best Girlfriend, too.

But Best Girlfriend needed to actualize herself in ways that never tempted me, career-wise, adventure-wise, relationship-wise. And, if I was going to love her like I loved no other woman on the face of this planet, then I was just going to have to let her lead her life in whatever way she needed to.

So, in a nutshell, it's not so much that I mind her being there; I just want her *here*.

10

"What the *fuck* do you think you're doing?"

Apparently, Best Girlfriend was not best pleased with some of the life decisions I was making.

"Are you fucking nuts, Scarlett?"

Having reached nearly the end of my quarantine period, I'd decided to call her up, looking for a little support, a little support that seemed to be sadly lacking.

"Oh, come on," I said. "Why don't you tell me what you really think?"

"Fair enough. Maybe that was a little harsh. But do you realize that what you're telling me sounds, uh—no, there's no nicer way to put this—slightly crazy?"

"Which part are you referring to?"

"Well, most women, when they get to be our age, put their efforts into making themselves look better, not worse. I'd say that pretty much covers the 'slightly crazy' part."

"I didn't say I was definitely going to do it."

"What then?"

"I said I was *thinking* about doing it."

"Oh. Well, that's radically different."

"Come on, be honest. Haven't you ever wondered?"

Best Girlfriend was the most beautiful woman I'd ever known who wasn't in movies. I know it may sound elitist to say this, but there's a real continuum of attractiveness. Someone has to occupy the high end; Best Girlfriend was at the very top, and I was close up there.

"Haven't you ever wondered," I asked, "what your life would be like, what your relationships with men would be like, if you didn't look the way you do?"

"No. I haven't." She said it so simply that I realized it must be true.

"Oh," I said.

"You never did say, Scarlett. Just what—or who—put this idea into your head?"

"Pam?" I winced.

"Oh."

Pam and Best Girlfriend had met once or twice, when Best Girlfriend flew into town for her occasional visits. While I'd had high hopes for those meetings—who, after all, wouldn't flat-out adore Best Girlfriend?—the meetings hadn't gone as planned. Pam had insisted on spending the entire time talking about mutual acquaintances that Best Girlfriend, living clear across the country, had nothing mutual with. And Best Girlfriend, usually so self-confident and secure, had been uncharacteristically miffed. The resultant conversations that began with "I don't know what you see in her" from both of them had been enough to keep me off the idea of ever willingly bringing the two together again. Maybe, if I ever finally got married, I'd need to have them

both in the same place again. But until such a time occurred...

"Oh," Best Girlfriend said again.

And then she changed the subject, and we talked about
politics and Israel and books and movies, and men of course.
It was our usual greatly fulfilling kind of conversation: we
got to solve the problems of the world, trade ideas on popular culture and remember yet again why we were and
would always be best girlfriends.

Naturally, none of that stopped her from obeying her in-
grained instincts by getting in the last word. I mean, she was
those few months older than me, after all.

"Just promise me one thing, Scarlett."

"Shoot."

"Promise me you'll really *think* about it before embark-
ing on this crazy road."

"Okay."

"'Okay' is not the same as 'I promise.'"

"Okay. I promise."

"Good. And one other thing?"

"Hmm?"

"Promise me you'll think twice before shaving all your
hair off?"

11

I believed in three things, beliefs I formed not while reading a book, but rather—gasp!—while watching a movie.

The movie, the name of which I no longer remember, had one character spouting off about Greeks, obituaries and passion, something along the lines of when a Greek man dies, his obituary isn't about what he's *done,* but about whether or not he had *passion.*

This is a wonderfully, wildly romantic notion of funerary rites that I have no way of proving or disproving, not having ever been to Greece or being much of an expert on Greek culture or even worldwide obituary practices in general.

"But," you'll say, raising your finger in the air as you make your indisputable winning point, "you *are* a librarian."

"True," I will concede.

"Surely," you'll go on, "you of all people should be able to place your finger on such information within moments. I mean," you reiterate, "hel-*lo!* You *are* a *librarian.*"

To which I'll finally have to respond, grumpily, "Fine. So maybe I don't want to know."

And it's true. I *don't* want to know if that stupid thing about Greeks/obituaries/passion I got from that stupid movie is true or not, particularly if it's not true. And, even if it seems unlikely that a culture foolish enough to center their dietary menu around things like lamb and massive olives should come up with such a vast improvement on our distillation of a person's entire life down into one short, fairly boring paragraph (plus inclusions about where to send flowers) by cutting right to the only thing that matters—whether a human being who lived had lived with *passion*—it seems equally likely that that same culture that built the Parthenon and that treats flying tableware as objects of joyful expression could have indeed accomplished such a thing.

Having admitted that I got the inspiration for my own life philosophy from a movie, here are the three things that I have chosen to stake my passionate claim on:

1. books
2. friendship
3. men.

The order changes from day to day; so sue me.

You probably can readily understand the books and friendship parts, at least why those things would matter to me so much, given what you already know about me. But here is where I take confession one step further. Here is where I tell you something about category three that you might not agree with, having perhaps grown too cynical.

I believe…I believe…I believe…

"Oh, God, Scarlett! Would you just fucking say it?"

Please don't ask where that voice just came from.

Fine. Here goes.

I believe, not only in being passionate about men in general—which I am, always have been, can't see myself ever not being—but I further believe that while you can go through an incredible number of men in a lifetime, and that there's nothing wrong in doing so, and it can even be an interesting way to live, and you can love them all, and you can even love two at once, I believe, really believe, that for each person there is only ever one true love, and that if you fail to find that love, then at the end of your life the Greeks will eulogize you by saying, "Yes, Scarlett did some things passionately, perhaps, but she did not have *passion.*" I also believe if you give up too soon, if you settle down and marry someone before locating that one true love, then that's exactly what you're doing: settling.

One true love.

One—in my case—man.

Only one.

And I got all this—fucking A, as we librarians are known to say—from some stupid movie.

12

The only great thing about owning a condo in Danbury is that you get the use of a huge swimming pool, at least at my condo complex. And the view's not bad. And it's nice not to have to worry about the lawn. And the neighbors who aren't psychotic are mostly okay. But other than that, I mean, come *on,* it's not like living in the Waldorf-Astoria or something.

But the pool certainly is a plus. At least, the way Pam and Delta and T.B. saw things, it was. And they put their money where their mouths were by showing up on my doorstep every Sunday morning between Memorial Day and Labor Day, like it or not.

Truth to tell, I suppose I did like it, most of the time. For one thing, it gave me a built-in excuse not to cope with my mother until much later in the day, and for another, it wasn't like I was seeing anybody special where it might make the disruption caused by three women showing up with a ridiculous quantity of paraphernalia on a Sunday morning after having had wild sex all of Saturday night, well, disruptive.

And they *did* always arrive with a ridiculous quantity of paraphernalia: the more normal items were sunblock, sunglasses, wide-brimmed hats, books, magazines, flip-flops. The less normal included yet more bottles of sunblock, only these had been emptied and rinsed thoroughly, making way for vodka apple martinis (Delta), since the condo rules were no consumables except for water by the pool. It was Delta's theory that the Absolut-filled brown bottles of Tropical Sun or Deep Hawaiian were less conspicuous than see-through water bottles. I failed to see the reasoning for this, but in our group, I was in the minority.

Yes, I know it's not very mature of us, still drinking so much as we age. What can I say? We were working on being Northern belles, except for Delta, who really was a Southern belle. Plus, whenever we went out, we appointed a designated driver—it doesn't do for attorneys to rack up DUIs—and whenever we drank at my pool, everyone stayed put afterward until they were sober enough to drive again.

The other less-normal items for poolside use consisted of whatever new outfits had been purchased in the interim week (Pam), the runway show from cabana to diving board commencing only when enough Absolut tanners had been quaffed; and four copies of the Sunday edition of the *New York Times* (T.B.), which might sound like intellectual overkill, but which T.B. brought every week in the hopes of getting us to compete in a four-way contest to see who could finish the puzzle in the magazine section the quickest. I was the only one who was ever willing to do this with her, but not because I felt the need to compete; it was more like that it was nice to enjoy what was traditionally a solo activity for me with company.

Best Girlfriend and I used to do the crossword together. And, even though she was a pencil-with-eraser person while I was strictly pen, sharing just one puzzle between us each day somehow worked.

"You think they think we don't know by now who 'architect Saarinen' is?" T.B. asked, not bothering to look up from her puzzle as she filled in the blanks.

"They must think we're stupid," I answered, filling in the same blanks on my own puzzle.

Truth to tell, of the three, T.B. would have made the best Default Best Friend—hell, if the job wasn't already filled until death us do part, she would have made a fine Best Girlfriend—but Pam had been so determined. Plus, T.B. was the only one of us four who was getting laid regularly by the same guy, and she wasn't about to cut into nooky time just to go hold my hand while we went to the mall to laugh at those stupid hip-huggers.

"Child, you white folks are funny the way y'all'll buy something just 'cause that skinny-assed Britney Spears is wearing it. You don't see black folks doing anything so *dumb.*"

T.B. was one of them black folks. And she and I loved to slip into "girlfriend" mode.

"No, that's right, girlfriend," I said, "ya'll black folks got your own dumb shit going on."

"We black folks like to do this just to confuse y'all," T.B. was fond of saying, "keep you on your toes, make you think we're going to steal your silverware—something fun like that."

"Gee, thanks, but you're a fun girl," I was fond of saying in return.

And then T.B. would laugh that rich beautiful laugh that I loved so well, the one that was like a swirling whirlpool made up of chocolate and which my skinny-assed Britney Spears self could never duplicate, not in a million years.

Now that you know just about everything else about T.B. worth knowing—that she was nice, smart and a *Times*-toting intellectual—you're probably wondering how she came by the name of T.B. Had someone in her family been hooked up to an iron lung machine a few generations back? Was it perhaps short for "Too Bad," as in "it's too bad for you, but I've already got someone else I'm doing regular-like"? No, it was neither as tragic as the former nor as rude as the latter.

T.B., quite simply, stood for Token Black.

When I'd first been introduced to her by Pam, I'd returned her warm handshake, responding, "T.B.? Oh, right. If my name was Terebinthia Butterworth, I suppose I'd just go by my initials, too."

"That's not what T.B.'s for."

"No?"

"It's for Token Black."

Since we were at a party at Pam's—it was amazing how many big parties Pam threw, given how few people she liked and how few liked her—where the current population consisted of approximately twenty-nine white men and women plus *her,* it wasn't all that difficult to guess where she might be going with this.

"Under the present circumstances, I can see what you mean."

"No, you can't."

"Excuse me?"

"You may *think* you see what I mean—Pam told me all about those liberal tendencies of yours—but you don't."

I know it was wrong of me to take offense at someone else's accurate assessment of the limitations on my experience of such things, but—what can I say?—I was offended anyway.

I puffed up: "Well, actually…" And I proceeded to tell her about my preteen best girlfriend, the one who came before Best Girlfriend, the one who was black, and about how once her sister had taken us and a carload of her friends—nine of us total, only one other white—to see a movie on the Fairfield/Bridgeport line, and how the movie theater was an every-seat-taken affair and the movie was a comedy and the only two whites in the whole theater were me and that other girl, and how downright *spooked* I'd felt when I'd been forced to recognize the truth: that some of the things we thought were funny were not perceived by those around us that way, at all, and that some of the things the majority found funny made me feel just a little intimidated. "So, you see—"

T.B. had the chutzpah to yawn in my face without making any real attempt to cover her mouth. "Oh, yeah, right," she said, when she'd yawned long enough to stop my self-conscious flow of words. "Y'all had one minority experience and now you know what it's all about."

"I wasn't saying that. What I was saying—"

"Look. Try taking your one lousy little experience and multiplying it by just about every day of your life. I didn't go to no *movie* once and have that happen. I *am* the movies, baby, and TV, too." T.B. shifted into street talk.

"Gee, you don't look like a movie."

"Well, I is. I's the judge and the pediatrician and the prosecutor and—"

"Well—" I stopped her "—you *is* actually the prosecutor."

She started to smile at me, and then made herself stop.

"I's the local color, I's the next-door neighbor, I's the best friend who gets killed so the star can get angry—" dramatic pause "—I's *expendable*."

"Naw," I said.

"Naw?"

"Ain't I sayin' it right?"

"Naw."

I shrugged. Well, *I* couldn't hear any difference between us.

"If I ain't expendable, then what am I then?"

"You's the glue. Without you, they ain't no story."

"No shit?"

"Naw shit."

"If you stop imitatin' me—" she smiled "—I'll let you be my friend."

"If you forgive me when I can't help myself or I just do it, anyway, I'll take you up on it."

"Well, I guess we'll just have to wait 'n' see how often you do it."

"Hey," I said, serious again and feeling foolish, but more serious about anything than I'd felt in years maybe. "I'm sorry."

And I could tell I didn't really need to explain, but she pressed me, anyway, her voice soft. "For what, baby?"

"For everything I had no part in creating, for everything I'll never change."

Still soft: "Me too, baby." Then much brighter: "But you know what?"

I shook my head.

"At least it'll give you and I something other than the usual 'being-a-woman-these-days-sucks-because-the-hem-lines-are-too-high' bullshit to talk about."

"True."

"Now, then. See her? See that one over there?" And she pointed her finger at the woman I would later come to learn was Delta from the Delta.

"You mean the one the men all seem to notice a lot?"

"Mmm-hmm."

"You mean the one with the hair teased so high it practically touches the ceiling?"

"Mmm-hmm."

"The one with the too-tight capris and the fuchsia chiffon scarf and the really big…"

"…acres of Tara? Mmm-hmm. That's be her."

"What about her?"

"She really talks like this."

"For real?"

"Naw shit."

"And ya know somethin' else?"

"What?"

"I actually *like* her."

"Naw shit?"

"Naw shit, baby."

And they *were* always disruptive.

Given that this was the first Sunday since getting the chicken pox that I'd been well enough to have them over for a swim, if anything, they were *more* disruptive than usual.

It's always struck me as funny how minigroups of like-situated people tend to cluster together. One of my male neighbors hadn't married until age thirty-four. Previously, he'd had a group of friends who were all of similar age, all unmarried. Then, when he fell, they fell, too. For the first year or two afterward, he'd still laugh about people he knew from work who had kids, their lives all occupied with Little League and ballet recitals. But then his wife had gotten pregnant and, like a row of dominoes redux, all his friends had followed suit.

Our minigroup's unifying theme was that we were all currently unmarried. T.B. had been married once and was still on good terms with her ex, Al, whom she even still dated occasionally, and who was in fact the person I'd been referring to earlier when I said she'd been getting laid regularly by the same guy. Delta had been married and divorced a whopping three times already, producing two bundles of mixed joy out of her efforts. Pam, like me, had never even said "I do" once.

I sat there in my lounge chair, a white beach robe covering my conservative olive tank suit. A sprinkling of faded pocks still marred my face and chest. Dr. Berg swore that they'd disappear completely in time, but I had my doubts. Unused to being blemished, I felt disfigured by the two spots that remained on my face, both on the left side, one just under my cheekbone, the other closer down to my chin. And my chest! Who would have thought that I, who had been previously bugged by all the attention the world paid to my unearned breasts, would be so bothered by having this smattering of flat, pale pinkish-red spots mar the previously creamy terrain? Well, even I was human.

As I sat there, I listened to my minigroup do the postmortem on their respective Saturday nights. T.B. had gone out with Ex-Al again, this time to a movie she'd badly wanted to see. To me this was a good sign of his earnest intent, since whenever a man consents to see a chick flick rather than a dick flick it means he cares enough to let his woman think Colin Firth is hotter than he is.

T.B. looked gorgeous in a strapless turquoise swimsuit, her long hair done in cornrows that she'd wrapped together in a matching turquoise scrunchie. I envied her the hairstyle (but knew I'd look like an idiot if I ever tried to imitate it).

"Are y'all possibly going to get back together again?" Delta voiced for all of us, readjusting her ample bosom with one hand to the chest of her ill-advised fuchsia two-piece suit as she knocked back a surreptitious mojito from her sun-tan-lotion bottle with her other. While I'd been ill, and with no pool to go to, mojitos had apparently taken my friends by storm.

"Naw," said T.B. "I don't think so. It's more like having a man who has the same tastes and can be depended upon for good sex whenever the need arises."

That didn't sound like such a bad arrangement. It'd be convenient, anyway.

Delta had had one of her three ex-mothers-in-law stay with her gruesome twosome while she and Pam had spent the evening at Chalk Is Cheap, the pool hall/bar we usually frequented when we went out together.

"Was it fun?" I asked wistfully, wishing I'd been out with them rather than spending the night at home with reality television, feeling sorry for myself.

"Naw," said Delta, "it wasn't so great. A pair of suits came in who Pam and I thought might turn out to be possibilities—"

"But then they turned out to be gay," Pam finished. Pam's choice of a sedate one-piece black swimsuit that could not begin to camouflage a world of sin indicated that she was still depressed from the night before. If she'd scored, she'd have been wearing the white one, in hopes of a wedding to come.

"Well," I said, "better you should learn that now than later."

"Ain't it the truth?" Delta laughed.

But Pam still looked bummed by the whole thing.

"So," I said, as if we'd been talking about what I really wanted to be talking about all along, "if I were to deliberately sabotage my own looks—you know, in order to see how the world treated me if I no longer looked the same—how would you suggest I go about it?"

Pam shot me a look of almost victory as she moved over to the aluminum ladder, lowering herself into the pool.

"You're not serious, are you?" T.B. asked, looking suspiciously over at Pam.

Was this a thing that my friends talked about behind my back? Strange to think that the paranoid voice in your head, the one that whispers, "People are talking about you," was probably right.

Whatever.

"I'm not sure how serious I am," I said, "but I am curious about what it would be like. And I'm also curious what y'all think I'd need to do."

Y'all? See how easy it was, when with T.B. and Delta, to lapse into the kind of phrasing they used? I didn't want to ask myself what it meant that, however much more time I spent in Pam's company than theirs, I never had the desire to sound like her.

Pam eyed me appraisingly. "You'd need to start dressing down," she said.

"Hah!" hah-ed Delta, the woman who'd never met an oversize piece of paste jewelry she didn't love. "If Scarlett dressed any more down, she'd be…she'd be… Well, I don't know what she'd be, but I just don't think it's possible. Maybe she'd be Toto."

I knew that Delta was referring to the fact that I tended to dress, um, anonymously. It really wasn't what you'd call dressing down—I mean, I was always clean—but my wardrobe mostly consisted of simple pants and shirts and dresses, things that were anti-fashion to the extent that I could have worn them ten years before, would be able to wear them ten years hence, and they'd never make a ripple of sensation. Timeless classics, I guess you would call them. But, like my condo, "lacking in personality or apparent ownership" is probably what Delta would call them.

As for the Toto remark, Delta, who had something nice to say about nearly everybody—well, she even occasionally found nice things to say about those two kids of hers, didn't she?—had always nursed a somewhat rabid antipathy toward the little dog in *The Wizard of Oz;* "Damn thing looks like the business end of a mop," she'd say.

"True," Pam conceded, referring to my wardrobe, not the little dog. Having pulled herself up onto a big black inner tube, she was lazing around the pool, using her hands to gently provide the motion. "But Scarlett's clothes still have some *shape* to them. She needs to go in the other direction." Then she looked at me, smiled. "I could help you out with that. I could take you shopping."

"Well," said Delta, leaning over to finger my raven mane, "the hair would have to go." She fluffed her own Dolly Parton-wannabe tresses. "Can't be trying to slum it with pretty hair."

"Oh," said T.B., getting into the spirit of things, although I could tell she didn't believe I'd ever do it, "and you'd need to get some glasses."

"I could do that," I asserted. "I wear contacts. I'll just switch."

"No heels," warned Delta. "Ever."

"Great," I enthused. I'd reached an age where I was tired of the pain of occasionally wearing heels, even if those heels were sometimes the only things standing between me and regular teasing by my gal pals at my lack of significant height.

"And no makeup," T.B. laughed. "Not that you ever wear any to speak of, anyway," which was true. A little lipstick in the winter, just enough so that the chapping wouldn't make me look like Linda Blair in *The Exorcist,* and I was pretty much well ready to face the world.

"Hey," Delta laughed, "and if you really want to make it challenging for a man to fall in love with you, you could borrow my kids for a while!"

"Um, no, thank you," I said. It wasn't that I was put off by the idea of kids in general so much as I was put off by the idea of Delta's kids in particular.

"Oh, come on," Delta encouraged. "Believe me, it'll make it nearly impossible to find Prince Charming, if you've got a couple of kids at home."

"Who ever said I was searching for Prince Charming?" I asked.

"Heh," T.B. laughed softly. "Ain't we all?"

"Well, no," said Delta, going all literal on us. "I don't think lesbians are looking for Prince Charming at all."

"Prince Charming, Princess Charming," said T.B., "it's the same thing."

All the while, Pam had been floating around in the pool, a smile playing on her lips as she tilted her face to the sun, eyes closed. She had the look of someone who was content to let others do her dirty work for her.

"Okay," I said, feeling that I needed to object to something, but reluctant to address the particularly objectionable things that they were saying, "let's say I do all this. What do I do about where I live, where I work?"

"Huh?" asked Pam, nearly falling off her float as she sat up too quickly.

"Think about it," I said. "I can't just show up at work one day looking radically different—people will think I'm nuts. I can't stay living in the same place after going from swan to anti-swan. Did I mention that people will think I've gone nuts? All my neighbors will think I've gone nuts. People would ask questions. I'd have to give explanations."

Pam shrugged, settled back, smiled. "So you'll get a new job. So you'll move."

"Just like that?" I asked.

"Sure." Pam shrugged again. "Why not?"

I thought about it. Would it really be that hard to do? I wasn't that attached to my job. I certainly wasn't that attached to where I lived. Except for the pool. But it would be Labor Day again before I knew it, which meant no more swimming for nine months, anyway. And leaving the library would get me away from Mr. Weinerman….

"You know," Pam said in a devilishly seductive tone, "you could also bind your breasts."

"I'm not going to bind my breasts!" I half shouted. Sheesh. A girl had to draw the line somewhere.

"Just a suggestion." Pam smiled.

"Well," I said, thinking about it all, everything, all at once, "if I do all that, I might as well change my name, too. People still do that sometimes when they get married or if they go Hollywood, so why can't I? I could even change it legally.

No sense in creating a new life, a new persona, and then keeping the same name."

"No sense at all," said T.B., in a tone that clearly revealed that she'd gone back to thinking me nuts.

"Naw," said Delta, "Scarlett's the name of a femme fatale. It's the kind of name men can't resist. We can't have that."

"So," asked Pam, "just what are you going to call yourself in your new life? Who is the new and de-improved Scarlett going to become?"

"Who the hell knows?" I answered.

"Are you really gonna do this thing?" T.B. asked a few minutes later, once Delta had joined Pam in the pool, the two others caught up in talking TV.

"Yes," I said. "I don't know." I thought about it some more. "Maybe?"

"But," T.B. said, "forgive me if this is a dumb-ass thing to ask—*Why?*"

I thought about how Pam had planted the seed when at the bar, had been planting the seed for years, that my luck with men was unearned. I thought about how having the chicken pox had harvested the seed that I might not be as lovable if I didn't look as good. I thought about my realization, while watching *Extreme Makeover,* that my looks might have brought me attention, but they hadn't brought me love.

"Because Pam's got me curious," I said. "Because for thirty-nine years I've done things one way, and it hasn't gotten me anywhere, not really. Has being attractive got me that Prince Charming you were talking about? No. So maybe doing something drastically different will get me what I want. Do I even want him? Who knows? Some days, yes. Some days, no. Maybe I want to do it because I worry that

Pam might be right, that my good looks have earned me a free ride. Maybe I want to do it because I want to prove something to myself, that I'm likable just for me after all. Or maybe I want to do it simply because," I finally sighed, "who the hell knows why? What can I say? I'm a confused and conflicted and ambivalent woman. I have murky motives."

"Ah," T.B. said. "I getcha now."

13

I stood before the mirror in my bathroom, studying my hair.

Yes, I know. That does sound a bit too much like navel-gazing. But I had a purpose to what I was doing. And, besides, it was hair-gazing instead of navel-gazing, so didn't that somehow make it okay?

Looking at all that long black hair, I thought about how long it had been a part of who I was. Ever since I'd been little, with the singular exception of a college flirtation with the shag, I'd always been the girl—now woman—with the long black hair. It was something I'd always received compliments on: from babysitters who had liked to play with it, turning it into long braids or trying to get it to take a wave with the curling iron, to men who had liked to see it splayed out against their pillows. Hell, there had even been a few women who had made passes at me because of it. Unlike some of my acquaintances, who were made uncomfortable by lesbian advances, I'd merely turned those women down in the same way I'd have turned down a man whom I wasn't interested in dating: "Thank you so much for the compliment, but I'm just not looking to date right now. What can I say? It's a character flaw."

Even my mother had always claimed to love my hair, calling it my "crowning glory."

Was I really going to get rid of it now?

I heard Best Girlfriend's voice, admonishing me not to shave my head.

But I wasn't going to shave it, just cut a dozen or so inches off. And besides, my local girlfriends had said that my hair was the first thing that had to go....

I went to the bedroom, lifted the receiver on the phone, thinking to call Helen at Snips & Moans, the combination styling salon and massage parlor I always went to whenever my split ends reached the unbearable point or when I needed to be touched by someone who would be unlikely to have sex as part of the agenda. The place was pretty rustic, and there was something vaguely scary about Helen, but in a pinch it worked.

But then I heard Pam's voice distinctly, as though she were right there in the room with me, saying, "But that's cheating, Scarlett! If you go to Helen, sure you'll get your hair cut, but you'll also be tempted to do something *stylish,* something that the world will approve of. Put down the phone!"

For whatever reason, I listened to her.

Having decided to listen to the voice of Pam in my head as opposed to—oh, I don't know—*reason,* I returned to the bathroom, looking in the drawers and cabinets for a decent pair of scissors. You would think I'd own a pair, but I never sewed anything, never hemmed anything that could be rolled up, so I was forced to settle on a teeny-tiny pair of gold scissors from my manicure kit.

Oh, well, I sighed, taking a hank of hair in my hand and holding it straight up in the air as I'd seen Helen do, watching my own reflected hand as it made the first decisive cut, *this is probably going to take all night.*

So…it didn't take all night. But by the time I got done with my self-styling, working one hank and snip at a time, it had taken quite a while, and left me with some pretty sore fingertips.

And what else was I left with?

Very short hair, that was what I was left with: a completely naked neck with very short hair, still all black and parted on the side, but now looking like an uneven patchwork quilt. I looked like a little kid who had gone wild in the bathroom while Mom yakked for too long on the phone. Except for the fact that I wasn't a kid and nobody was yakking on the phone, I looked exactly like that.

Oh, well, I sighed. The goal had been for me to look radically different….

Now, let's see. What was next on the list?

I got out my contact lens case, removed my lenses, gently stowing them away as though they were a beloved pet I was sending off to the Great Rover Beyond.

Looking in the mirror, I saw…absolutely nothing but a blur. Without any assistance, I was blind as a bat, unable to pick O.J. Simpson out of a lineup of dwarves.

Reaching for my eyeglasses case, I removed the pair I wore at night before bed and first thing in the morning. They were on the small side, with tortoiseshell arms and gold rimming just the top half. Anne Klein II, maybe? I can never remember these things without looking.

I put them on, hearing Pam's voice again in my head, only this time, it was from a dinner we'd had the spring before. Suffering from an eye infection, I'd worn my glasses for once. Pam had looked at me over the top of her menu.

"You know, Scarlett, I've never missed work because of a hangover or lack of sleep in my life. But if my only two choices were calling in sick or being seen in public with my glasses? I'd call in sick."

Unbothered, I'd merely pointed out, "That's what makes the world go round. People like us being so different and yet not killing each other." Then I'd ordered the salmon.

I looked at myself in my glasses. I didn't look too bad…did I? I'd always thought my glasses looked kind of neat on me. But then I tried to think of movie stars whom men made passes at, despite their glasses, and I drew a blank. Nicole Kidman had put on a big nose to be Virginia Woolf, but that was hardly the same thing.

Sophia Loren!

There was one, I thought, tamping down my own enthusiasm an instant later. Somehow, I doubted that the same sort of people who were drawn to Sophia Loren were going to be drawn to me. Besides, her glasses were a lot different than my glasses. I'd look silly in her glasses.

I tried to tell myself that the short hair looked good on me. I tried to tell myself that the glasses made me look like a funky kind of chic, if not necessarily a Sophia Loren kind of chic.

Then I called my mother.

★ ★ ★

It had been long overdue. Calling my mother, that is. Having been unable to face her while I was sick, now that I'd been well more than a week, it was time to bite the mother bullet.

My mother, *Mom,* was the kind of woman for whom the phrase "She means well" was originally coined.

Meaning well, in this instance, however, meant me meaning well and going to see her for lunch in her oversize house on Candlewood Lake—at least the swimming was good, theswimmingwasgood, *theswimmingwasgood!*—so that she could ply me with the homemade chicken soup that I'd cheated her out of plying me with when I'd been really sick.

As I eyed a suspicious-looking piece of chicken bone floating around in the greasy liquid, I refrained from telling her I thought that maybe I liked ramen better.

Needless to say, Mom's a lousy cook.

But she had been living in a great home, ever since Dad died, and I liked visiting there, if not too often, liked gazing out her big picture window at the sun shining down on the lake, the children playing near the shore, the boats in the distance.

Mom had changed a lot in the seven years since Dad had died. Sure, she'd loved him—or seemed to, in the way that people who have been married a long time often do—but once he was gone, it was like some sort of door had opened for her. She no longer wore jeans, having adopted polyester for the duration; she'd stopped dyeing her hair, letting her short cut go steely, which somehow complemented her brown eyes; and she'd taken to decorating parts of her home in what I could only think of as "*TV Guide* Style." No, I don't mean she got inspiration from decorating articles in

TV Guide. Are there any? I mean she decorated *with TV Guide.* She'd done a quarter panel of one living room wall from floor to ceiling in *TV Guide* covers as well as the support pole in the garage. Somehow, whenever Sam Waterston got his picture taken, I doubted he pictured himself ending up here.

She'd also taken to paying extra for any and every sports station cable had to offer.

"Your father always hated sports," she'd said the first time that, having picked up the clicker, she'd turned on the TV during one of our dinners.

"Um, yeah," I'd said, thinking I had after all known the man for more than thirty years, "I did know that."

"Go Yankees!" she'd yelled at the screen, apparently not hearing a word.

And, somehow, since Dad's death, she'd also grown taller.

"How did you *do* that?" I'd asked her once, looking slightly up at her as we'd stood side by side at services on Rosh Hashanah the autumn before. I was sure she used to be shorter than me. "Aren't women supposed to get shorter as they age? You know, osteoporosis?"

"Who knows?" she'd said. "Maybe I was slouching all those years? Anyway, shush, the rabbi's glaring at us."

As I spooned my chicken soup, watching her watch the game, it was as though she were reading my mind.

"And you'll go to services with me again this year? The High Holy Days will be here again before you know it."

"Do I have to?"

Sometimes, I could sound soooo *twelve.*

"No, you don't *have* to. If you don't want to be religious anymore, that's between you and God."

"Good."

"So, I'll buy tickets for both of us?"

"Okay."

"Are you seeing anyone special?"

"No."

"Still working at the library?"

"Well, it is my job."

"Feh."

What I didn't tell her was that I was in the midst of a two-week leave. Having decided to devote myself to My Transformation, I'd put in for the vacation time I hadn't taken yet that year. True, they didn't love the idea on such short notice, but they did feel bad I'd been so sick, and I had worked there for a long time and was a good employee.

"You could always change your job," my mother suggested.

"We'll see."

A commercial came on, something involving talking fruit that could also dance pretty good, and my mother finally tore her eyes away from the screen.

"Omigod," she said, "there's something different about you."

Hard to believe, we'd been together for an hour already. You'd think she'd have noticed when I first walked in the door, but the TV had been on. With one eye on the game and the other on the pot, she'd served up my bowl of chicken soup without looking at me once.

"What?" I asked, hopefully. "Maybe I look taller?"

"No—" she pooh-poohed the suggestion "—you're still shorter than me."

Rats.

"Omigod," she said. "Your hair! It's…gone!"

I waited, dreading to hear her cry over the loss of my "crowning glory."

Then: "I *love* it!" she cried. "Where did you get it done? I want to get a cut like that!"

Oh, God: it was even worse than having her cry over the loss. Apparently, I was now sporting my polyester mother's ideal haircut.

I told her I'd done the snipping myself, but she wasn't listening. She was already on to something else.

"And those glasses!" she enthused. "You just look so…kind-of *smart*."

"Thanks, Mom."

"Oh, are they going to love you at synagogue this year!"

In part to make myself feel better over the fact that my mother now wanted to look like me, I accepted Pam's suggestion we spend the evening at Chalk Is Cheap. Besides, I needed to try out my new look in the Real World, didn't I?

Chalk Is Cheap was somewhere on the middle of the continuum between the high-end pool halls that refused to admit anyone wearing a leather jacket and the grunge bars I'd frequented when I was younger; there was plenty of leather in sight but the carpeting was still intact, there was only minimal risk of getting shot, and the police never raided the place after hours for allowing gambling.

As I sat there at a tall but tiny round table with Pam, I noticed there was something different about her.

"Your hair!" I said.

Indeed, her hair. Apparently, I wasn't the only one who'd been doing some changing. In place of her previous overdone-for-nights-out-on-the-town coif, Pam was now sporting a look that would have been at home on any of a number of sexy sitcom stars: an uneven part separated the strands that had been tinted in pretty col-

ors ranging from a white gold to chestnut. The hair itself had been straightened, with just the ends turned up
in a perky flip.

"You like it?" she asked, preening.

"Yes," I said. And I did. It was beautiful hair.

"Thanks." She smiled. "You know, I just figured, why not?
Why not shake things up a bit?"

Her hair wasn't the only thing Pam had shaken up, I noticed, peering at her more closely in the dim light. She'd also
done something new with her makeup, her previous too-
much attempts having been muted down to a pretty and
tasteful technique that made her eyes pop without looking
as though she had pop eyes. I would have complimented her
on that, too, but I've never felt comfortable complimenting
other women on their makeup, the underlying message akin
to: "I'm glad to see you're getting professional help. You look
sooo much better now!"

"I had the girl at the Macy's counter do me," she said, answering my unasked question. "Usually, when I do that, I
don't buy anything afterward. But she did such a good job
on me, that I bought it all. Good move, you think?"

I thought.

Too bad she hadn't done something about her clothes.
Still determined to look like a Joan Collins throwback, she
appeared to be wearing every sequin in her collection for
her night on the prowl. I, on the other hand, had on a pair
of old tight jeans—no way was I going to engage in the
belly-baring low-riders that had taken the nation ill-advis-
edly by storm—and a tight white T-shirt that bore the faded
pink legend "National Cha-Cha Champion"; not that I'd
ever cha-cha-ed, but the cotton felt good.

"Your hair looks good like that, too," Pam said, returning

the compliment, although her smile seemed a little wicked. "I like the glasses, too. They're, um, very anti-chic."

"Thanks. I think."

Two rounds of drinks later and Pam was brooding that no men were approaching us, not that that's what I was there for at least, so I put some quarters down on the pool table and waited my turn to shoot.

When my quarters finally came up, the usual kerfuffle ensued, meaning some guy I'd never seen in there before approached me, assuming—wrongly—he could con the table off some *girl*.

I, of course, wasn't having any.

"Just because I have ovaries," I said to the guy, who might have been attractive if his eyes weren't so red with drink, "doesn't mean I can't remember where I put my own quarters." We librarians can be tough. "See this blue chalk mark across the face of these quarters?" I held up the two in question close to his face so he could see. "Did you put that chalk on these quarters?"

Of course he hadn't. I'd put the chalk mark there—hey, chalk is cheap—knowing this kind of con attempt was more likely to happen as the night wore on and people got drunker, ruder.

He shook his head, sheepish.

"No, of course you didn't." Librarians can be pedantic, too; we get a lot of practice at work. "*I* did. Now move it." I gave him a gentle I-mean-business shove. "I've got a game to shoot here."

As I bent down to put my coins in the slot, I heard from behind me, "Whoa! Nice butt!" This was from Cute But Too Drunk Guy. And then, from farther behind him, "Ah, *shit*." This, of course, said in disgust, came from Pam.

And so the evening went.

No one paid attention to Pam and me as a duo, no one approached with offers to buy us drinks, but whenever I took my turn at the table, whenever I bent over to take a shot, someone would comment on my backside, some offering invitations, all of which I declined.

"Ah, shit," Pam said again at the end of the evening, as we divvied up the bar tab. "You still have an unfair advantage. We've really got to do something about that wardrobe."

14

The Danbury Mall in the evening, particularly in late summer, never feels the same as it does during the daytime, when the mothers and young children rule the skylight-covered lengths, or the weekends, when the fathers have been added to the mix. Like some kind of netherworld, it becomes overrun with teens, the whole place taking on an edgy quality, as though something could happen at any moment, although, truth to tell and Danbury being a relatively safe city, it never had the few times I'd been there on a weeknight.

Based on what had happened the last time we'd been in Chalk Is Cheap, Pam had decided it was time to take my extreme makeunder to a new level.

As we met in front of the carousel, debating where to grab a bite to eat before shopping, we discussed the merits of Sbarro's versus the brick-oven place.

"Sbarro's," Pam decided for us. "I want to get a big salad."

"You? Salad?"

"Sure, why not?"

I shrugged. She'd never wanted salad before.

As we walked past the other tables and stood in line, I felt Pam put her hand on my arm, leaning in to whisper, "Omigod! Did you see how that…*boy* was looking at you?"

"What boy?" I asked, ordering a slice of plain cheese and a large diet soda.

"Him." She turned back toward the tables, indicating with her chin the one she meant.

There was indeed a boy back there—well, okay, he was probably at least nineteen, but to us he was a boy—sitting with a group of friends and looking our way. He had dark hair, pants that were way too loose for my taste and soulful eyes that looked like he might have at least read a book in his life. If I'd been twenty years younger, I might have gone over to say hi. When my eyes met his, he blushed, having been caught staring, looked away, then boldly looked back to see if I was still looking. I smiled to be polite, the kind of smile you give to the convenience-store clerk whenever he gives you the right change *and* remembers to thank you, and turned back to pay for my dinner.

"He's probably just a very friendly person," I said to Pam. "I'm sure he smiles that way at everybody."

"Hah!" she hah-ed, paying for her salad and water. "Look at you."

"What about me?"

"Look at how you're dressed."

I had on my white summer short-shorts and red tank, a pair of skinny gold sandals that had seen better summers adorning my feet. No slave to the current trends in sloppy fashion would ever dress this way, but hey, I'd grown up in a time when short-shorts were the norm and the look worked for me.

"It's summer," I said. "It was hot outside today." I certainly wasn't about to defend my inalienable rights to life, liberty and the wearing of comfortable clothes in seasonally hot and humid weather.

"I'm just saying," she said. "It's not like anyone can miss how...*you* you are when you're dressed like that."

Again, I wasn't about to debate this with her, but I did kind of know what she meant.

For as long as I could remember, going to the mall meant selectively ignoring a certain kind of attention: men, sometimes ancient and sometimes too young to know what puberty was, passing me by, their eyes staring too long at things like, oh, say, my breasts. Truth to tell, I didn't mind the young ones so much as I got older—I thought it was kind of funny, kind of flattering. But the old ones? I did wonder what possessed men, because they always looked as though they thought it was possible, however remote, they might have some kind of a chance, which was kind of icky. If, when I'm seventy, I go through life always staring at the penises of forty-year-old men, looking as if I expect to get some, don't you think someone might lock me away?

But I wasn't about to change the way I dressed. Nothing I wore was ever overly suggestive—okay, maybe some things were a little tight, but nothing overly suggestive—and I did have the same rights as everyone else to wear whatever I found comfortable.

"See?" Pam smiled, grabbing us a small table. "We're doing this just in the nick of time."

"How's that?"

"We're *saving* you from yourself, Scarlett. Don't you think it's time you find out how the world treats you when it's no longer staring at your breasts?"

"What do you suggest," I asked, taking the plastic knife and fork and, with much effort, cutting the large slice right down the middle, "purdah?"

She ignored my question, watching what I was doing to the pizza instead. "You always do that," she said, "cut your food in half. Why?"

I shrugged, raised the half slice I intended on eating. "I've been doing it for years. It was something I read once."

"What? A diet book?"

"No. I think it was Muriel Spark's *A Far Cry from Kensington.* This woman loses a lot of weight simply by cutting everything she eats in half."

"Sounds like a great book."

"Well, that wasn't really what it was about. Anyway, ever since then, I never say no to anything I want to eat. I just eat half."

"Sounds efficient."

I shrugged again. "It's only ever really a problem when what I want to eat is a whole pound of M&M's."

I was tired of the microscope always being on me. "What about you?" I said a bit defensively, indicating the salad. "What's up with that?"

"Oh. That." I could have sworn she blushed. "Well—" she squirmed around a little, self-consciously playing with her new pretty hair "—I just figured, while you're busy deglamorizing yourself, why can't *I* try to improve my appearance, to see how the world treats me if I look different?"

Why, indeed?

★ ★ ★

A half of a scoop of mocha-chip ice cream for me and a cup of black coffee for Pam, and we were contemplating where to shop first.

"Eddie Bauer?" I suggested. "J. Crew?"

"Sears," Pam said.

"Sears?" Even non-materialistic me was horrified at this.

"Oh, all right," she conceded, "we'll compromise: Filene's. At least there I can get some new things, too, and it won't all be about you-you-you."

Sometimes, I wondered: just who *was* this all about?

As I fingered the price tag on a deep purple silk blouse—it would be great for work with a gray wool skirt I had, plus I could tuck it into jeans for an eclectic look on Saturday nights—Pam tugged on my arm.

"Come on," she said, stowing me in a vacant dressing stall. "I'll *bring* you things. Sheesh! No way can you be trusted to pick out your own clothes."

She made me feel like my ten-year-old self out shopping with Mom: *"No, Scarlett. You most definitely can*not *have that tube top. You need to wear a bra."* Then, snagging a passing salesgirl: *"Foundations? Don't you sell foundations here?"*

Pam made me feel just like that.

For the next half hour, I stood in the stall as Pam brought me armload after armload of clothes.

"Just think of the favor I'm doing you," she said brightly. "You do need a fall wardrobe, don't you?"

"Well, maybe one or two items," I muttered. "But, no, I hadn't planned on doing a whole new wardrobe this season."

I pulled one of the dresses, all of which looked remarkably similar in shape, even though the colors were slightly different—olive, forest, beige, tan—over my head.

Looking in the mirror, I saw that it had long narrow sleeves and a loose Empire cut with a long skirt touching nearly to my ankles. Across the back, there were two strings to tie, which—take your pick—made me look either asexual or pregnant, in that the whole effect somehow made my breasts look like nonstarters while the rest of me now looked like there was perhaps much more to me than there really was.

Well, I thought, feeling the material against my skin, at least it was one-hundred-percent cotton.

"Isn't this, um, a little big?" I asked Pam tentatively, fiddling with the tag to check the size. "Hey!" I answered myself before she could say anything. "This is three sizes bigger than what I normally wear!"

She shrugged. "Just think of how much more comfortable you'll be this fall. Now wait here—I'm going to go get you a few more things."

Going to get me a few things took her far longer this time. What? Had she stopped for a snack? But as she knocked on the pink door and entered, I saw that, in addition to two more tent dresses for me—mauve and orchid this time, so she was branching me out—she was carrying a Filene's bag with a paid receipt stapled to the top.

"You bought me something?" I asked, slipping into the mauve dress.

"No, I bought *me* something." She carefully pulled apart the receipt closure and removed a stunning cashmere wool sweater dress with gently folded turtleneck in an off-white that looked soft as a bunny. Throw in a pair of decent pumps, and I'd wear that dress.

As she held it against her body, I saw that something was wrong: the dress was so much smaller than Pam—more my size, really—I *could* wear that dress.

Apparently, Pam was able to guess what I was thinking. "It's all right," she said, not at all bothered. "I'll just hang it in my closet until my body is ready for it."

"Right," I said, "the salads."

"You know," she said, eyes sparkling, "while I'm losing weight, you could be gaining weight!"

"Uh, *no,*" I said emphatically. After all, I had to draw the line somewhere. "Who do I look like to you—Renée Zellweger? Are you going to pay me twenty million to do this?"

"No," she conceded, "I guess not. So maybe that was too much to ask."

"Uh, *yeah,*" I said, still miffed as I turned to check out my mauve reflection, *"maybe."*

The mauve dress looked exactly like the olive dress had, only mauve.

"Um," I said, realizing even as I said it that I'd suddenly become the kind of person who said "um" a lot, "don't all these dresses look, um, remarkably the same? What is this supposed to be, um, my new uniform from now on?"

"Exactly!" said Pam. "Are you sure you're not willing to bind—"

"No!" I half shouted, crossing my arms protectively over my breasts.

"No need to get so touchy. I was just asking." Pam surveyed my reflection in the mirror with satisfaction—the shapeless mauve dress, my short hair, my glasses—the same reflection that caused me such unease because I felt as though I didn't *know* this woman. "Empire waists—" she smiled "—what a wonderful thing. They're the next best thing to bound breasts!"

Having persuaded me to wear the new clothes home— Pam: "Might as well start with the New You tonight"; Me:

"But it's hot out"; Pam (winning): "Oh, don't be such a baby"—our next stop was the shoe department. Well, since the mauve dress did look ridiculous with my gold sandals, I realized Pam was right; I needed new shoes.

As I looked at the fun boots that were out for fall—soft leathers with heels that were architectural marvels—Pam picked out a pair for me.

They were brown. They laced up above the ankle. They had a clunky heel.

"Don't these look, um, military?" I asked, trying them on.

"They're perfect," she said, putting on a pretty pair of pumps to go with the new dress she had in her bag.

Hey! I wanted those pumps! Who cared how much they made my feet hurt? Besides I was lying when I said I didn't want to wear high heels anymore.

Then she selected a new bag for me: a nondescript pleather thing that was more book bag than fashion statement.

"It's perfect for the librarian in you," she said.

Finally, she took me to a store where they sold only sunglasses.

"Here," she held out her hand, "give me your old pair."

Feeling like a robot, I surrendered my Wayfarers.

Not my Wayfarers!

"Here," she said again, handing me those clip-on sunglasses made for the visually impaired who can't handle contacts. "Tomorrow, when the sun is shining, you can put these on."

I glanced in the tiny mirror: I looked like an idiot.

Not that there's anything wrong with people who wear clip-ons. It's just that on me, they looked idiotic.

Then Pam put on my Wayfarers: she looked, if not great, almost cool in them.

All in all, it really was worse than shopping with Mom.

Since Pam was now on a diet, and I had lost my appetite, rather than having a snack, we headed back to the carousel. At the top of the ramp leading from the mall to the parking garage, I saw the young guy we'd seen earlier when having pizza and salad, the one who'd been checking me out. He was still hanging out with his friends, sharing a cigarette. As we walked by them, his eyes briefly met mine, but there was no spark of recognition as he moved his gaze onward.

It was as though I wasn't even there.

The tide, apparently, was already starting to turn.

It was as though a fairy godmother had come to visit, only she'd been an evil fairy godmother; instead of waving her wand and giving me a ball gown and a royal coach, she'd left me in rags and bare feet.

Best Girlfriend wasn't going to like any of this.

Just then, I heard a voice yell out of the relative darkness of the parking lot, "Yo, mama!"

Pam and I both turned reflexively, being the only two mamas around. Pam actually preened a bit.

"Yo, mama! You in the big dress! I'm talking to you." It wasn't the guy who had looked at me before, but it was one of his friends.

If preening could be said to dim, I saw Pam's preening dim.

"I *like* a woman in a big dress," he said.

"Oh, *shit,*" Pam muttered. "It doesn't matter what I do to you, does it? Someone still finds you attractive."

15

Best Girlfriend did not like any of it, had said as much during a long phone conversation recently, and she certainly wouldn't like what Pam was telling me now.

"It's your breasts."

"It is *soooooooo* not my breasts."

"It's your breasts."

"And if it were, what do you propose I do…bind them?"

I couldn't believe we were back on this subject again. Pam had dropped by, unannounced, and we were sitting in my living room, drinking the wine coolers she'd brought. People might not think anyone still drank wine coolers, but Pam did.

"Hey…" Her eyes gleamed.

"Oh, no. What in the world are you thinking about? Did I ever mention how I hate it whenever you get that particular look in your eye? I positively *hate it* whenever you get that look in your eye."

"Listen, Scarlett, believe it or not, there are days I don't completely love you, either. But this isn't about that."

"You're talking about talking me into binding my breasts, and it has absolutely nothing to do with the fact that there are times you don't completely love me?"

"Who said anything about binding your breasts?"

"Uh, *you* did," I said. "You said it that last time we were at the pool with T.B. and Delta and you said it again when we were shopping at Filene's."

"You must be mistaking me for someone else. I never said anything about binding your breasts. I mean, how gross. How geisha-y. How *Asia*."

"Now, there's a whole continent you don't completely love?"

"Put it like this—are you going to ever go there?"

I thought about my bank account; did some quick mental calculations. My bank account was actually in good shape, given my father had left me nearly as well off as he'd left my mom, but still: "Probably not."

"Me, neither. See what I mean? Why bother?"

The sad thing was, I did kind of see what she meant, which made me feel very small and very much like I was a part of what constituted the least attractive part of being born an American, like maybe I was still on the flag, but I was the star that had gotten mustard spilled on it at the baseball game or something. Know what I mean?

"Hello, Scarlett. Earth to Scarlett. Is anybody still at home?"

"Ouch," I said, fending her off. "You don't need to tap on the side of my brain like that."

"Maybe if you stayed with me, I wouldn't. But as T.B. always likes to say, 'You *does* like to wander.'"

Somehow, hearing Pam mimic T.B. never seemed the same as when I did it or when Delta did it, especially since we knew T.B. hammed it up for us, anyway. And in Delta's case, she wasn't exactly mimicking. Regardless, T.B.'s voice coming out of Pam's mouth seemed just plain *wrong* somehow, making me feel like I used to feel when I was a kid and I'd run into a teacher in some out-of-school place like the grocery store or the town pool or whatever and I'd think to myself, "What's wrong with this picture?" only to answer my own question: "Everything."

So, yes, everything was wrong with T.B.'s words, real or mock, coming out of Pam, but, like with those wandering teachers who wouldn't stay where they belonged, it was nothing I could articulate to other human beings, certainly nothing I could ever properly articulate well enough to still sound sane.

"Well, Pam," I said, finally returning to her definition of Earth, "if you could ever just once tell me what it is you're thinking from start to finish, it might make it easier for me not to get distracted or even completely lost in the details."

"Do I need to keep spelling out in so many words that nothing I'm about to suggest has anything remotely to do with binding your breasts?"

I reflected for a moment. "Yes," I finally decided, "you do need to keep spelling it out in so many words. Until we reach a point in this conversation where at least five minutes have passed without the words 'binding' and 'breasts' appearing together in the same sentence, you absolutely do need to keep spelling out in so many words that you're not going to suggest that."

"Fine." She looked at her watch, started timing herself.

"This is what I've been trying to suggest, if you'd only just let me get the words out."

"Yes?"

"Except for the breast-binding part, how would you feel about giving me your looks for a while?"

16

"Who *are* you—the devil?"

It'd taken me longer than the five minutes Pam was supposed to be timing her success at not simultaneously using "breast" and "binding" in the same sentence—a success that had turned out to be a complete failure, I might point out, as evidenced by that last question of hers.

"And, by the way," I added, "wasn't having me moderate my appearance what we've been doing all along here?"

I don't know why I was so bugged exactly. Maybe it was simply that I'd never felt she'd voiced her idea, her plan, in such cold terms.

"No, I'm not the devil," she said, answering my first question and ignoring my second. "I'm your friend. I'm trying to help you find out if people like you merely for what you look like and not who you are. Besides, what kind of a devil would offer you a deal to make yourself look worse? It seems to me, that all the devils I've ever read about only make people deals that will make them look better."

"Yes—" I tried to sound sage and mystically in-the-know, but only succeeded in sounding like a complete and utter ass, even to my own ears "—but you might be the cleverest devil of all, the devil that does the exact opposite of what all other devils have ever done so that no one will ever suspect that you're the devil, and not just any devil, but the real one, the tricky one, which is what you are, the realest and the trickiest."

"Whoa, you really need to stop watching the same supernatural shows that all of those preteen girls get hooked on, Scarlett." She held up her hands defensively, looking like she was going to go for the garlic next. "Watching them like you do is really starting to turn you into some kind of flake."

She was my Default Best Friend. You'd think she'd have known I didn't watch those shows.

"Oh." I hands-on-hipsed her. "And, like, suggesting that an American woman compromise what looks she has is such a completely *un*flakey thing to do?"

"Relatively speaking."

"We can talk like this all day, going in circles, can't we?"

"Pretty much."

"Any time you want to start explaining…"

"Any time you want to start listening…"

"We're doing it again."

"Yeah, but you started it."

"Did not."

"Did too."

"Did not."

"Did too."

"Omigod! Sometimes, I don't even know which one of us is talking anymore!"

Pam gently—very gently, for her—removed my hands from over my ears. "That person—" she wince-smiled "—that person who just screamed? That person was *you*, Scarlett."

Is it possible to feel both mollified and mortified at the same time? "Thanks for clearing that up," I said.

"Don't mention it."

17

I wasn't sure if it was Pam's idea or my idea, or if maybe it was simply me domino-reacting to Pam's ideas but Pam and I had decided to switch places in life by switching faces.

Well, sort of.

"You be nuts," said T.B., seeing my haircut, glasses and new clothes for the first time, and hearing Pam's Official Plan, as she'd finally spelled it out for me during her impromptu visit to my home.

"She be right," added Delta.

"You both be annoying," said Pam, sounding completely wrong somehow, and prompting me to say, "I wish we all be stop talking like this. It's giving me a *Fat Albert* headache."

We were all seated on the floor around the coffee table at Delta's, site for that month's edition of our book club.

For a few months, after Pam had initially introduced me to T.B. and Delta, they'd both taken to attending the once-a-month book-discussion group that I was moderator for at the library. Pam had been an attendee for some time and she pulled the other two in. This made it nice for me, since it kept the numbers up and made the program look like one that was worth the library maintaining, which was further nice for me since I preferred to spend a portion of my hours preparing for that rather than staring endlessly at Mr. Weinerman. But a few months into it, the glow had worn off. Oh, it wasn't anything so mundane as them finding my discussions too mundane. I mean, really: how could such a thing be possible? No, rather, it had to do with the fact that the library forum wasn't fulfilling the function that we all wanted in a book club together: a reason to meet other than specifically for food or drink, where we could spend five minutes pretending to be literary and then spend the rest of the time talking about our usual girl stuff, the group feeling self-satisfied in having engaged in a communally cultural activity. So we spun off from the library group (which I still moderated).

That night, we'd discussed Anita Diamant's *The Red Tent*—Delta's choice since she was this month's host—for five rip-roaring literary minutes, and now we were back to our favorite topics: us, men, life, and how to be satisfied with any and all combinations of those three.

Delta was the only one of our merry little foursome who had ever taken on multiple marriages and kids. The marriage part was now a dead issue for her, two of her three long-gone exes being card-carrying members of that widening circle of men known as deadbeat dads. True, with Delta's legal talents, she might have run them to earth and demanded some kind of support, but as she so wisely put it, exhibiting a hard-won wisdom that her twin pigtails belied, "Sure, a person can try to get blood from a stone, but whyever would you want to bother? A stone with blood in it, on the other hand—now, that'd be the kind of man I could still do something with."

If the marriages were a permanent thing of the past, the two children they had produced were still permanent things of the present.

A half-century ago, Tennessee Williams would have called Mush and Teenie no-necked monsters, and his depiction would have been wholly accurate. The no-necked part was a result of regular consumption of the standard American child's neo-diet of a super-sized Big Mac, fries and milk-shake combination; I cast no aspersions on the notion of body fat in general by relating this, but rather, I'm merely pointing out that they were already well on the road— through no witting choice of their own—to becoming part of a sad national statistic. Mush was exactly what his name stated, while Teenie was anything but. As to the monster part, trust me on this: they just were. And that simple fact— that they were in fact monsters—made it a little difficult for them to come across as sympathetic characters to me, never mind the fact that so much that was awful about them had been created within them by events and circumstances over which they'd had no control.

Plus, any time we were all over at Delta's, which we certainly did all try to avoid, they were always underfoot.

"Let go of my Lego!" yelled Mush.

"Uh-uh," countered Teenie, snatching what little hold he still had on it out of his reach before somehow managing to *squeeze* herself between T.B. and me, and then *squeeze* herself under the coffee table. "The only way I'll let go of this Lego is if I decide to shove it up your butt!"

Ah, children.

Okay, so maybe it's just possible that those of us who have never *squeezed* a child out of our bodies, or adopted or made one in a test tube or whatever, don't have the accumulated natural sympathy necessary to see the charm in a sentence that includes the words *Lego, shove* and *butt,* all arranged in the worst possible order. Delta, on the other hand, having *squeezed* these particular children out, saw things differently.

"Ain't they just the cutest little things whenever they do like this?" she asked with the absent air of a mother who, hoping to get something done for an hour, informs her kids that it's okay to play in the street so long as they remember to keep an eye out for cars.

"Yeah, real cute," said T.B., who sounded as though she really meant it, until Teenie, still under the table, bit down on T.B.'s gold-painted toenail, giving the toe beneath the nail a healthy bite in the process and caused T.B. to shriek, "Ah, son of a bitch! That goddamned little Teenie bit my toe!"

Even Delta couldn't let this one slide by. "Teenie! Get your butt out from under that table!" Now, we all knew where Teenie had gotten her curious grasp of the English language from. "What the hell do you mean by biting your Aunt T.B.'s toe for?"

Teenie looked a little puzzled; maybe even she herself wasn't completely certain of why that impulse had come over her. "Uh," she asked her mother, "because I wanted to see if black people's toes taste any different than Mush's stupid dirty ones?"

"Shit, Teenie! That ain't no reason to *bite* her! My God. You think my friends come over to see me so that they can get *bit* by you just because you take it into your head to perform some kind of weird *sociology* project on them? If you'd wanted to know such a stupid thing, you could have just asked one of us, and we'd've told you. Of course black people's toes taste different from Mush's toes. They taste *better.* Hell, everybody's toes taste better than Mush's, that ain't no big mystery. Now, then, say you're sorry to—"

"Hah!" yelled Mush, having snatched back the Lego from Teenie while Teenie was busy being chewed out by Delta. He raced, as best as he could race, toward his bedroom door, shouting over his shoulder to Teenie, "The only way you'll ever see this Lego again, is if you're willing to reach up my butt to get it back, 'cause that's where I'm gonna be hiding it from you!"

The over-the-shoulder-shout technique soon proved to be a tactical error on Mush's part, when the side of his face crashed into his own doorjamb.

Five minutes, one washcloth filled with ice cubes and a single admonishment to "stay in this room until my friends are gone and I don't care if y'all kill each other in here because if you even think about coming back out into that living room and interrupting us again I'm going to be up both your butts" later, Delta was back among us.

"Lord," she said, flopping down on the couch, wineglass in hand, "y'all have no idea what it's like to have kids."

Uh, yeah, we do, I wanted to say but didn't. *We got a real good idea from watching you. And what we see makes us think maybe we'll all procreate like…uh…let me see, now…never?*

Delta eyed me suspiciously. "Did you just say something, Scarlett?"

"Me? Uh, no."

"Huh. I don't know why, I could've sworn you just said something about having kids. Oh, well." She shrugged it off, tilting her head to rest her neck on the back of the couch, two fingers massaging the inner corners of her eyes. "Never mind."

"Well, you sure do make it look easy," T.B. spoke softly, hoping perhaps to give Delta the necessary confidence to soldier on, even though T.B. was the one who was going to need a rabies shot after tonight.

"Oh, right," Pam snorted. "Nobody could make being those kids' mother look easy."

"Pam!" I cautioned.

"Well, it's true," she insisted.

Well, of course it was *true,* but *still—*

But Delta waved me and T.B. down before we could stage a credible defense of her offspring.

"Pam's right, you know," she said.

"Now," T.B. said in an effort to lighten the moment, "there're two words—*Pam* and *right*—a person doesn't hear uttered in the same sentence every day."

"Fuck you," seethed Pam.

"Fuck you right back, Pam," smiled T.B. "Oops," she added, "I just made it twice in one day."

"Can y'all save your natural animosity for one another for a day when I'm not in the middle of a personal crisis?" Delta asked. "I'm *trying* to talk to y'all about my *life* here."

"Sorry," said T.B. "You were saying? I believe it was something about Pam being *right?*"

"Well, she is," said Delta. "You know, when you get pregnant, nobody ever really tells you, in any way you could ever possibly grasp, just how hard it's gonna be to *squeeze* a baby out into the world."

There was that squeeze *word again,* I thought.

Delta went on. "And then, once you've had the baby, nobody ever really tells you just how hard those squeezed babies are going to make the rest of your life. Oh, I don't mean that it never makes me happy. Hell, being Teenie and Mush's mama makes me happier than anything else I do in this life—"

It *does?* I translated the looks Pam and T.B. and I flashed to one another.

"—but it's harder than anything else in my life, too. And you know what the hardest part is?"

Removing Legos from their butts? was what I wanted to ask but didn't.

"Dating. That's what. You have no idea how hard it is to meet some nice man, some man I think I might *like,* have him ask me out, tell him I was already married once before, have a good time, want to get to know him better, invite him back here, finally get up the nerve to tell him I've got two kids from three previous marriages, have him tell me that's just fine, and then…and then…have him meet… *them.*"

"I can imagine," said Pam.

"No," said Delta, and her gaze was rock steady, "you can't. You really and truly cannot even begin to imagine."

Despite the fact that it was no fun seeing the usually bubbly Delta feeling so dejected, it was nice, for once, to have the conversation shifted away from how nuts I was to be doing what I was doing, this plan Pam had concocted. Or was it my idea, too? See? It was too confusing to think about and a relief to be thinking about something else.

"Hey!" Suddenly, Delta was looking much happier. In fact, she looked so happy as she looked at me, I could swear her pigtails were dancing. "I've got an idea, Scarlett. If you ever *really* want to test if some beau really wants you for yourself, you could always borrow Mush and Teenie!"

Well, *she* thought it was hysterical.

18

Best Girlfriend really was worried about me.

"I don't like these turns your life is taking," she said during our regular Sunday-night phone conversation. "And I really don't like the idea of Pam having so much control over you."

This was an old story: Pam hated the very idea of Best Girlfriend and Best Girlfriend was eternally suspicious of Pam. Oh, to be loved by too many women...

But if Best Girlfriend was worried about me, I was worried about Best Girlfriend, too. When we'd first got on the phone, she'd mentioned that she'd been feeling in crisis lately. She wasn't sure if photography was the right profession for her.

"But it's what you've wanted," I said, "ever since we were children."

"People change," she said. "Plus, I've realized it's not everything I thought it was going to be."

"How so?"

"It's hard to say. But I think that, sometimes, getting your dream is worse than not getting it."

"How can you say that?"

"Uh, because I just did?" But then she must have decided that sarcasm wasn't the most effective approach here. "It's kind of like, as long as you have the dream, you have something to shoot for, you can keep telling yourself, 'Once I get X, I'll be a happy person. My life will be great.'"

"But then you get it—" I started.

"—and you're still not a happy person," she finished softly.

And then there are no excuses left. I was sure we both thought this, but neither of us had whatever it would have taken to speak the words aloud.

So when she started trying to shift the focus of our conversation on to me and Pam, naturally I rebelled.

"Can we not talk about me and my problems for once?" I said.

"Then what would we talk about?"

"You."

I heard her sigh. From hundreds upon hundreds of miles away, I heard her sigh.

"I'm just not *happy* anymore, Scarlett. I'm not happy with work. I'm not happy with Bob," she referred to the man she'd been living with for five years. "I'm just not *happy*. I'm thinking of moving."

"Where to?"

"I don't know. Maybe Canada?"

Best Girlfriend and I had been friends for what sometimes seemed like forever. Both being only children, it was more like we were each other's families than two people who shared no common blood.

Peculiarly enough, it was the only relationship I had in which the balance of power shifted in the other direction, meaning that Best Girlfriend was so drop-dead gorgeous that men literally fell at her feet. All through high school, all through college, I did fine for myself where guys were concerned, except for when she was around. When she was around, it was like guys couldn't push me out of the way fast enough to get to her. Well, except for the ones who, as part of their strategy, became my friends so they'd have an excuse to hang out with her.

Did this bother me? Did I resent it?

No, I honestly thought I never had. After all, I thought Best Girlfriend was the most amazing female who ever lived. I mean, I'd made her Best Girlfriend after all, right? And if I thought that, then why shouldn't everyone else?

But, yes, it could sometimes make a person feel just a little insecure, like a dying star trying to hang out with the Northern Lights. Sometimes, I wanted to say to some of those guys, "Hello! Don't you see another girl here? Don't you see how great I am? Besides, Best Girlfriend is so busy…" So, I guess, in a way, having grown up to be something of a Northern Lights myself, I could kind of understand what bugged Pam so much.

But I still believed—I had to believe, despite the niggling doubts Pam instilled in me—that people liked me for me, just like once upon a time people had liked Best Girlfriend for Best Girlfriend.

19

Quitting a job that you no longer love, a job in which you are required to be with Mr. Weinerman forty hours a week, is just as easy as it sounds. Having taken advantage of the four weeks' worth of vacation that I still had coming to me, was I going to devote that time to finding a new job?

Nah. I wasn't worried about that. For some reason, any profession that has to do with reading can always make room for one more person who is good at what she does.

I was going to use all of that free time to work on becoming as much not like me in appearance as I possibly could. If not a female version of Mr. Weinerman, I could at least make myself a little less good-looking, a little less in shape.

I would become a sloucher.

Okay, so maybe there wasn't much I could do about the spectacular breasts, but I was determined to level the playing field between Pam and me, to tilt the scales of dating justice more firmly in her favor, so that, at the end of the day, I could still prove that it was *me* and not my looks that attracted other people.

After I was done with that, *then* I could worry about finding a new job.

"Frump," Pam declared, holding up a brown wool skirt.

"Frumpier," she said with delight two minutes later, lofting a beige shirtwaist.

"Frumpiest," she concluded triumphantly. The object in question? Something that looked suspiciously like a housedress.

"I can't believe it," I said.

"I know." Pam shook her head, the disillusionment apparent. "Who would have suspected something like *this*—" she indicated the unlikely garment "—could be found in a place like *this?*"

"Oh, I'm not talking about that," I pooh-poohed her.

"What then?"

"It's just that, I can't believe what I'm doing here. I can't believe I keep letting you take me out to purposely select clothes that will make me look less attractive. I mean, isn't that the opposite of normal female behavior or something?"

Even though I'd said that I wanted to prove that it was me and not my looks that attracted people, to purposefully be seeking out the frumpiest… What can I say? Not only did I have murky motives, but I was fickle.

She shrugged her shoulders. "Not if you're self-destructive, it's not."

"But I'm not."

"But you do want to prove some kind of point."

"Wait a second here. Isn't it *your* point that you're having me see if I can disprove?"

She shrugged her shoulders again. "Details."

My life had become some sort of weird Halloween party where I was seeking to costume myself as anything *but* the fairy princess.

There was an ad in the paper from Bethel Library, looking for an entry-level librarian. Bethel is a small town bordering on Danbury and I figured this was the chance I needed to start somewhere fresh.

But how to keep the person I'd been at Danbury Library and the person I was going to be at Bethel Library, provided they gave me the job, separate? After all, if I gave Danbury as a reference, the person Danbury described would be far different from the person Bethel would be getting.

Delta had the solution.

"I'll doctor your transcripts," she offered.

"You can do that?" I asked.

"Sure," she said, between keeping Mush from killing Teenie, or maybe it was between keeping Teenie from killing Mush. "Just give me your school transcripts. I'll just change the dates, so it looks like you just got your degree."

"But wouldn't that be, um, deceptive?"

"Well, if y'all want to be *technical* about it."

"Can you really distinguish between technical and non-technical deception?"

"Oh, who the hell knows?" Her attention was momentarily deflected by: "Teenie Beauchamp! Stop pouring pepper on your brother's Pop-Tart. It ain't nice." Then she turned back to me with a shrug. "Look at it this way. In actuality, Bethel'll be getting a librarian with twelve years' experience, but they'll be thinking they're getting someone at entry level and, unfortunately, will probably pay you same.

How bad off does that make them? Actually, sounds like a pretty good deal to me."

When she put it like that...

"So, I'll kind of be offering them the librarian deal of the century?" I asked.

"Exactly!"

I suppose it should have given me some financial pause to be considering taking a job at entry level, but I did have that money my dad had left me and the job was full-time, so there would be good benefits.

"There's just one other thing," I said.

This was when I told her about wanting to change my name to fit my new identity. It just seemed, oh, I don't know, *fitting*.

"So," she said, finally grabbing the pepper from Teenie, "you're going to go from being Scarlett Jane Stein to being who exactly?"

I'd given this a lot of thought.

I took a deep breath. "Lettie Shaw," I said.

Well, at least she didn't laugh at me. She laughed at something Mush was doing to get back at Teenie. At least, I *think* she was laughing at Mush and not me.

"You're going to go from being a Scarlett to being a Lettie?" But then she looked at my new hair, my glasses, my clothes. "Yeah, I guess Lettie sounds about right now. But *Shaw?* What the hell's your Jewish mother going to say? You are going to go on being Jewish, aren't you?"

"I hadn't really worked that out yet," I said, and I hadn't. "I mean, I'm still going to go on being Jewish. But Mom? Oh, hell. I'll just tell her that the name change has to do with meeting men. She'll be all for it then."

"You still haven't said. *Shaw?*"

"Oh, that. It's a nod to George Bernard. I know what I'm doing is the opposite of *Pygmalion,* but, somehow, it's still the same thing."

Feeling a little like I was making a deal with a counterfeiter, I got my transcripts and left them with Delta, who promised they'd be ready the next day, in time for my interview at Bethel Library.

"You're a little, um, *experienced*—" I was sure the director wanted to say *old* "—to have only just decided on a career in Library Science, aren't you?"

"My mother always said I was a late bloomer," I said.

He eyed me, obviously concluding that my mother was right, about everything.

We were in the Bethel Library, of course, that beautiful white building with black shutters that sits on the corner of Greenwood Avenue—Bethel's version of Main Street— and Library Place. I loved the old building: its large white pillars out front, its brick walkways. It was so different from where I'd come from.

The director, Roland James, looked to be only about five years or so older than me, with fading blond looks that had an "I coulda been a contenduh" air about them. He also wore glasses, not all that different from my own, and a lean body that was either the gift of metabolism or the result of some serious effort,

Once upon a time, I would have expected a man in his position to give me a different once-over than this critical one he was doing. Sure, it wasn't politically correct, that I'd become accustomed to men in power pleasantly ogling me, but what one is accustomed to and political correctness do not always go hand in hand.

"Perhaps," he said, "but I was hoping to get someone with a bit more experience. Uh, I mean," he amended, obviously recalling his earlier remark, "*practical* experience. It's so much more trouble, training someone from scratch."

"But I thought this job was entry level," I said.

"Well," he looked embarrassed, "the pay is…"

"I'm a quick learner," I said, feeling as though I were selling myself.

"A late bloomer *and* a quick learner?" he laughed. "Maybe if you'd learned quickly first, you wouldn't have bloomed so late."

I laughed at myself right along with him, hoping that amiability would be a selling point. Then, for good measure, I crossed my legs.

Well, shameless as it is, it had always worked for me in the past.

But I'd forgotten that I'd become A Wearer of Long and Shapeless Garments. So my crossing of my still-in-great-shape-for-thirty-nine legs didn't even cause a ripple in the office. The man didn't even look up from his perusal of my falsified records.

"Well," he finally said, perhaps deciding a woman like me couldn't possibly do any harm, or, more likely, that the town would save a lot of money by hiring someone like me instead of someone experienced, "when can you start?"

"Whenever you want?" I offered, feeling surprisingly meek.

"Good. You can start in Circ, see how it works out."

20

To go with my new job, I needed a new place to live.

"Isn't this, um, taking this thing a bit too seriously?" T.B. had asked when I'd told my friends about it.

"I don't know," I'd said. "I've already qualified for Loon of the Year, so why stop now? Besides, I never really felt like I lived in the condo, no matter how long I'd lived there, you know? Why not start fresh?"

As the Realtor showed me places in Bethel, I wondered what kind of place Lettie Shaw would buy.

"No, definitely not a condo," I told the Realtor, Sue Buchanan, when she pulled up in front of one.

"All right," she said, in a tone of voice that indicated she thought I was the stupidest woman who ever lived. "But condos are really hot right now and they represent the best value for a person living alone."

A person living alone. That had always been me. Sometimes, I thought it always would be me.

Sue had taken my future salary, my current savings and the projected earnings from the sale of my Danbury condo, plugged it all into her calculator, added some more mumbo jumbo, and decided I could actually afford quite a bit of house.

So, of course, she tried to show me quite a bit of house.

"This is really more than I want to spend," I pointed out, looking at the mini-McMansion she showed me.

"What?" she sniffed. "You mean you'd like some pin money left over?"

"Maybe." It was getting late in the day. If I was going to get home in time to change for services with my mother, this being the eve of Rosh Hashanah, I was going to have to move quickly. When I said as much, Sue's eyes brightened with recognition.

"Oh! You're *Jewish!* I guess the Shaw name confused me. This explains everything."

"Excuse me?"

"Well, you do seem to be savvy about numbers…."

It really was late in the day, too late for me to find a new Realtor before sundown, or I'd have fired her sorry ass.

"Given that you're so, er, *finance-conscious,*" she said, "I've got one more place I think you'll want to see."

The one more place turned out to be a tiny house, more like a cottage really, set far back from the road on a half acre of land. Tall trees lined the property, and the house itself was made of naturally stained shingles and had peaked roofs and a covered porch held up by four wooden posts. As we walked through, I saw that on the lower level, there was a cozy living room with a stone fireplace, in front of which was a wooden rocking chair, a Mexican throw over the back. There was also a small dining room with a Shaker dining set and an even tinier country kitchen.

Natural wood stairs and banister led up to a recessed loft bedroom on the second floor. The design of the bedroom echoed the southwestern accent of the Mexican throw down below, with a big ash bed that looked as though it had been handmade, covered in a spread of aqua and coral. Off the bedroom, there was a small but perfectly modern bathroom with a skylight over the marble tub.

I wondered: would Lettie Shaw live in a place like this?

Lettie would, I decided, she really would.

"It's charming!" I said.

"Oh, it is, it really is," Sue said eagerly, seeing the end in sight. "It's the perfect place for someone like you to live."

I didn't dare think what she meant by that.

"There's just one catch," she said.

"Catch?"

"The owner's in Europe for a year, working on a book. He's not sure he definitely wants to sell it. So, for now, it's just a rental with a possible option to buy at the end of the year."

I felt so disappointed. Having decided to change my life, I wanted to make a total change.

"But I was looking to buy something. Why would you show me a rental?"

"Because it's *perfect* for you!" Sue had gone back to being perky. "And besides, you know how writers are."

I did?

"In a year," she said, "he'll probably have fallen in love with Florence so much that he won't want to come back to Bethel. He'll probably sell long-distance!"

She was right about one thing: it was perfect for me. It was certainly perfect for Lettie.

"So all the furniture stays?" I asked.

"Definitely," she said.

I looked at the walls, which were kind of dingy. The one thing wrong with the place was that it could really use a fresh coat of paint on all the interiors.

"But what if I wanted to paint it?" I said. "The owner probably wouldn't like me changing anything, not until he's completely sure he doesn't want to move back here again."

"Oh, sure you can paint it." She dismissed my concerns. "He's a writer. You know how they are—so oblivious. If he ever comes back home again, he probably won't even notice the difference."

21

"Where did you get that dress? I love it. Maybe I'll go to the same place to get one."

"Shush, Mom, the rabbi is talking."

We were in the United Jewish Center on Deer Hill Avenue in Danbury, the pale blue walls and white trim of the sanctuary providing a feeling of, well, *sanctuary.*

"I just love these changes you've made," my mother said.

Apparently, there was to be no shushing her.

"Oh, Scarlett," she said, "you look like *such* a librarian."

I was outraged. "I *am* a librarian!"

"Yes, I know. But now you look so…*Amish.*"

"And that's good?"

"*Shush,* the rabbi is talking."

When I was growing up, my mother had not been much for synagogue, only going on the High Holy Days. But ever since my father had died, she'd taken to coming nearly every weekend, claiming that it gave her some kind of peace she couldn't find anywhere else.

"And the little food get-togethers they have right after services, with those minipastries and desserts? Yum," she always said. "Where do you think they find those tiny éclairs?"

Of course, I still only went on the High Holy Days. And, even then, I only went because it would have hurt her feelings if I didn't. Sure, I still considered myself Jewish. But, for me, it wasn't tied to anything like regular attendance; I'd been Jewish all my life and, for me, I couldn't see ever being anything else.

Naturally, going every week as she did, my mother had social relationships, however tenuous, with all of the regulars. Naturally, only going a handful of times a year like I did, my relationships with people there were secondary; myriad people would say to Mom, "It's so nice, Scarlett coming with you each year," and she'd reply, as I stood mutely by, "Scarlett's a good girl."

So why should this year be any different?

"Scarlett?" the rabbi peered at me closely, questioningly, having greeted my mother first, as the congregation all gathered for little plastic cups filled with Manischewitz and apples and honey in the little room off the main synagogue.

"Er, no," my mother hastily corrected him. "This is Scarlett's cousin from out of town, Lettie Shaw."

I couldn't believe this: my mother was lying to the rabbi!

"Shaw," he said, "Shaw…That doesn't sound…?"

"Of course it's not Jewish. It's from her father's side of the family. You know—" and here she leaned in closer to him so she could whisper behind her hand "—intermarriage."

When I'd told T.B. about the name change, she'd said, "You want to change from your cooler-than-cool name to something that sounds like you got left over from the Grand Ole Opry? That's your problem. But don't expect me to be calling you Lettie. That dog just won't hunt with me."

"Are you sure you guys are lawyers?" I'd asked her and Delta. "You talk weirder than Anna Nicole Smith, even if the accents are different."

"We're having great careers—" Delta had smiled "—we really are."

Of course, I'd had to tell my mother, too.

"Why in *hell* would you want to do that?" Delta had asked.

"I be wanting to do that," I'd said, "because she is my mother. What if she needed me for some kind of emergency or something, and she called up the Bethel Library, only to have them tell her that they'd never heard of Scarlett Jane Stein?"

"Or," Delta had said, "what if she came by your new house once you find one and move in, started going through the mail on your table while you were in the bathroom, and concluded from the name on the envelopes that either something weird was going on or you were living with a woman she'd never seen?"

"That too," I'd conceded.

As I'd predicted earlier, when presented with my new name as being a way somehow for me to meet a man and settle down—not that I had a clue as to what I meant by that—my mother had been thrilled with the idea of the name change.

"Well, of course," she'd said, "it makes perfect sense. As Scarlett Jane Stein you've been a complete romantic washout, so why not shake things up?"

Why not shake things up, indeed. But I'd never expected her to…

"Mother!" I hiss-whispered, grabbing on to her arm as the rabbi excused himself to go talk to other congregants. "You just lied to your rabbi!"

"Lied, schmied. If being Lettie Shaw finally gets you married in the end, he'll dance with me at your wedding."

I wished there were a way I could convey to her how uncomfortable her talk of marriage and a wedding was making me.

Instead, I knocked back another plastic cup of Manischewitz. What it lacked in refined taste, it made up for in alcohol content.

But, I had to remind myself before reaching for a third, I wasn't a kid anymore. No one would think it funny if I got tipsy and started dancing the hora by myself in the corner.

"Oh, Scarlett," my mother said. "I mean, *Lettie*—" she winked "—I can't wait to see your new home once you move in, meet all the new people where you're going to work." She was practically clapping her hands like a seal.

"What's so great about it?" I was feeling surly and my words were starting to slur a bit. Maybe just the two glasses were getting to me?

"I think it's *wonderful* the way you're reinventing yourself. It's just like Madonna or Fergie or something. Everyone should do it at least once in their lifetime. Maybe *I* should—"

"No, Mom—" I stopped her, scared of what she might transform into should she also try to reinvent herself "—you're perfect already, so why would you ever want to change?"

I thought I saw her eyes mist over. "Oh, that's so sweet," she said. "Thank you, dear. But isn't this great? Look how differently people are treating you here this year than on previous years."

It was then I noticed that, since the rabbi had moved off, no one else had approached us. In previous years, I'd been the centerpiece for the matchmakers, every yenta in sight trying to persuade "Scarlett" to take the number of her son, her grandson, even a few ex-husbands! But now…

"See what I mean?" my mother said. "Isn't this better?"

"Well, it's better for me," I said. "It's certainly quieter. But how is this better for you? I thought your lifelong dream, because you keep telling me it is, is to see me settled."

"Of course. But who can hear Mr. Right with all of the noise that was going on before?"

"Oy."

"Oy? You never say oy."

"Can we stop with the Mr. Right, Mom?"

"Oh, look," she said, leaning in, "but don't look!"

"How am I supposed to—"

"David Gladstein is looking this way."

"But I can't marry David Gladstein! Then I'd be Scarlett Jane Stein-Gladstein!"

"Don't be ridiculous. You'd be Lettie Shaw-Gladstein."

"Oh," I said. "Well, that's certainly much better. Now, which one is David Gladstein again?"

"Over there," she said with a nod.

How could I have forgotten? David Gladstein and I had gone to Hebrew school together, although he'd been two years ahead. Everyone, parents and children, had known who David Gladstein was: if the rabbi needed someone to help out on the pulpit, as David had indeed done just that day, he called on David Gladstein; if a kid needed an ounce of pot for the weekend, they also knew who to call. Extended pot usage having robbed him of any kind of maturation regarding his personality, David Gladstein was kind of like a yeshiva version of one of the more stupid permutations—Vinnie Barbarino, perhaps?—of John Travolta. Naturally, none of the parents had ever caught on, decades later still thinking he was the greatest catch a girl could find.

In previous years, he'd ignored me on the High Holy Days, because, well, I was too good at stringing words together.

But now?

Now, apparently, he didn't recognize me as the woman I'd been before. Now he was eyeing me across the apples and honey like I was the hottest gefilte fish in the sea.

My mother, in her excitement, grabbed on to my arm. I really wished she'd stop doing that; my arm was starting to hurt. "I think he's coming over here!" she cried with joy.

Oy.

22

To look at my mother now, with her commitment to polyester and her love of my new asexual wardrobe, you'd never guess that she was once a floozie.

Well, maybe *floozie* is too strong a word. Let's just agree then to call Mom a *party girl*.

Long before she'd met my dad, she'd been declared the prettiest girl New Fairfield had ever produced. Many felt that she should have gone the Hollywood route—which would have made her the Meg Ryan of New Fairfield before Meg Ryan was ever the Meg Ryan of Bethel—but being elected Homecoming Queen had proved to be the extent of her aspirations regarding any kind of public arena.

But she did love the parties she was endlessly invited to, loved being the prettiest girl in whatever room she ever found herself in, loved having men fight over her.

It's always kind of weird, thinking of your mother as the kind of woman men once fought over.

Once Mom married Dad, whom she was as madly in love with as he was with her—I'm nearly sure of this—people expected her to settle down a bit. After all, her friends had all settled down with the men they'd married.

But Mom wasn't ready to settle down. She was only twenty when she got married and she liked the hippie clothes that soon burst on the fashion scene (even if she couldn't pick Vietnam out on a map), she liked all the blue makeup (even though electric-blue mascara looks silly on a brown-eyed woman) and she liked the parties where the lines were blurred as to who came with whom (okay, maybe I wasn't there, so I don't really know, but I'll bet I'm right).

Dad, on the other hand, wore suits every day and hated those parties, which he could only be dragged to because he was so besotted with Mom. I mean, of course he hated them—the man sold insurance! (This was also why he was smart enough to be so heavily insured that, when he died, Mom was so well taken care of that she'd been able to afford the house she'd always wanted on the lake.)

Anyway, I remember them going off to those parties, Dad dragging his feet all the way and Mom all merry, and then, lying in bed later, hearing them come home, always arguing, the arguments always being about what men Mom had been talking to for too long, standing too close to, what men she'd disappeared for a while with.

For years, I tried to tell myself that Dad was just a jealous guy; that he was seeing things that simply weren't there.

But somehow, deep down inside, I knew that wasn't true. Somehow, I knew that Mom had cheated on Dad—and that she'd done so repeatedly. She'd cheated repeatedly because she liked the attention, couldn't give up on her idea of herself as being the prettiest girl who every guy wanted.

Naturally, I never discussed any of this, either with Mom or Dad, but I was always aware of his love and his pain. I would have liked it if things could have been somehow different for him.

Of course, in rebellion against her, I'd grown up makeup free, almost daring the world to like me without the gimmicks. But somehow, along the way, I'd come to rely on gimmicks, even if I'd been unaware of them, even if all my gimmicks amounted to was a contact lens here, a high heel there.

And how did Mom go from being the party girl to being the chicken-soup wielding maven of practical shoes she now was? Who the hell knows?

I'd tried to ask her once, not long after Dad died, but all she would sadly say was: "You know, Scarlett, sometimes you just get tired of being the same person after a while. Everyone needs change."

I had my own theory, albeit a warped one: without the audience of my dad, who was the best audience she ever had, it was no longer any fun playing dress up.

Needless to say, between Mom and Best Girlfriend, I'm conflicted on the subject of women's appearances, both in terms of what it does to the women themselves and what it does to the world. I'm certainly conflicted about my own appearance.

Two hundred years from now, some anthropologist will dig me up and wonder, "Was she bothered by having great breasts? Was she proud of them?"

Okay, I know that will never happen; I'm going to be cremated. But still, somehow, they're worthwhile questions, even if I may never know the answers.

23

I was shopping the Super Stop & Shop in Danbury, looking for cake mixes with which to christen my new home. The Queen of England may use champagne over the bow to break in a new battleship, but we girls from Danbury know that it's Duncan Hines chocolate cake mix and Betty Crocker Ready-to-Spread Instant Buttercream Frosting that make up the real blessing of choice.

Of course, I wasn't a Danbury girl anymore, I was now a Bethel girl, and so should more properly have been shopping my new local store, but old habits die hard. Just ask any politician.

So there I was, looking at the back of the box to see how much oil and how many eggs I'd need, since it had been so long since I'd pulled out my limited culinary talents to make a cake from mix that I'd forgot, when I heard an allergic sneeze and looked up to see a familiar head of hair over the bow of my cart.

Old-fashioned pageboy of black hair, pretty brown eyes: it was Sarah, the girl who'd given me the chicken pox, only now her complexion was cleared up, she was wearing the red-and-blue school uniform of a coed Catholic school in Danbury, including navy knee socks, and, lordy-lordy, she now had hairy knees.

She sneezed again. Weird how in a world where only a few people used to suffer from allergies, now nearly everyone I saw had problems with them. But of course there wasn't anything wrong with the environment.

"Gezundheit, Sarah," I said.

She shot me a quick look, confusion on her face.

"It means God bless you." I answered her look.

"Not that," she said warily, looking around for the safety of other shoppers as if I might be about to snatch her. "How did you know my name?"

"From Danbury Library," I said, hopefully allaying her fears. "Your mother brought you in over the summer to get books from your reading list."

She still looked puzzled.

"I helped you with the list," I said. "I recommended some books for you."

"You?" She looked shocked.

"Me."

She looked at me more closely and I knew what she was seeing: the much shorter hair, cut weird, the glasses.

"Huh," she said, "I'd have never recognized you. But why did you…?"

"Hey, I see you got over the chicken pox!" I said, not wanting to answer what I knew her question would be— why had I deliberately sabotaged my own looks?—perhaps because I wasn't sure I even *could* answer it, not even to myself.

"Oh, yeah," she said, completely forgetting me and re-membering herself, just like any kid would. "It was awful!"

"Tell me about it," I said, trying to be companionable. "I caught it from you."

Now she looked horrified.

"But it's okay," I said, putting my hand on her arm. "Hon-est. It wasn't bad at all," I lied, "and it gave me a great ex-cuse to stay home from work for two weeks and watch TV."

"Hello, do we know you?" I heard the feminine voice first and then turned to see the woman I recognized as Sarah's mother, with the toddler she'd had in the library with her now in her arms. A part of me had been wondering who Sarah was with and where they'd gone to, since she wasn't old enough to be doing the family shopping alone. From the look of the diaper bag over her mother's shoulder and a slight whiff of something less than appetizing in the air, I guessed she and the toddler had needed to make an emer-gency trip to the Super Stop & Shop bathroom.

"I'm Lettie Shaw." I introduced myself to her, hand out-stretched, figuring she'd never known my old name, so I might as well introduce myself with the new one. "I helped you with Sarah's summer reading list at Danbury Library several weeks ago."

It was obvious that Sarah's mother, a once-pretty woman with brown hair and a tired smile, was as puzzled by my change in appearance as her daughter.

"Nancy Davis." She reluctantly shook my hand, as though whatever had made me suddenly look worse might be catching. Then she added brightly, "Those were great suggestions you gave Sarah. She loved the books. We'll have to come back and see you…"

"Oh, no," I cut her off. "I'm afraid I don't work there anymore. I'm at Bethel Library now."

"Oh, well…" Nancy Davis's voice trailed off as if there was nothing left for us to say.

I looked at Sarah. Damn! But with that black hair and those brown eyes, not to mention the hairy knees, she looked like a mini-me. She also looked like she could use a friend.

"Hey," I said to Sarah, "if you're ever in town…"

24

As I navigated my way through my new job, as I decorated my new home, I found myself constantly wondering: "What would Lettie do now? What would Lettie say about this? What would Lettie *want?*" It was weird, like there was more than one person living inside of me, or maybe like I was finally getting in touch with a part of myself that I hadn't even known existed before.

T.B. had offered to help me paint the dingy walls. Pam had claimed that paint fumes always made her queasy and Delta couldn't find anyone to stay with Mush and Teenie for an entire Sunday—no surprise there—so it had fallen to T.B. to be my sole partner in brushes.

"I like this sienna color you picked out for the dining room," said T.B., watching as I swirled the paint in the can. "Makes it feel like you're going to Italy without having to pay the plane fare."

"I don't know," I said. "Do you think the owner might

mind it being so dark, whenever he gets back from wherever he is?"

"Naw, I think he'll like it. Why wouldn't he?"

"I don't know," I looked around me at the dingy walls,
still the color of funky urine. "Maybe he likes the subway-
station look. I just figured that Lettie would like—"

"I gotta tell you, Scarlett, it creeps me right out, the way
you talk about Lettie like she's some kind of real person."

"I'm just trying to get into the spirit of things." I
shrugged, bending to dip my brush in the can, rising to put
the first neat stroke on the wall. What I couldn't admit aloud
to her was that Lettie had indeed become very real to me.
Mostly, I was curious as to what Lettie would be like, once
she completely became herself, and I also really did want to
know just exactly what Lettie wanted from the world.

"What'd you do last night?" I asked, hoping to deflect
conversation about my weird and sort-of fake life by talking about her real life.

"I went out with Al," she said.

I turned to look at her, but her back was to me as she
worked the other side of the room.

"You went out with Ex-Al *again?*" I asked. "What's up
with that? I swear, you've been out with him nearly every
weekend this month."

"He's safe," she said softly.

"Safe?"

"And fun. He's a lot of fun."

"So why'd you ever divorce him in the first place?"

"You know why—he was unpredictable and he made me
miserable."

"So now suddenly, what, he's changed his spots?"

"I don't know. It's different when you're married."

"I wouldn't know," I said, wondering idly if Lettie wanted to get married.

"Lucky you," she laughed.

"How's it different?"

"Tough to say. But it's like you start expecting your spouse to be someone other than who they are."

"So, you expecting Ex-Al to be a, I don't know, dependable husband sort of forced him into acting unpredictable?"

"Well, when you put it like that," she laughed. "But, yeah, in a way, yes."

"What are you talking about? You mean that what you wanted made him somehow feel like rebelling?"

"I don't know. 'Rebelling' is such a strong word."

"What then?"

"I think he just felt like he had to assert himself, to be seen."

"And to assert himself he had to make you miserable."

"It's not that simple, not that syllogistically 'if X, then Y.' Love's never that simple."

I nearly dropped my brush. "We're talking about *love* now? You don't think you'd marry Ex-Al again, do you?" I asked, thinking the absolute worst thing about that would be that I wouldn't have the fun of calling him Ex-Al anymore.

"Marriage? Who the hell's talking about marriage?"

"Then what?"

"I don't know."

I could have sworn she blushed.

"Maybe we'll just live together this time around," she said.

"Really? No shit?" I felt like the little dog scampering annoyingly around the big dog in the cartoon. "Do Pam and Delta know about this yet?"

"Who the hell knows if I'll do it or not, Scarlett? And you best not be talking to Pam or Delta about it. I'm not ready to have the harsh light of girlfriendship shining its nasty little glow on what I'm thinking about."

"I best won't tell them," I said, unable to prevent a smug smile from sneaking its way onto my lips. "I best keep your secret." Then, I started singsonging, "T.B. might be moving in with Ex-Al, T.B. might be..."

"And don't you be singsonging that schoolyard crap at me." She pointed her brush at me like it was a weapon, but I could see she was fighting back her own smile. "Besides, who are you to be laughing at someone else's weird life? Aren't you the one who's painting your house the colors you think will please some weird little alter ego in your head named Lettie?"

This was true.

"Just so long as those voices you're hearing don't go telling you to shoot somebody."

Just so long.

25

Getting used to being Lettie at home was somehow easier than getting used to being Lettie in my new job.

At home, it was somehow comforting, channeling Lettie, trying to figure out what kind of drapes she'd like to hang (lace curtains), what kind of food she'd like to eat (nothing too rich, but the occasional éclair was okay), what she liked to watch on television (surprisingly, or maybe not so much, a lot of Lifetime).

But work was harder.

The director insisted I call him Roland, which was fine since I was used to dealing on a first-name basis with anyone I worked with. But Roland insisted on looking at me—during the daily morning staff meetings or whenever I passed by his office on my way to the lunchroom or to fill out my time sheet—with a certain looking-straight-through-the-nonexistent-new-worker kind of air that was somewhat less fine. I was not yet used to men not reacting to me in a positive way, and his lack of any reaction to me was disconcerting, like I was some kind of tabula rasa, waiting for the world to write a more interesting story on me.

My friends had been right about one thing: the new women I worked with—and they were all women, save for Roland and Pete, a guy who worked part-time in Reference—were absolutely thrilled at how little training I needed. The first day on the job, when the person I was working with in the morning, Jane, switched places with Pat, the woman I'd be working with in the afternoon—most of the other workers were part-timers—I heard Jane say, "You should have seen her! The computers went down, and without even asking me what to do, she just called Bibliomation and got it fixed," to which Pat had replied, "Not much to look at, though, is she?"

That last stung a bit, I'll grant you, but I tried to remind myself that this had all been part of the exercise. After all, wasn't the point to prove that people would still like me for myself no matter what I looked like? Still, I supposed that, without realizing it, I'd grown used to the personal sense of validation I'd gotten from people I worked with complimenting me on the little things (like how pretty my hair was) or seeking out my esteemed opinion (on how to catch men). It fast became apparent that at Bethel Library, neither of those things was going to happen, since my hair was now as plain as could be (at least someone could compliment me for washing it) and I no longer looked like I'd had much experience with the latter.

Not that Jane and Pat were any great shakes. Both had been made grandmothers more than once already and were deeply committed to the large stash of minichocolates we at Circ kept stashed in a Danish cookies tin beneath the counter. The chief distinctions between the two were that Jane was much taller and wore her long gray hair tied in a braid on top of her head, while Pat was, obviously, not as nice.

Not five minutes into my first shift with her, having seated herself to call patrons to remind them that they had books on hold and that we'd only hold them two more days, Pat asked, "Never been married, huh?"

It had struck me before that there's a certain kind of woman, devoted to watching daytime talk shows, who believes that anyone she meets is fair game, right away, to be asked the rudest questions; as though life were some kind of studio setting, with her being the audience and everyone else panel guests up on the stage.

"Uh, no," I answered.

She looked at me for a long moment, considering. In fact, she looked at me so long that I began wondering if she were waiting for Oprah to pop in and ask me what kind of diet I was following. Finally:

"Does that bother you?" Pat asked.

"Only when people like you ask me if it bothers me," I answered, not thinking to stop and channel Lettie before letting my mouth speak what I really thought.

"Huh," said Pat, picking up the phone and punching in the numbers of the next patron on her list, "who would've thought? There's more spunk to you than meets the eye. Not much, but some." Then she turned her attention to: "Mrs. Calloway? Bethel Library here…"

You'd think that a library in a small town would be different from a library in a small city, but not really. Once you made allowances for the differences in square footage between the two buildings—okay, the bigger library, by definition, did have more stuff in it than the smaller one—it was all basically the same. People, to a certain degree, are the same anywhere you find them. Sometimes, there's just fewer of them, like maybe only 20,000 instead of 80,000.

In Bethel, I quickly found, just as I'd found in Danbury and in my years in the bookstore before that, there were certain people who liked to play games; people who liked to say that they had no idea how they could have amassed twenty dollars in fines and that they'd never taken out the latest Richard Gere movie, much less sixteen times and failed to return it on the last, no matter what the computer said. There were also mean people, people you could never move quickly enough for, people who were never pleased, people who were looking for someone to blame for everything that had gone wrong in their lives and tag!—the taxpayers are paying you, aren't they?—you were it. But these were, thankfully, a tiny minority, and there were also the nice ones, the ones who loved books and people, the ones who reminded you of why you had become a librarian in the first place.

26

"Why in the world did you ever choose to become a librarian?"

I sighed upon hearing this question I'd heard so often, but had hoped to never hear from this particular quarter.

It was odd, after all, being asked that question, in this of all places—the library—by one of the patrons. It was like if a prospective client of Pam's were to ask her why in the world had she ever chosen to become a lawyer. It was the kind of question that smacked of doubt, as though the questioner was assuming that either the questionee was not properly equipped for the job or had chosen poorly. Either way...

Remember when I said before that good-looking men are never found in bookstores or libraries?

Well, I was wrong.

All right, so, maybe the guy standing on the other side of my counter—with his thick auburn hair, kind of shaggy on the edges and parted on the side, his warm brown eyes, his orthodontist-somewhere-in-the-background smile, his paint-spattered shirt opened just enough to reveal the optimum amount of chest hair and his tight-jeans-clad hip pressed lightly against my counter—wasn't about to give Tom or Brad a run for their box-office money, but for a guy in a library, he looked pretty damn okay.

I looked at the name on his library card—Stephen Holt—before scanning it into the system and processing his order: a pulp mystery (he had low-brow tastes), an older Rushdie (he had high-brow tastes), a coffee table book on trompe l'oeil (who knew what that said about him?).

Putting prestamped cards inside the flaps of his books, I was finally ready to answer his question. But how was I going to answer it: as Scarlett or Lettie?

Deciding the Borscht Belt approach would be best in this situation, I answered the overly familiar question with a wincing question of my own. "Because the job of supermodel of the decade was already taken, and besides which, I wouldn't have qualified, anyway?"

He looked puzzled. "Why would anyone want to do *that* for a living?"

I repeated the Stein family motto: "Be-*cause*—the pay is good, thepayisgood, *thepayisgood?*"

"Is that ever sufficient reason to do anything?"

What planet was this man from? I was beginning to get the sneaking suspicion, a really scary suspicion, that maybe the planet he came from was *my* planet.

"Okay," I said, "how about this for a reason, then. As supermodel of the decade, you get to wear *all* of the awful new fashions before anybody else?"

"Now, *that* I really don't get."

I didn't get it, either, but I just didn't feel like letting on, so I changed tack.

"Why is it hard for you to understand why I became a librarian?"

"Because you don't look like one?"

Now I felt really offended. I'd worked hard, damned hard to attain the frumpiest look I could achieve (without doing any irreversible damage, of course). Hands on hips, I guess you'd have to say I orated at him. "How *dare* you imply that I don't look sufficiently like whatever your narrow-minded conception of what a librarian should look like is. What's wrong—huh? Is my skirt just a little too short?" I knew it wasn't. "Is my bun a little too loose? Is it that I'm not wearing support hose and black orthopedic shoes?"

"Your skirt's not short at all and you don't have enough hair for a bun," he countered.

"Well, then, what is it?"

"You're too alive."

I did a little hand-flapping thing then, the kind of thing that you see game-show contestants do when they want to think of an answer badly but can't, like "Who were the other two presidents besides Kennedy and Lincoln to be successfully assassinated?" and they start fanning themselves rapidly like Melanie Wilkes on amphetamines. It was that kind of motion, and I'm sure it looked excessively over-the-top, but I was that frustrated and that was exactly the motion I made while straining to get out the one word I so desperately wanted to say, which was…

"*WHAT?*"

"What 'what'?"

"What *WHAT?*" I hand-flapped some more. "What are you *talking* about?"

He pointed at my hands with a "eureka" gesture of his own. "Yeah," he said, "that's it right there."

"What's it right there?"

"That thing you're doing with your hands. I've never seen any librarian do anything like that before."

"So? You just made me feel so fucking frustrated and…"

He eureka-pointed again. "And that, too. You just did it again."

"Did what again?"

"Acting too alive. And swearing. I've never heard a librarian get so emotional that they couldn't stop from swearing before."

Now I was really exasperated. "We *swear*. We just do it in the staff lunchroom, that's all. But of *course* we swear. What do you think a librarian is?"

"I don't know." He shrugged. "Someone really intelligent who's too scared to use her intelligence someplace else. Someone who's supplementing someone else's income. Someone who's playing it safe." He paused, looking like he had more to say but hesitating as though fearful to offend. "Someone who wants to hide. Someone who's decided it was easier to settle."

This time I didn't hand-flap at all. This time, I just gave him the hands-on-hips, steely-eyed, out-of-the-corners-of-my-eyeballs glare. "Oh…that is just soooo…inaccurate."

His eyebrows shot up. "It is?"

I sighed, giving in, relenting. "You want to know the real reason why I became a librarian?"

"Yes."

"Fine. I'll tell you." I couldn't believe I was going to actually do it, I couldn't believe that I was finally, for the very first time, going to tell another human being the honest-to-God truth about why I'd chosen the profession I had.

He waited, expectantly.

"I became a librarian because, to me, anything, *anything* to do with books—except for burning them or banning them, of course—is the noblest profession there is."

There went those eyebrows, rising up again. "No shit?"

I stood my ground. "No shit."

Then he stared at me for a long time and then he smiled, and when he smiled it was the biggest—you heard it from the librarian first, folks—shit-eating grin I'd seen on his face yet. And, if I wasn't mistaken, there was just the barest hint of awe mixed into all the joy in that grin.

"Omigod," he whisper-smiled.

"What?"

"I think you're the most romantic woman I've ever met in my life. Will you please go out with me?"

I was in no mood to be mocked by this guy. Whether I was Scarlett or whether I was Lettie, I was in no mood to be mocked.

"Don't I hear your mother calling you?" I demanded rather than asked. "Don't you have somewhere else you need to be right now?"

He tried to stare me down, but I wasn't having any of it. Still, it was something of a shock to realize how unintimidated he was by my best steely librarian's stare.

"I guess," he admitted with a slow grin. "But I'll be back."

"How's that?" I asked, feeling as though I were being threatened somehow.

He waved his pulp, his Rushdie and his arty stuff in the air over his shoulder as he walked away. "I'll have to return these in a few weeks, won't I?"

"Maybe I won't be here that day," I muttered.

"We're not really supposed to swear at the patrons" came

Pat's voice from where she was seated at the desk behind me. Stephen Holt had ruffled so many of my feathers, I'd forgotten they never let me work alone since I was so new.

"I know," I said, only half wondering if she'd report me to Roland.

"You said 'fucking' to a patron, Lettie," she said. "The town that employs us kind of frowns on that sort of thing."

"Did I really?" Even I was shocked at me.

"It was kind of funny," she said.

"Thanks. I'm glad you liked it."

"And he did kind of have it coming."

"You think so?"

I couldn't stop myself from wondering: Was he a Stephen or a Steve?

"Not that you'd want to make a regular practice of that sort of thing," Pat cautioned.

"Of course not."

"But you are kind of, oh, I don't know what it is exactly, but you're *different* whenever you forget about yourself."

"Uh, thanks, I think."

Stephen? Steve? Stephen? Steve?

"And that sure was one good-looking piece of man," Pat said.

"You think so?" I looked at her closely, wondering if she'd seen something I hadn't seen. I mean, he'd looked *okay*…. "Really?"

"You mean to tell me you didn't notice?"

"I just assumed he looked so good because of the context."

"How's that?"

"It's just that we're in the library. I'll bet that if we ran into him out in the real world, he wouldn't look half so good to us."

Pat pondered this.

"Besides," I added, "he's rude."

"Yeah, well."

27

In order to celebrate my new job—any excuse for a celebration—my girlfriends decided to take me out to dinner and then out partying.

"We'll go to that new Italian place," T.B. had said. "Mama Rosa's? Mama Italia? I don't know. Mama *Something*. Whatever it's called, I'm sure it'll be good—it's Italian."

Mama Something turned out to be a clichéd little Italian place with a menu—*prima* this, *seconda* that—that was trying a little too hard to be someplace other than Danbury.

"Well, *I* like it," Delta insisted as the Andy Garcia-ish waiter seated us at a table for four, taking our drinks order: a bottle of—what else?—Italian red to be shared.

When it came time to order food, I ordered a large salad (I knew I'd be drinking more later and didn't want to fill up), Pam also ordered a salad (she looked like she'd already lost about ten pounds), T.B. ordered the fried calamari (she never worried about what she ate) and Delta ordered the eggplant parmesan (on general principle, even though she claimed not to be hungry, because Delta was the original anti-dieter).

As often happens when a group of friends go out to dinner together, in the beginning we made general conversation that everyone could participate in: talk of my new job and how I was dealing with the very different personalities of Jane and Pat, not to mention Roland; talk of whatever latest thing Bush had done; talk of the weather, which had for once turned seasonably cool heading into October. For some reason, I chose not to say anything about Stephen—Steve?—Holt.

But, as the meal wore on, we broke off into smaller conversations, with Pam and T.B. talking about some high-profile case that was currently working its way through the Danbury court system, while Delta and I talked about…her kids.

"I wish I could go on with you all to Chalk Is Cheap afterward," Delta sighed into her wineglass, picking up her fork to make a determined stab at her eggplant, "but the sitter would only agree to stay with Mush and Teenie for three hours, tops."

I could understand the sitter's reasoning. Mostly, I was amazed that anyone would sit with Mush and Teenie at all. But of course I couldn't say that, so aloud I said, "Well, it is a school night. Maybe the sitter's got class in the morning?"

Delta ignored this, spearing more eggplant, apparently determined to eat her way through her apparent misery, whether she was hungry or not. "You-all don't know what it's like," she said, "being single with two kids in the house."

I was never completely sure of the distinction between her "y'alls" and her "you-alls," but I thought I had the gist of it this time: she was telling me that I couldn't possibly know what her life was like. Having already spent more time with Mush and Teenie than I'd want to in a lifetime—the bond of friendship does require certain things—I could certainly understand her fatigue.

"Men don't exactly flock to women with kids," Delta said.

Now this I couldn't understand. Since I really did believe that people fell in love with each other for themselves, it seemed to me that if the emotions were real, nothing would get in the way. But I couldn't say that, either.

"A couple of weeks ago, I met a new guy," Delta said, "and he asked me out. So, last weekend, we finally go out, we have a good time, he takes me to dinner, he's real nice, I can tell he's not an ax murderer, I ask him back to my place, I dismiss the babysitter, and then…"

"And then?"

"And then we're sitting on my living room couch, we're starting to get all snuggled up. My motor's purring like the engine on a '48 Packard—"

I had no way of knowing if this was a good thing or a bad thing.

"—and then Mush gets out of bed and comes on in." Delta finally laid down her fork, dejection written all over her, leaving two pieces of eggplant on her plate.

"Well, but," I said, "I'm sure you must have already told him that you had kids, right? Surely, they were no surprise."

"Honey, Mush is *always* a surprise."

She had me there.

"But that ain't it," she said. "It was what Mush said."

I wasn't really certain I wanted to—

"He said," Delta continued, deciding for me that I did indeed want to know, "'Excuse me, sir, but if you plan to be hammerin' on my mama, do you happen to have an *extra* rubber on you?'"

I tried hard not to wince, failed. "Well," I said, trying to bright-side it, "at least he said, 'Excuse me, sir,' so the kid's got manners."

"Scarlett, my eight-year-old *son* asked my *date* about rubbers!"

Mush was eight? How old was Teenie?

"So he's health-conscious," I tried.

"My date didn't see it that way."

"No?"

"No. He left, said he had an early day, would call the next morning. Never called again."

"Aw, I'm sorry," I said, covering her hand with my own. "Was he nice?"

"Of course he was nice," she huffed. "He was nice right up until Mush—"

"I know, I know," I soothed, reluctant to hear the words "Mush" and "rubbers" in the same sentence again.

"I just don't know how I'm ever going to attract another man to stay longer than dinner. The older Mush and Teenie get, the harder it is to convince people that they're really cute."

As Andy Garcia made his way over to the table with our check, Delta perked up a bit.

"Oh, but *he's* cute," she said, still checking out our waiter. "I would definitely risk the embarrassment of Mush if I thought I could get him to come home with me. I do love a man in a tight black uniform. And have you noticed how much extra attention he's shown our table?"

Now that she mentioned it, I realized that Andy had been very attentive.

As he set the check down, he reddened a trifle, looking embarrassed.

Had he heard Delta? I wondered.

"What's up?" Pam gave him a sly smile, having retouched her ice-pink lipstick for the occasion.

"It's just," he said, blushing furiously and then looking straight at me, "I have this big *thing* for women in large dresses. Maybe it's the Italian in me?"

"Oh, crap." Pam threw down her napkin, sought assistance from the others. "Do you see what she's doing? Can anyone else figure out how she does this? How does she do this to me every time?"

Having dropped off Delta to the sound of Teenie's greeting—"Mama! You didn't have to come home from getting drunk so early! We weren't doin' *nuthin'* to the baby-sitter"—we headed over to Chalk Is Cheap, and walked in.

"Don't you people ever think about going anywhere with any color?" T.B. asked, surveying the, um, whiteness of the joint.

"Not really," I replied. "That is to say, I don't purposely avoid…"

"It's just that we never thought to actively look…" tried Pam.

"Don't worry about it," T.B. laughed, "I got Ex-Al. Just get me a Scotch," she added, taking a tall seat at one of the high bar tables.

Pam and I sidled up to the bar, ordering T.B.'s Scotch plus another wine for me and club soda this time for her since she was driving.

"You ever notice," I asked, "how hard it is to be politically correct at every given moment?"

"You ever notice," she said, "how easy it is to fuck up?"

"You ever notice how everyone else notices it whenever you do fuck up?"

"You ever notice how no one ever notices the other twenty-three hours and fifty-nine minutes a day when you don't fuck up?"

I laughed. Funny: I almost never remembered the things I liked about Pam.

Our drinks came.

"Cheers," Pam said. "I'm glad I got the club soda. Not only am I driving, I've also got to watch my girlish figure. Oops," she added, giving me a once-over, "I almost forgot. No one can see yours anymore."

Pam.

She left me to pay for all our drinks, moving off to join T.B. at the table.

As I turned to pay, He walked in. Note that capital H there? Not too many men rate one, but some do and He was one of them.

I'll stop now.

As he stepped up to the bar, I immediately saw that he was blessed with that rare stop-you-in-your-tracks quality of looks, the kind that are just as startling out in the real world and not just startling in a library setting. He had almost-black hair, dark brown eyes and a set to his jaw as if he'd never heard the word *no* directed at him: certainly not from any woman and probably not from life, either. He also had the kind of body, underneath a black turtleneck and jeans, that was just begging for someone to rip his clothes off. With teeth if necessary.

But, really, it was the strong jaw that got to me. Really.

As I stood there, half a bar away from him and painfully

aware of the fact that he had yet to notice me breathing him in there, I decided to just go for it.

Historically speaking, I'd never been shy about approaching guys. From a very young age, I figured that if I saw something I liked, I should make my liking known rather than sitting back and hoping it would come to me. It might not be an approach all women would be comfortable taking, and I was sure that there were men out there who would be put off by a woman making the first move, but I'd also always figured that any man who was put off by my forwardness was, by definition, not a man I'd want to waste time on, anyway.

Wineglass in hand, I approached my goal with my usual boldness. But, as I did so, a curious thing happened. Looking down at my feet, catching sight of my sensible shoes, I felt different all of a sudden, hesitant, like I was someone other than the person I'd always been.

I tried to brush the feeling off, climbed up on the stool next to…Him.

"Um," I said, feeling more Lettie than Scarlett, "so, you like beer, huh?"

Shit, my inner voice hit my inner self on the head. *That was smart.*

He raised his glass to his lips—oh, those lips!—and sipped. Then he licked the foam from his upper lip—oh, that tongue!—and smiled. But it was the kind of smile you dish out with a fair regularity to marginally cute little puppies, not the kind of smile you reserve for the one woman you desperately hope will become the love of your life.

"Um, yeah," he said, still smiling.

Um, was he mocking me?

"Um, you ever come here before?"

"Um, no. Is there a reason I, um, shouldn't?"

"Um, well," I said, "if you make a habit of mocking the regulars, um, I might have to kick your butt."

There was the old Scarlett charm!

A good way to judge the character of any man is to find out if he can laugh at the absurdity of a situation.

Apparently, from the size and generosity of his laugh— oh, those teeth!—this man had character.

I began to feel more like myself immediately, like maybe I could even speak a whole sentence without using the interjection "um" even once.

But as I asked my next question—"So, what kind of work do you do?"—I realized I wasn't myself at all. I was still some paler version of me. It was as though someone had taken the more vibrant version of Scarlett—the one who was capable of approaching any man with confidence—and what had been left in her place was now a watercolor version, all verbal cautiousness plus sensible shoes with only the occasional glimpse of a fighting spirit.

"I'm an investment adviser," he said.

"Tough market these days," I sympathized.

He shrugged. "All the more reason for people to need my advice."

"Do you like what you do?" I asked.

It occurred to me I was asking all the questions here. Who did I think I was, the quizmaster?

"I wouldn't do it if I didn't," he said.

I liked that answer.

"Plus," he added, "the pay is good."

And I understood that answer.

"How about you?" he asked.

Omigod, I thought, *he's finally asking me a question! He— of the lips, tongue and teeth—was curious about me!*

"How about me, um, what?" I asked.

"What sort of work do you do?"

"I'm a librarian."

"Ah," he said in what sounded to me suspiciously like an "ah, I should have guessed" kind of tone.

"I like it," I said, not waiting for him to ask. "You could say it suits me."

"Yeah, you could."

Over his shoulder, I caught sight of my friends. T.B. was holding up a napkin on which she'd lipsticked something in Certainly Red. I squinted: "YOU GO, GIRL!" Beside her, Pam appeared less happy as she looked at her watch and then looked pointedly at Him—I still didn't know what his name was—and me. I got the odd feeling if I didn't do something that would prove successful soon, Pam would make a move to move us all on out the door.

"What's your name?" I blurted.

"Saul," he said, taken aback. I wasn't sure what was causing that effect: the suddenness of my blurt or his realization that I hadn't asked this earlier. "Saul Waters."

"Lettie," I said, extending my hand, feeling not unlike the young girl whose pa has been killed shaking hands with John Wayne in *True Grit*. "Lettie Shaw."

"Ah," he said again.

"Now, what's that supposed to mean?" I demanded, Scarlett taking over. "I can understand your ah-ing my job, sort of, but my name? What's so *ah* about my name?"

"Oh, I don't know." He looked kind of ashamed. "It just suits you somehow."

While one party being ashamed hardly seemed the basis

from which to springboard to a lifelong romantic entanglement of cinematic proportions, I was forced to go with what I had.

"Give me your number," I said, all Scarlett. "I'll call you sometime."

"You'll…? Whoa, little lady! Isn't that a bit strong for a…for a *librarian?*"

"'Whoa, little lady?' Who are you supposed to be, John Wayne?"

From the look on his face I could see that, clearly, he had not been privy to my earlier *True Grit* fantasy.

Whatever.

"Fine," I said, all business, taking a pen from my sensible bag and scrawling my name and number on a bar napkin, putting the napkin in his hand. "You call me then, if you want to be old-fashioned about it."

He looked at the napkin, looked up at me. "Scarlett Stein?"

"Oh…here," I said, blushing furiously, grabbing the napkin back as though this were somehow all *his* fault. I scratched out Scarlett, replaced her with the woman I was now supposed to be.

"What can I say?" I wince-explained. "I get a little confused sometimes."

"Well, uh—" he let out a little explosion of breath "—sure, *Lettie.* Whatever you say."

I moved to rejoin my friends, feeling Pam's leash tighten. But not before throwing over my shoulder, "Don't forget to call me. You won't be sorry."

28

Despite my seemingly cocky throwaway line to Saul Waters, I woke the next day with a feeling of dread.

I'd never worried once before that some man I wanted to call me might not call me.

Not once, Scarlett? you ask, understandably skeptical.

"Not once, Lettie," I answer.

Yes, well, er, um, it does get confusing sometimes, knowing just whom I'm talking to.

Anyway, I woke the next day, certain that Saul would never call me, not even if he were desperate and I was the last librarian on Earth. I mean, I didn't even do the "Do you think he'll call me? I don't think he'll call me. But he could. What do you think?" nervous dance I'd seen other girlfriends do from time to time. I was simply dead certain that I'd seen the last of him.

(But who knows? Maybe he'd call.)

Feeling thoroughly depressed by this novel state of affairs, not to mention feeling unpleasantly wine-headed, I lurched at the first opportunity to cheer myself up; upon arriving at the library, Jane mentioned needing to go to the post office to send some things down to a few of her grandkids in Florida. What was wrong with her family? Didn't these people know that the kids were supposed to stay up here and *she* was supposed to move down there?

Whatever.

In order to cheer myself up, I offered to take Jane's package across the street to the post office.

"But there's really no need…" she said.

"It's no problem," I said, smiling as I held the large package out in front of me, jauntily backing into the glass door with my butt to open it rather than pushing the automatic door opener. "I'll even treat. Really. I love going to the post office."

And I did love going to the post office.

Okay, so maybe I didn't love the physical act of going to the post office, but I liked playing post office.

And okay, by "playing post office," I don't mean what you think I mean, but I still liked doing it.

Playing post office was something I'd been doing for years, ever since I turned thirty. It was a little game I played—a contest, if you will—with, well, whatever other women happened to be in the post office whenever I happened to walk in.

Rules of the Post Office Game:
1. Go into post office.
2. Stand in line.
3. Check out other women in post office—those ahead

of you, of course, but don't cheat by neglecting to account for those coming in behind.★

4. Figure out where you rank among those women in the room on the continuum of physical appearance.

5. Go away happy.

(★The women behind the counter don't count, since it's unfair to expect women to compete when they're wearing that blue uniform.)

Okay, okay, I do realize that this doesn't sound very nice, but I swear I'm not the only woman who does this. (Who knows? Maybe you do it, too.) I used to feel guilty about this little game until one day, during a conversation with Best Girlfriend—I forget which one of us introduced the subject—one of us made an allusion that made it clear she played the game and the other said, shocked, relieved, "Omigod! You, too?"

And somehow, as so often happened, Best Girlfriend made me feel better about some human smallness of mine.

"It would be one thing," she'd said, "if you gloated afterward. Gloaters don't deserve to get that little extra lift that can only be achieved by realizing that you're still outpacing over half of the woman race. But so long as you keep it to yourself, so long as you leave the post office as humbly as you entered, then yes, it's perfectly fine behavior to count how many people you're better-looking than while you're picking up stamps."

And, anyway, it wasn't like I was so vain that I played this game everywhere: I didn't do it at Super Stop & Shop, didn't do it at the movies, didn't do it at Chalk Is Cheap. Really, for some reason, the only place the game was played, because it was the only place the game worked, was in the post office.

When I walked into the post office, there were already four people waiting on line: two teenagers with low-slung jeans and Britney waists (no way was I going to beat them), plus a woman, about my age, who looked like she lived in the gym (shitshitshit), and a man (which meant he didn't count in this particular contest, but damn, he looked better than me, too).

I stood there with Jane's package in my arms, convincing myself there was still hope. Right up until I stood at the counter paying for the shipment, anyone who came in behind me would still count as contestants.

For once, I prayed for a slow-moving line. This was a contest I'd never lost before, it was a harmless game that had always made me feel better about myself; I was determined that this time should be no different.

I heard footsteps on the dusty linoleum behind me, indicating that someone else was getting in line. Resisting the temptation to turn around and check—was the new person in line better-looking than me? Or, please God, worse?—I decided that I would keep my eyes peeled on that gray counter until I laid Jane's package down on it in order to pay. Only then would I allow myself to turn around and see who the new contestants were.

I heard four more sets of footsteps behind me before it was finally my turn. Stepping up to the counter, I put Jane's package down and steeled myself in preparation for looking over my shoulder. The way I figured it, I needed to beat all five of the sets of footsteps, since beating only four would put me into a tie with the people who had been ahead of me in line, whether I counted the guy or not. Of course, anything less than four, or if a couple of the new people turned out to be guys, would mean sure defeat.

Finally, I looked over my shoulder, and saw, looking down the line…

Two old ladies. Yes! Yes! Gray power! I practically pumped my arm in the air to show my solidarity. There just weren't enough old people in the world. Old people should be *everywhere*. It really was a shame they couldn't be fruitful and multiply themselves.

And I was better-looking than they were.

Behind the two old ladies there was…

A really old lady! Yes! Yes! Everyone should live to a hundred! If everyone lived to be a hundred, the world would be a better place for me, me, me! Well, at least until I got older.

Still, I had her beat by a sixty-year mile.

I was now running neck and neck: I was worse-looking than three of the people who had been in line ahead of me (I'd decided definitely not to count the man because he was a man and, besides, he was better-looking than me and threw my net score off) and better-looking than three of the five people behind me. Just two more to go. I was sure I could do it.

Behind the really old lady there was…

A man.

Bzzz.

But, I decided after my initial disappointment, that was okay. Since I was much better-looking than this man, who had a nose where most people had a face, he officially and fairly canceled out the good-looking man from before.

Just one more to go; just one more and I would be home free.

I craned my neck to see behind the two old ladies, the one really old lady and the man's nose. Well, mostly I just had to crane to see around the nose.

But I couldn't look just yet. I was beginning to think it might not be such a bad thing if the last person turned out to be a man. So if it turned out to be a draw—how bad was that? A draw at age thirty-nine wouldn't be such a demoralizing loss.

I realized that I couldn't put it off any longer. I had to look. Hopefully, it would be another old lady.

I looked.

The fifth person who had gotten in line behind me was a woman. She was under thirty, about five-and-a-half-feet tall, with perfectly nice breasts, narrow waist, tight jeans over decent hips. She had honey-colored hair, long and parted on the side, clear skin, green eyes, and when she smiled— yup—all her teeth. She looked like a glamorous author photo on the back of a book, the kind of pic that would make cynics ask, "Who'd she sleep with to get published?"

A few months ago, I could have easily given her a run for her money, despite the advantage she had by being ten years younger. But now? In my present incarnation?

Earlier, I'd been anxious, experiencing the uneasy feeling that I was starting, at long last, to lose the game.

But this was worse, much worse. Because, as long as there had been anxiety, there had still been a weird kind of hope of winning that had run concurrent with it.

But now?

Now I was filled with a deadening dread, for I was no longer merely losing the game. I had, in fact, *lost* the game.

"Excuse me," asked the postal clerk behind the counter, "but would you like insurance for this?"

"Oh, who the hell really cares," I said dejectedly, for the first time in my life swearing in front of a sister public servant other than Pat. "It's not even my package."

★ ★ ★

I walked across the street from the post office to the library, feeling depressed. When I got to the parking lot, I saw a familiar figure locking her bicycle to the metal bike rack. It was Sarah, the reluctant chicken pox giver. She had on a long-sleeved purple T-shirt in honor of the slight nip in the air. Underneath the T-shirt, it was impossible to ignore the fact that she was sprouting breasts; I'd been right in my prediction. She also had on faded jeans with holes in the knees. I didn't look closely to see if they were still hairy, but somehow was sure they still were.

"Hey," I said, "what are you doing here? Aren't you kind of far from home?"

"Not really," she said. "We live off of Shelter Rock Road."

The street she named wasn't far from where I used to live, was on the Bethel side of Danbury, so only about two miles from the library. Not such a long ride after all.

"Oh," I said, brilliantly.

"We have the day off from school," she said, "some Catholic holiday."

"Oh," I said, again brilliantly.

"So I thought I'd come visit you."

"Oh!" I brightened. "Well, I do have to go back inside now, but if you want to come with me, maybe talk for a bit…"

I walked with her into the building, figuring we'd be safe until the shifts changed and I exchanged nice Jane for not-nice Pat.

Once inside, I started to walk around the corner of the Circ desk, while Sarah just kept on going toward the door that led upstairs to Reference one floor up and the Chil-

dren's Department and staff offices above that. We were like
a small train whose cars had suddenly broken apart. When
she realized she'd lost her caboose, she turned around.

"Don't you work up in Reference?" she asked.

I shot a nervous glance at Jane, who was seated on one
side of the twin tables that served as our work area when
we weren't working at the actual desk. "Uh, no," I said. "I
work here."

"Why would Lettie work in Reference?" Jane asked,
puzzled. Then, without waiting for an answer, she added
with a smile, "Besides, I always like to keep the good ones
here with me."

Bless her grandmotherly heart, I thought, the woman
liked me.

I pulled up the two high swivel chairs we used when we
were working at the desk, which was really as high as one
of the bar tables at Chalk Is Cheap. "Here," I offered Sarah,
"sit."

Then I pulled out some new card applications and began
the process of entering the information into the computer
system before making up the plastic cards themselves.

"You can talk to me while I work," I said, hoping the conversation wouldn't distract me so much that I'd make mis-
takes, like making a six-year-old boy a sixty-year-old man
or anything Dewey-decimal cataclysmic like that.

"So, tell me," I said, "what's up?"

"Up?"

"Well, you didn't come here on your Catholic holiday off
from school just to watch me work, did you? And what holiday did you say it was again?"

"I didn't."

"Oh."

I studied my work seriously, as if I might actually be serious about it, figuring that if she wasn't worried I was looking at her, it might be easier for her to tell me whatever it was she wanted to tell me. And I was sure she wanted to tell me something.

"My mother won't let me shave my legs!" she blurted out.

"Ah," I said, waiting for more—there's always more—and I could almost hear Jane's ears perk to attention behind me, like a happy schnauzer. Well, it had to be more exciting than going through computer printouts of patrons with overdue books.

"And there's a Sadie Hawkins dance coming up!"

Oh, to be ten again, when every utterance required an exclamation point. But wait a second. Wasn't ten a little young for dances?

"How old are you?" I asked.

"Twelve," she said defiantly. "How old did you think I was?"

Well, I sure wasn't going to tell her I'd thought she was ten. So maybe my certainty that she was a mini-me had been a bit off. After all, at ten I'd already needed…

"Hello? Lettie? Are you still there?" she asked.

"Sorry." I blushed. "Where were we?"

I saw her start to look preteen irritated and cut that short with: "Right—hairy legs and dances. Go on."

"The kids call me Monkey!"

Now I was on familiar territory.

"And I want to ask Jeff Polanski!"

"But he calls you Monkey, too?" Jane couldn't resist asking.

"No," Sarah turned to her in disgust. "But his friends do!"

Ouch.

"And," Sarah added quietly, looking down at her budding breasts, "when they don't call me Monkey, they call me Jiggles."

Double ouch.

"When's the Sadie Hawkins dance?" I asked.

"A few weeks," she said dejectedly, "on Halloween."

"Then we have time to think of something to do," I said positively, not having a clue as to what that something might be.

What I really wanted to do was to tell Sarah that none of this mattered—the hairy legs, the budding breasts with no bra, the kids that were too stupid or too jealous or just too plain ill-mannered to know any better. I wanted to tell her that she was a special girl, of course she was. Hell, I even liked her, and she'd given me the chicken pox! I wanted to tell her that this was all surface bullshit; ten, twenty, thirty years from now, none of this would matter. She'd be so far ahead of anyone who was giving her grief now that none of it would matter. And instead of wanting to shave, she'd probably hate to shave! But of course, looking at her, I realized I couldn't say any of that. Because of course it mattered. To her, it mattered.

"We have time to think of something," I said again.

Sarah looked woefully down at her chest. "We may have enough time for me to change," she said, "but I don't think we have enough time to change my mom."

29

"Roland hired a new woman for Reference," Jane announced when I arrived late in the morning for my shift, having drowned my sorrows the night before at losing the post office game in one too many glasses of Chardonnay and stayed up too late watching one too many Lifetime movies.

I'd known that Roland was looking for someone to replace an experienced worker who'd left unexpectedly and I'd been sorely tempted to ask for the job. Reference was my personal love in the library and I would have given…I would have given… Shit, I'd realized. I'd given so much up lately, what was there left to give? Okay. I'd have given my mother's right arm to get back behind a reference desk. But the key word in Roland's job description was "experienced." And I was supposed to be the new girl who didn't know anything yet, even if I'd been wowing Jane and Pat and even Roland sometimes with everything I seemed to just instinctively know. So I'd let the golden opportunity pass, rather than blowing my cover.

"What's she like?" I asked.

"Why don't you go see for yourself?" Jane suggested. "I can handle things here. We're not busy right now."

I looked up and saw that the only other people in the room were a patron reading the day's newspapers and another patron browsing the video racks.

I decided to take her up on it. I may love being a librarian, but we librarians still need to take our excitement where we can get it.

Just a half flight of stairs separated Circ from Reference, and in no time I was doing my best Nancy Drew, peeking my head around the corner to get a glimpse of the woman who'd won the job that should have been mine.

Her back was to me as she worked on the computer, but I could see that she had honey-colored hair and was a little overdressed for our casual library, wearing a sea-green jacket that looked like it was the top half of a suit. Oh, well. People often overcompensate in the beginning, trying to make a good impression. And look at me: I was wearing dresses to work every day. But, of course, that was for an entirely different reason.

I heard Pete, the part-time Reference guy, say, "Kelly," just before he came into view, "was this what you were looking for?"

In his hand, he held out a blue binder. But from where I was standing, I couldn't read what the spine said. It could have been the binder with staff procedure in it or the binder for volunteer work or just about anything. But that didn't matter, because at that moment She turned in the chair.

Yes, that's right, she was a She with the capital *S.*

She half rose from her chair to take the binder from Pete; Pete, who lived at home with his parents, wore his pants too high, and who could never be bothered to answer me if I asked him a question during the morning staff meetings; Pete, who was now smiling at her like he was applying to be her personal lap dog, as her half rising revealed an ultra-short skirt to match the sea-green jacket and a pair of legs that even tempted me. In fact, the legs were so perfect that it took a moment before I tore my eyes away, traveling them upward, only to find…

Shit! *Shitshitshit!*

It was the woman from the post office, the woman who'd come in while I was playing the game, the woman with the green eyes, the woman who'd caused me to lose the post office game for the first time in my life.

I must have either gasped or at least muttered one of those "shits" out loud, because both Pete and the woman's head snapped in my direction. Not up to introductions at the moment, like the mouse I suddenly felt like, I scampered back down the stairs and resumed my breathless place behind the Circ desk.

"Didja seer?" Jane asked, in that two-words-for-the-price-of-one pattern of speech that we New Englanders like to sometimes affect.

"Yup," I answered in kind, still stunned.

"Her name's Kelly Seaforth. Can you beat that?"

"It fits her," I said. And it did.

"You think a woman like that gets a lot of action?" Jane asked, surprising me.

"How would I know? I guess. Probably."

"Good," Jane said, "then she'll fit right in."

"Excuse me?"

"Oh, hell, Lettie. It's only in books where you always see these uptight librarians who are repressed and never get laid. But in real life? Librarians are *hot*. Hell, we should have our own swimsuit calendar."

Everyone likes to talk to the guy who paints the shop windows. It's kind of like the guards at Buckingham Palace: people like to see if the artist can maintain his focus, his creativity, while being interrupted by all kinds of inane bullshit.

There I was, walking along Greenwood Avenue in Bethel, minding my own business, asking myself for the gazillionth time: *Where did I know him from?*

I was wondering, of course, about the guy who was painting the windows outside of Mister Caffeine, the coffee shop where I was going to pick up my lunch—turkey sandwich on whole wheat, mustard, no mayo—the guy, I realized, was Stephen (Steve?), the guy who himself had wondered why too-alive me had ever chosen to become a librarian, the guy who'd asked me out and whom I'd turned down.

Ever since that day, I'd been wondering where I knew him from, since he had that oddly unsettling, vaguely familiar look of someone I should know, but not like someone famous, because what would someone famous be doing in Bethel Public Library, unless of course it was Meg Ryan and she were to return to Bethel, but if she did, I doubt she would come to Bethel Library. And, anyway, if I was certain of one thing, it was that he wasn't Meg Ryan.

Am I rambling here?

Now *you're* the one who's probably wondering, "Scarlett, why the fuck did you ever turn that guy down? Sure, he was kind of insulting about your chosen profession. Sure, it was a little bit potential-psychotic-in-the-making, the way he asked you out in such an over-the-top romantic kind of way,

but isn't that what most women want, some kind of authoritarian/sensitive combo platter, a Schwarzenegger/Lauer
hybrid?"

Maybe.

Maybe.

I *said* maybe…okay?

Of course, if the guy in question has unbelievable legs,
legs that look even more unbelievable in cutoff shorts—the
kind of shorts that *real* men used to wear when I was growing up, the ones that show off a guy's, um, *manhood,* like the
guy with the strawberry patch who used to clean my best
friend's pool when I was ten, not like these too-loose things
that the guys have taken to wearing since the entire fashion
world has gone insane—and if he wears those shorts even
though it's pretty crisply cool out on a mid-October day,
coupled with a bright orange sweatshirt as he paints storefront windows in preparation for Halloween…

I snapped my fingers. Of course! *That's* where I knew Stephen (Steve?) from! He was the guy who painted the windows whenever the seasons changed or whenever a new
holiday was coming up. It seemed to me that there had been
a time when kids painted the storefront windows and then
an adult had taken over, which seemed like an odd job for
an adult to have. Why hadn't I ever noticed him before?

I certainly noticed him now, as he stood there, palette in
hand, painting pumpkins and witches and tombstones with
tall grass growing around everything, all the while fending
off questions from passersby—teenagers, late-afternoon
drunks, early-quitting-time businessmen trying to masquerade as nice people by talking to someone not wearing a tie—
himself looking attractive enough to be the subject of an
artist's work as he brushed his brow with the back of his

hand, paintbrush poised, brushing a second time in a vain effort to control uncontrollable wavy auburn hair.

I certainly noticed when he took the time to stop what he was doing to answer the questions of any really tiny questioners, in other words anyone who looked like they were still young enough to go at Halloween without cynicism. God, it was cute, how patient he was with them.

I certainly noticed—

Oh, my God—I certainly didn't want *him* to certainly notice *me* certainly noticing him! So, naturally, I did the only thing that any self-respecting librarian in my shoes would do:

I ducked behind the nearest tree, pressed my back into the bark and pretended to be invisible. Peeking out from behind the tree a moment later, having realized that there was not much point in sticking around if I wasn't going to actually see anything, I saw him hand his brush to a little girl, encouraging her to use the paint on it to add to a big red-gold maple leaf he'd already started.

Damn, he was good with those kids.

But then I wondered: What kind of guy becomes the guy who paints the shop windows?

In Bethel, it seemed like the windows were always changing and that it wasn't enough to merely change the displays inside; the outside had to be thematically painted as well. Was this quaintness a New England thing? Did they do it elsewhere as well? Was someone doing it right that second in Boca?

So many questions, but the one I kept coming back to was: What kind of person does such a thing?

Years ago, I'd known a mime; not a famous mime, like Marcel Marceau or anything, just a guy who was a mime on weekends—children's birthday parties, town fairs, that kind of thing. From Monday to Friday, Joe was a mason, a respectable-enough job, if a bit cold in the winter. But Joe didn't really care about masonry. If it were up to him, if someone would let him design a better universe, he would have had that mime makeup on seven days a week. And, in Joe's perfect universe, he wouldn't even get paid for wearing the makeup and white gloves; he'd be independently wealthy, just giving his mimehood away for free.

I knew Joe from shooting pool at a bar that had been an earlier incarnation of Chalk Is Cheap called Minnesota's. In Minnesota's Joe and his mimehood had achieved a weird sort of respectability. You'd think the discipline would be the kind of thing that might make other, bigger guys want to beat him up, but people seemed to take Joe's hobby like just any other hobby, like weekend softball leagues or paintball or, well, pool. To them, Joe's thing was just like their thing, only different and with different accessories. Plus, Joe was a helluva mime. Everyone said so.

And Joe had liked me. A lot. And he kept asking me out. A lot. And everyone kept telling me how cool Joe was, how nice he was, how honored I should feel, how I should really go out with Joe. And don't get me wrong: I liked Joe, I really did, because he was a nice guy. But…but…but…*the guy lived to be a mime!* Who does such a thing?

There was just no way. No way in hell that I could go out with a guy who was voluntarily a mime, someone who sought out mimehood like it was a good thing. To me, miming, with those teary-looking black-and-white clown eyes, was something that a person should only do if they had absolutely no other choice, like if they belonged to the mime family equivalent of the Flying Wallendas or if being a mime would somehow feed Africa. (Not that I'm being judgmental here or anything.)

So to find out that Stephen (Steve?) Holt was a painter of holiday storefront windows...

But, I told myself, this was different. For starters, painting isn't miming—can't argue with me there. Plus, the kids that were watching Stephen (Steve?) were actually *enjoying* watching him work, which was a far cry from miming, which, in my experience, always served to make kids, well, cry. And who could blame them? Miming was so creepy; it certainly creeped me out. Painting, on the other hand, wasn't.

"Nice leaf."

Stephen (Steve?) turned at the sound of my voice.

"Thanks," he said, looking surprised, maybe even pleased, to see me standing there.

"It looks so, um, autumny," I said.

"Thanks again." He waited, as if expecting something more.

Sucking it up, I thrust out my hand. "Lettie," I said, "Lettie Shaw."

He shook my hand. "I knew that already," he said.

"You did?"

"Yeah. When I went in to the library to return my books, I asked after you, and that woman you work with—"

"The mean one or the nice one?"

"The mean one."

"Pat."

"Well, Pat said you were off for some Jewish holiday."

"My mother likes me to go to synagogue with her."

He smiled. "That's nice of you."

"I guess."

"I was a bit surprised. Shaw doesn't sound much like a Jewish name."

"Yeah, well…"

"Steve Holt, by the way," he said.

"I knew that," I said, "from your library card. But it's good to know about the Steve part. I hadn't been sure about that."

"Would it have been bad if it was Stephen?"

"Huh?"

"Well, you said it was good that it's Steve."

"No, either one is fine. It's just good to know which."

The grouping of little kids who'd been watching Steve paint were giving me hostile looks. Apparently, I was interfering with their entertainment. Particularly hostile was the little girl he'd given the brush to. I suspected she'd developed a massive crush on him the minute he'd put that brush in her hand.

The little girl insinuated her little body between me and Steve, gazing up at him with adoring, if demanding, eyes.

"Can you paint a witch?" she said.

"Sure," he said, getting to work with black and green, "I can paint you a witch."

I don't know what I was expecting, something scary probably, but that wasn't the kind of witch he painted. Sure, he used the black and the green, but what came out of his brush was a completely unintimidating witch with long black hair that kind of looked like mine used to and a warm smile, laughing eyes. It was the kind of witch intentionally designed *not* to scare any little kids, however small, who happened to walk on by. I would have liked to have known that witch.

It certainly wasn't the kind of witch any mime would paint.

"Is that good?" Steve looked down at the little girl.

"It's perfect!" She clapped.

Who could blame her?

"So, um," I said, "you like Halloween?"

"Of course." The little girl gave me an accusing look, a combination of "you're stupid" and "why are you interrupting my moment with Steve?"

But Steve seemed to understand that I'd been talking to him.

"My favorite holiday," he answered, smiling wide, "that and all the others."

An equal-opportunity holiday-lover.

"How about you?" he asked. "Do you dress up for it?"

The question struck me as odd, since in a way my entire life had now become a game of dress up, but he didn't know that.

"It's weird," I said, "but as old as I get, I still love Halloween. My friends and I dress up every year, go out to bar parties or have parties at one another's houses. As a matter of fact—" I didn't know I was going to do this until I said it "—I'm planning on having a party this year. Would you like to come?"

Why did you just do that? the voice in my head demanded. *You're not even sure you like this guy! He's the guy who insulted your job!*

He smiled at me, a little sadly. "I'd like to," he said, "but I can't."

The little girl looked at me with smug satisfaction. I could have sworn she was dying to stick her tongue out at me. *So there.*

"My older brother's divorced and has two small kids," he went on. "He's got custody. He lives in one of those big houses on Deer Hill Avenue in Danbury."

"Wow, he must have money."

"Does that matter?" Steve asked abruptly.

"No." I shrugged. "Why would it?"

"Anyway, I promised I'd go over there and hand out candy while he took Tim Junior and Sally around."

"Ah."

"But," he brightened, "we could still go out sometime."

I thought the little girl was going to haul off and kick me in the shins.

"You remember," he said, "I asked you out once before?"

Of course I remembered. What I also remembered was feeling at the time as though he was teasing me, mocking me, like he couldn't possibly have been sincere. No man, I was sure deep down inside in a place I couldn't admit to anyone, would sincerely want to go out with me the way I had become.

And now? What did I feel now?

I didn't feel like he was mocking me anymore, definitely not that. But, I don't know, I thought that maybe he was asking me out because he somehow felt sorry for me. After all, what kind of adult woman works in a library, wears shapeless dresses, stops to talk to the guy painting the storefront windows and throws Halloween parties?

"Um, no," I said, backing away, letting him off the hook, letting the little girl have the playing field free and clear, "that's okay. I only asked you to the party because it was going to be an, um, group thing. But we don't have to…"

"No, but—"

"Really," I said, "that's okay. But, hey—nice leaf. Really. A mime couldn't do any better."

God, I was an idiot sometimes.

30

Kelly Seaforth was making her debut at our morning staff meetings. Seated to the left of Roland, she had on a cherry-red version of the sea-green suit she'd worn the first day. If she'd been a television anchor, it would have been called a power suit.

Still trying too hard, I thought.

These daily meetings were held before we opened for business for the day. There were also monthly meetings, more formal, to which even those who had the day off tried to attend. At either the daily or monthly meetings, there was always plenty of coffee going around the group of twenty and someone usually brought in doughnuts or some other sugary snack.

"Would you like some coffee?" Roland offered Kelly, *just* Kelly.

"Here, I'll get some for you," Pete said, before Kelly had barely had the chance to get the entire one-syllable "yes" out of her mouth.

Jeez, I thought, *you'd think those two had never seen a woman before, as if there weren't seventeen other women in the room.* At my very first staff meeting, nobody had fallen all over themselves trying to get *me* a cup of coffee.

Roland turned on the tape machine to record the meeting. Later, Celia, his administrative assistant, would transcribe the notes and put them in a permanent binder so that anyone who'd missed the meeting could find out what was going on. For more immediate reference, the department heads—Diane from Children's, Susan from Reference, and Kathy from Circ—all took notes so that part-timers not coming in until later in the day or week would know whatever relevant details they needed to know.

It seemed early in the year to be talking about the annual Holiday Can Drive—collecting cans of food for disadvantaged families—but Roland felt like talking about it, so we did.

"I think that's wonderful," said Kelly, "that you give something back to the community on top of the public service you perform daily here."

Roland was so pleased, his glasses steamed up.

Other than the "yes" to coffee, these were the first words I'd heard Kelly speak and I discovered that her voice was uncommonly lovely; if she weren't working here maybe someone would offer her a contract to sing the soundtracks for Disney movies or something.

Diane wanted to talk about story time in the Children's Department.

"It's going great," Diane said, "and is a very popular program. There's just one problem. Occasionally we get a parent who thinks we've offered to babysit his or her child for the hour. The parent leaves the building, goes out for coffee or to run an errand, and before you know it, that's the one child we're having problems with and we can't find anybody."

"Oh, how awful," Kelly sympathized, as though she'd never heard of such a thing. "Perhaps if you put a note on the flyer," she gently suggested, "something along the lines of 'Program only available to children able to sit quietly without their parents, however one parent must remain in the building at all times' you could avoid that situation?"

Diane was writing furiously. "What a fabulous idea!" she said, as if no one else had ever thought of the idea, as if there weren't already a similar sentence on all the flyers about story time in the library.

Then Kathy wanted to discuss how, with the colder season upon us, it got chilly for the workers in Circ, the station being right next to the front door, which, naturally, kept opening and closing.

Celia, whose desk was upstairs in front of Roland's and thus far from the draft, got a little acerbic with Kathy.

"Gee," said Celia, "isn't the whole *point* of a public library to have the public use it? Don't we *want* the front doors to be opening and closing a lot?"

Naturally, the staff offices where Celia worked were upstairs, and, since heat rises, the area where Celia worked was always way too warm in the cold season, a fact she was quick to point out.

Before Roland could speak up to mediate, Kelly stepped into the breach.

First, she turned to Kathy: "Perhaps you and your staff could wear layers to work? If you don't have enough, I have some sweaters I knitted I could bring in."

Then she turned to Celia: "And couldn't you wear layers to work and then take some off once you get here? Sure, it's too hot upstairs now for a sweater, but I'll bet a nice cool Oxford shirt would be just the right thing."

Celia, who was preppy in the extreme and who had never met a J. Crew catalog she didn't like, was clearly pleased with the idea.

"What kind of yarn do you knit with?" Kathy asked Kelly, leaning across the table. "I'm allergic to one-hundred-percent wool, but if it were a blend…"

Oh, jeez, I thought, *why not just let Ms. Gorgeous Whiz Kid run the whole place?*

Then Susan wanted to talk about a problem they were having in Reference and, of course, Kelly had the solution.

"Wow," said Susan, slumping back in her chair. "I should just take my month's vacation now and let *you* run the department."

See what I mean?

And the most annoying thing was that Susan didn't even look peeved when she said it. She looked *grateful!*

Still, I didn't think Susan should take it so lightly. From the look on Roland's face, he'd have loved nothing more than to be able to lay Susan's job at Princess Kelly's feet.

Roland looked at his notes, then looked around the table. "Well," he said, "I've got everything covered that I wanted to talk about today. Anybody else?"

There were no takers.

"More coffee, Kelly?" Roland asked.

Kelly shook her head, which kind of surprised me, since she seemed like the kind of woman who just looked for opportunities to let men do things for her. She probably even carried her own supply of suicidal hankies, so she could surreptitiously throw one on the ground and wait for a man to pick it up, always relying on the kindness of strangers.

"Wonderful!" he said. "I've never had a staff meeting go so smoothly." Then he turned to Kelly. "Thank you so much for all your insightful input. I can see that adding you to the staff was a wise decision."

The meeting adjourned.

Five minutes later, the room cleared of the rest of the staff and the front door opened for business, Jane and I were at our stations behind the Circ Desk.

"So what'd you think of her?" Jane asked.

I knew who she was talking about right away. I tried not to make a face, failed, grimaced. The most charitable thing I could think of to say was: "She seems to be trying too hard."

"You think?" asked Jane, clearly astonished at my response, which was clearly different from hers. "That girl's the bee's knees, and then some." Then she paused for a moment, considering. "I wonder what color sweater she'll give me?"

The impossible had happened: Saul Waters called and asked me out, the sheer wonder of it immediately ejecting all concerns over Kelly Seaforth out of my head.

Phone pressed to my ear, having passed through my initial reaction, which was to hold the phone away from myself in shock upon realizing who was calling me, I was nearly dancing with glee in my kitchen. It was all I could do to keep from saying what I was really thinking: *Are you fucking nuts? Why in the world would you want to go out with me?*

"So, I was thinking…" he said.

You were thinking that you're fucking nuts and that you've changed your mind? my mind continued to taunt.

"I was thinking," he said, "that we could go to Bethel Cinema, maybe grab a bite to eat afterward. That is, of course, if you're not busy tonight."

How could I be busy on a Saturday night now that I was Lettie? Well, of course I'd told Pam we'd do something. But she'd understand. Having seen Saul the night I'd met him in Chalk Is Cheap, she'd understand.

And, oh, how this would vindicate me. After all, this gorgeous man had met me as dowdy Lettie and he *still* was asking me out, he *still* couldn't resist the woman underneath. I'd been right all along: it was me that men had been attracted to all my life, not the surface packaging that rendered me as one of life's swans.

I was so busy stroking my inner crow that I nearly missed the details involving what movie we'd be seeing, something either produced or directed by Clint Eastwood. Whatever. Just so long as he wasn't taking his shirt off—Clint, that is, not Saul. Saul could take his shirt off. And the only reason I didn't want Clint to take his shirt off wasn't that I was ageist but because I was sick of a system in which it was acceptable for a seventy-year-old man to take off his shirt in front of millions of people, but if a seventy-year-old woman did it...

Well, actually, that's the point: a seventy-year-old woman *wouldn't* be allowed to do it, and probably wouldn't even be in the film.

Be that as it may...

"Pick you up at seven?" Saul asked.

"Perfect," I said, thinking, *What kind of adult asks a woman out for a first date at a movie theater? I hadn't been on one of those since before I turned twenty.*

I couldn't wait to call Pam, tell her the news.

"So," she said, and I had the weirdest sense she was angry, like I could see her with one arm crossed defensively under her breasts, the back of her hand propping up the elbow of the hand that held the phone, as she beat an irritated tattoo with the toe of her high-heeled boot against the floor.

Just a hunch.

"So," she said, "that gorgeous guy you met at Chalk Is Cheap *actually* called you up and you're *actually* going on a date with him tonight?"

"Actually? Yes."

I don't know what I was expecting. Perhaps that a woman I considered to be one of my closest friends, my Default Best Friend, would be happy for my good fortune?

I tried to brush off the feeling that every time I succeeded, my Default Best Friend died a little death.

"Yes, Pam, he actually did and we actually are…and I'm so excited! I'm trying to decide what to wear. If I go with jeans, I'll feel too casual. But if I go with a short skirt, I'll feel like I'm pushing it, since it's getting cold out, so why would I be wearing a short skirt, unless I was trying to let him see—"

"You can't wear jeans or a short skirt."

"I can't?"

"No." And now I thought I heard her smile. "You have to wear your uniform."

"No!" I practically shouted, horrified. "Don't make me!"

"But you really do have to, Scarlett. After all, how will you know if he really likes you for you?"

With a sunken heart, I realized that, of course, Pam was right.

If Saul really wanted to go out with me for me, it shouldn't matter to him if I didn't go to any extreme measures to look better than I had when we first met. With that in mind, then, I did the best I could, given the confining rules of the game I was playing: I put on a fresh shapeless long dress, rust-colored this time, wiped off the lenses in my glasses, washed my face and washed my short black hair.

Well, at least I was clean.

For good measure, I put some lip balm on my lips. Surely, taking that single measure as a preemptive strike against looking like Linda Blair in *The Exorcist* must be permissible under Pam's stringent rules.

When I opened the door for Saul, I was perversely relieved that he'd taken no efforts to look any different during this, our first planned date meeting, than he had on our first accidental meeting. He still was committed to the idea of black being the color that suited him best. And it did.

"Great place," he said, poking his head into the living room. "It's so cozy in here. I've never been much good at doing the cozy-home thing myself."

"Yes, well…"

I looked around, taking in the room as he must be seeing it: the table I'd added next to the rocking chair, piled high with books waiting to be read; the couch with the overstuffed cushions; the delicate curtains letting in the early evening light; the Halloween decorations I'd already put up around the big fireplace. I was tempted to tell him that I'd never been much good at doing the cozy-home thing, either, that this was all Lettie's doing.

But I couldn't tell him that.

"Ready?" I smiled brightly.

When we got to Bethel Cinema, I fished my wallet out of my big bag. Even though it had been months since my last date—a longer dry spell than any I'd had since hitting puberty—I still remembered my own etiquette of offering to pay my fair share until I knew the lay of the land.

But Saul wasn't having any.

"Put that away," he said, smiling. "I had a good week at work. It's my treat."

Okay, so maybe I'm archaic, maybe I'm the kind of woman who needs someone else to burn a bra on her behalf—well, I certainly can't go braless—but I've always been charmed by men who insist on paying. I don't mind carrying my financial weight, not at all, but I like men who don't go through life with mothballs in their wallets, I like men who hold doors for you, pull out chairs.

"Popcorn? Candy?" he offered.

I said no to the popcorn, figuring the last thing I wanted were popcorn kernels stuck in all my teeth when it came time for him to kiss me later.

"M&M's," I finally said, figuring they were the perfect non-messy thing for the occasion. How is a girl like a green M&M, indeed?

Apparently, Saul wasn't at all concerned about the prospect of popcorn kernels interfering with our kissing later on, since he ordered himself a large bag with butter and a bottle of water.

As we sat in the darkened movie theater, I tried to concentrate on the movie—was there a murder? was there a river? and where the hell was Clint Eastwood?—but I just couldn't force my mind to focus on it. I was too busy wondering about the more important things in the world, like, should I lean my shoulder far enough to the right so that it made contact with Saul's, thus hopefully inspiring in him the conditioned response of putting his arm around me? Was his thigh resting against mine a conscious effort on his part or was it the natural result of his having long legs and needing to do something with them in a small space? And where the hell was Clint Eastwood?

I hadn't felt this rattled, this insecure, this completely and totally first-date heebie-jeebie weird since…since…I'd *never* felt this way!

By the time the credits rolled, I honestly couldn't have said if I'd been watching Sean Penn or Elmer Fudd.

Saul looked like he'd enjoyed himself, so I said, "Wow, powerful stuff," hoping I'd hit the mark. For good measure, I added, "I really liked the director's use of the color blue," since the one lasting impression I did have was that the film had had a lot of blue in it.

He looked at me strangely, then smiled. "Would you like to go get a coffee and some dessert?"

I wasn't much of a coffee drinker, except for maybe once or twice a year; I couldn't imagine he was still hungry after downing that whole thing of popcorn; and I certainly didn't need more dessert to go on top of the M&M dessert I'd just had, but I was grateful he wanted to extend the evening. I mean, sure, I was anxious for our first kiss to take place— oh, how I wanted him to kiss me!—but we hadn't really done any talking yet, other than about my decorating skills, who was going to pay, what we were going to eat and the director's use of blue. Surely, he was right: we should do some more talking before we got to the kissing.

As Saul pulled his blue Lexus into a spot out front of Mister Caffeine, I experienced an immediate sense of nervousness, half expecting to find Steve Holt in there as Saul held the door, all covered with Steve's Halloween painting.

But there was no Steve inside, just other after-movie people and a half-dozen teenagers, waiting to be old enough to go to a proper bar on Saturday night rather than a coffee bar.

Remembering the rule that states that even if you're not hungry or thirsty, if your date is interested in eating and drinking you must engage in same, because otherwise you look weirdly ascetic or like a potential eating disorder and most men really don't want a girl who is no fun or who they have to visit in the hospital while she's being force-fed through an IV, I ordered a small black decaf and a slice of mudcake I could fork around my plate. He ordered a large mocha-something and apple pie, which seemed like a strange combo to me, but what did I care? He was going to be kissing me soon. First dates always ended in kisses at the very least. I'd never had one that hadn't.

Perhaps, feeling overly enthusiastic and anxious about the kissing yet to come, I blurted out, "I can't remember the last time I was on a first date that involved going to see a movie! I was probably fifteen the last time—"

Something about the way he dropped his pie fork cut me off mid-anecdote.

He reddened slightly, looking unsure about what to say. Then: "You thought this was a *date?*"

"Well, I…" I became flustered, no doubt reddening some myself.

"When I called you up and asked you what you were doing tonight, you assumed I was asking you out on a *date?*"

"Yes, well, that usually is the way that…"

"I'm sorry, Lettie," he said, looking more embarrassed now for me than for himself as he covered my hand gently with one of his beautiful hands. "This isn't a date."

"Oh."

"It's just that…"

"Just that what?"

"When I met you at Chalk Is Cheap, you just seemed so lonely, like you could use a friend."

"Oh, I see. You just had a free night and figured you would, oh, I don't know, do me a favor."

"Don't make it sound like that. It's not like that at all." He paused, perhaps looking for the right words to explain what it *was* like. "I like you. I really do. And everyone can use friends. Even me. I just thought we could be friends, you know, do things together occasionally. You seem like the kind of woman who'd make a great friend."

It's hard to remove your hand from someone else's without appearing either dismissive or wounded, but I decided to risk giving both of those impressions as I disengaged my hand from his.

"That's okay." I forced a good-natured laugh. "Did you think I was serious before about that first-date stuff? Well, I wasn't. I was just joking around, that's all."

And, in order to salvage my pride, I proceeded to spend the next hour being the best sport I could be. I encouraged him to talk about himself, about his work, his family, his favorite sports teams, smiling at everything he said, all the while thinking on the inside, *When the evening's over, when he takes me home, he's not going to kiss me. Of all the things that might happen tonight—a fender bender, a falling star landing at my feet—the one thing I know for sure that is not going to happen is that he is not going to kiss me.*

While we were talking, I could see he genuinely did like me. Well, what wasn't to like? I was a good listener and I made him laugh. It seemed a shame, really, the idea of a world in which someone like him would never kiss someone like me.

When the time came to leave a tip for the pie he'd eaten

and the cake I had not, I tossed a generous twenty-five percent on the table. When he tried to stop me, I said, "No way.
Friends share expenses." I even made myself smile when I
said it.

As he dropped me off in front of my house a few minutes later, I looked for a falling star, didn't see any. A good
sport to the end, I asked, "Are you busy for Halloween?"

"No," he said, a bit surprised. "Why?"

"Because I'm having a little party here that night and I
thought you'd like to come. You know, as just friends."

"Thanks for asking me," he said. "I'd like that. I haven't
dressed up for Halloween in years."

31

Ever since her first visit to see me at Bethel Library, Sarah had taken to stopping by regularly when she got off school or sometimes on weekends, just to chat. When she came in the afternoons, she even got along with Pat—not an easy thing. But Sarah was a nice girl (despite the fact that she'd given me the chicken pox) and impossible not to like. She'd even become one of the library's volunteers, making sure the alphabetization of the books remained an exact science and not an approximate art, to justify to Roland the inordinate amount of time she spent there with me.

I'd promised her, on her first visit, that I'd help her find a way to get around the problem of her changing body and her mother's reluctance to let her take appropriate measures, but as the Halloween deadline drew near I still hadn't done anything. Now that Saul had accepted the invitation to my party, however, the thought came to me that it was now do or die.

But what to do, what to do…?

Well, I was a research librarian by trade, wasn't I, even if a former one? Surely, I could figure out *something*.

While Pat was on break and Sarah was off making sure Ross Thomas never got ahead of D. M. Thomas again, I went into the library's computer system, looked for patron information on Nancy Davis in Danbury.

There she was.

Feeling like I was doing something wrong, I looked around me for witnesses, saw only one patron looking at the video racks and picked up the phone, punching in the Davis phone number.

Sarah's mother picked up on the second ring.

"Ms. Davis, you probably don't remember me. This is Lettie Shaw. We met when—"

"Of course I remember you," she said. "You're the librarian, the woman Sarah told me she's been working for over at Bethel Library."

"Well, she doesn't exactly work for me…"

"Oh, no? That's not what she says. She loves it there, by the way."

"Well, yes, libraries can be great places."

"She says she's become invaluable to you."

What to say to that? The woman was probably jealous I was usurping her place with her daughter or something; I knew my mother would have been.

I looked up at the ceiling. "Yes, well…"

"Hey," she said, "don't get me wrong. I think it's great."

"You do?"

"Sure, if not for you, she'd probably be hanging out at the mall, getting into all sorts of trouble, buying inappropriate clothes like all her friends."

"Funny you should say that...Ms. Davis, would it be all right if I took Sarah shopping?"

"Shopping?"

I explained to her, as delicately as I could, about the Sadie Hawkins dance and Jeff Polanski, hairy legs and no bra, Monkey and Jiggles.

"They call her Monkey and...Jiggles?" she asked when I was done. I could almost see her wince through the phone.

"I'm afraid so."

I could hear her thinking now.

"And you say you'll take her to get whatever she needs, so that nobody calls her Monkey or Jiggles anymore?"

"Yes," I said, letting out a big breath I didn't know I'd been holding. "Everything."

"But no push-up bras," she warned, "no bikini waxes."

"I promise," I swore.

"How much do you think this will cost me?" she asked.

"Never mind that," I said. "It's my treat."

"Gee," she asked, "if you take her to get the things she wants, do you think this Jeff Polanski will say yes to her invitation?"

"Who knows?" I said.

"Oh, lordy, lordy," she said, "her dad'll probably kill us all."

As soon as the clock ticked five-thirty, Sarah and I locked the doors on the library and hit the shops. Rather than the mall, I planned to take her to some of the boutiquey places that lined Greenwood Avenue. It being Thursday night, many were open late.

In a lingerie shop called Underthingies, we had her fitted for a bra. I could tell she was uncomfortable with the saleslady measuring her, just like I'd always been uncomfortable whenever my mother had yelled, "Foundations? Foundations? Do you sell foundations for my daughter here?" But we laughed through it, and in the end bought her a couple of pretty snow-white bras with tiny satin flowers at the cleavage. They weren't exactly Victoria's Secret Naughty Collection, but they were a far cry from the trainers my mother had bought me and would hopefully put an end to Jiggles.

Then I took her to the Bethel Underground and bought her something funky to wear over her new bra: a long-sleeved, eerily greenish-yellow T-shirt with an image of Paris on it that had opaque red sleeves, and *almost* low-slung black jeans that I thought were icky but knew from what I saw teenage girls in the library wear, her friends would envy.

Then I realized something. "Hey," I said, "isn't this Sadie Hawkins dance supposed to be on Halloween? Shouldn't we be getting you some kind of costume instead?"

"Nah," she said, "they only hold it on Halloween because they think Halloween is bad for kids. My school doesn't believe in Halloween."

"So they think it's better to just have a dance where the girls ask the boys and everyone tries to make out when the chaperones aren't looking?" I asked, remembering my own young days.

She rolled her eyes at me. "I guess." Every now and then, I'm sure I was just another stupid adult to her.

We hopped into English Drug and picked up a razor for later—we were going to do the deed at my place—before heading over to Snips & Moans. I hoped Ms. Davis wasn't going to mind, but I'd arranged for Helen to do something about that old-fashioned pageboy. It just had to go.

Forty-five minutes later, we were on the way to my place,

a very young Audrey Hepburn at my side. Without all that hair weighing her down, it was possible now to see Sarah's gamine features. I couldn't help but think, too, that her new haircut looked kind of like my new haircut, only hers didn't look ragged, as if she'd done it all by herself with a pair of tiny gold scissors.

Back at my place, we squeezed into the tiny bathroom off my bedroom upstairs.

"So, how do you use one of these things?" Sarah asked, studying the pink plastic razor as though it might be a tiny alien.

I shrugged. "You just scrape it along your legs."

She looked at me doubtfully.

"Why don't I just leave you alone?" I offered, inching out the door. I mean, I liked Sarah, but I didn't necessarily want to watch her shave.

"Ouch!" I heard a minute later.

"What?" I opened the door.

On Sarah's legs were three tiny drops of blood.

"Are you really sure I'm supposed to dry-shave, Lettie?" she asked, baleful and accusing at the same time. "Isn't there a reason they invented shaving cream?"

"Sorry." I winced. What did I know? When my mother had finally grown tired of my own complaints at being called Monkey, she'd tossed me in the bathroom by myself with a similarly Pepto-colored razor. Of course I cut myself a lot at first. But, over the course of the intervening thirty-plus years, I'd managed to learn how to do it without drawing blood every single time. "Maybe if you used soap and water?" I winced again.

Another fifteen minutes, some soap and water, and a few tiny Band-Aids later, found us on my couch, sharing a tub of Ready-to-Spread Frosting with two spoons. They'd only had chocolate the last time I'd gone shopping, which had started to taste more plasticy the past few years, but what the heck.

"Gee," said Sarah, "do you think Jeff Polanski will say yes?"

All of a sudden, I couldn't believe what I'd let myself become a part of. I'd encouraged Sarah to think that if she made just a few cosmetic changes, she'd get what she wanted; as if those cosmetic changes were the most important thing in the world and not the girl underneath. But she looked so hopeful....

"If he doesn't," I said, "then he's an idiot."

32

It was a pretty poor excuse for a Halloween party.

Unable on such short notice to get together much of a crowd, we were going to be eight in number. Pam, Delta, T.B. and Ex-Al were all coming, plus my mother. Hey, it was a holiday; my mother had always insisted that all holidays be spent with family—she even made me come for Easter every year, even though it was not our holiday and we traditionally ate meatless lasagna rather than lamb or ham—and I hated the thought of her being alone. I'd put up an open invitation on one of the cabinets in the staff room at Bethel Library, but the only one to RSVP with a "yes" had been sour Pat, which was okay with me, since I'd been worried that Kelly might say "yes" and there was no way I could disinclude just one person from the staff. When Kelly told me she couldn't come "—I always like to stay home and hand out candy by myself on Halloween—" she'd added, "But I really hope you and I can have lunch together someday soon, Lettie. I think we could be real friends."

As if.

Oh, and Saul Waters, the man who only wanted to be my friend, was coming, too. And me, of course.

To make up in decorations what we didn't have in numbers, I'd added to the Halloween decorations Saul had seen on his previous visit. The living room was festooned in black-and-orange streamers and a gazillion pumpkins of all sizes, each painstakingly carved into jack-o'-lanterns with a different face—happy, sad, silly, scary and even one that looked astonishingly like a young David Letterman. I had enough different-size orange candles burning to qualify me as a psychopathic serial killer waiting to entrap my next victim, and I'd even lined the walk leading up to the front door with those little candle-in-paper-bags things. I can never remember what they're called. Something French. Papiers? Candliers? You'd think a woman who used to be a reference librarian would know such a thing. I'd always thought those things looked vaguely dangerous whenever I'd seen them at other people's houses. Weren't they some kind of fire hazard that should be against the law? But, I figured, if the fire department showed up, it was all to my good. After all, it seemed to me that women in stories were always finding their one true love in the shape of a hunky firefighter who'd caught them in the act of doing something truly stupid.

Not much of a cook, having inherited my mother's sucky-cook gene, I'd settled for a bunch of frozen mini-pizzas. Nobody really came to these kinds of parties to eat, right? Besides, the nice thing about having predictable friends was that I knew that even though I'd told them not to bring anything, that I had the food situation covered, they would all bring something, knowing how lacking I was in any discernible cooking skills. And, just in case they disappointed me, I'd put together a kickass vodka punch that would make everyone quickly forget the lack of food. Feeling like Martha Stewart in her better days, I'd used orange food coloring to obtain a hue that looked like the pee of someone with a serious vitamin deficiency. The drink itself, though it looked preschool appropriate, was almost pure alcohol. For festivity's sake, I planned to serve it in little glass cups with curved handles that had black cats painted on them for good luck.

During my years in the condo, I'd grown used to having about two hundred kids troop up to my door over the course of each Halloween night. But a talk with one of my new Bethel neighbors, the only neighbor who'd ever really said hi yet, had revealed that it wasn't likely to be busy here. A lot of people took their kids to community celebrations instead, plus the street we lived on had only a few houses, set far apart. Just to be on the safe side, I'd called the party for 9:00 p.m., figuring that if there were any trick-or-treaters, the only ones who would still be out then would be of the thug variety, the teenagers without costumes who expect you to give them something *just because,* and that if I got any of those, it would be a good idea to have a group of people behind single ol' me.

An acquaintance who'd lived on Long Island in a similar setup to my Danbury condo had once told me about how, one year, she hadn't locked her door yet, only to come back downstairs to find a large teenager in army fatigues sitting at her dining-room table; apparently, he'd let himself in. This had impressed my acquaintance as being rather, um, *odd.*

Freaking out internally, she'd called back upstairs to an imaginary husband, "Honey! We've got another trick-or-treater and we're all out of candy. Do you think maybe you could run out to the store and get some more?"

Upon hearing this, my acquaintance's uninvited guest rose to his feet and said, "Uh, that's okay. I'll catch you guys next year."

My acquaintance had thought she'd been smooth, getting herself out of a potentially tricky situation where she could have turned out to be the treat, but I had thought, *What a screwball! What if the uninvited guest had said, "Sure, I'll wait while your husband goes to get my candy"?*

Anyway, to set the mood for my own Halloween party, I'd put together a tape so that my guests would be treated to a constant loop of "The Monster Mash," lots of Warren Zevon, and an old Hollies song, "Long Cool Woman in a Black Dress." Even though I wasn't *long,* I was determined to be the *cool* woman in the black dress in the song. While I was dying to know what everyone else was going to dress up as, not wanting to reveal my own costume in advance, I'd made everybody swear not to reveal theirs until the night of the actual party. Growing up, I'd noticed a trend in the costume choices of boys and girls: a large percentage of girls wanted to be princesses, while a large percentage of boys wanted to be something scary. The whole Women Are From Disney, Men Are From The Black Lagoon thing confirmed my belief that females cared more about pleasing, while males wanted to intimidate. Of course, we were all adults now. But I still believed that a choice of Halloween costume said something about the person doing the choosing.

Ding-dong!

As I moved to answer the door, I spared a thought for Sarah, wondering how her Sadie Hawkins dance was going, if Jeff Polanski had said yes.

I would have bet any amount of money the first guest would be my mother, a woman for whom tardiness was the equivalent of adultery with your best friend's husband, but—surprise!—it was T.B. and Ex-Al.

T.B. looked positively soignée, decked out in a matching fuchsia belted top and pantsuit, circa midseventies, her hair poofed up in a mushroom shape with bangs that looked more like a black helmet than hair. Beside her, Ex-Al, bearing a plate of what looked like stuffed artichokes beneath the cling wrap—did I know my friends or what?—was dressed in a boring business suit, his black hair dusted with powder, his black face painted as close as he could get it to white.

"Um," I said, taking the plate of good food, inviting them in, "y'all are supposed to be…?"

"Tom and Helen," said T.B., like I was supposed to know.

"Who?"

"Tom and Helen," she repeated, "the mixed marriage from *The Jeffersons.*"

"T.B. wanted to be Lenny Kravitz's mother," said Ex-Al, referring to the rock star, "but neither of us knew what Lenny's father looked like, so this was the closest we could get."

As I looked at how ridiculous Ex-Al looked, and all to please my friend, I wondered yet again why she had ever divorced this man.

"But never mind us," T.B. said, taking in my own getup, "oh, is Pam gonna be pissed when she gets a load of you."

Ding-dong!

Saved by my mother, something I never thought I'd be.

"Mom…um—"

"I'm a Jewish princess!" she said, thrusting a plate of chopped liver in my hands I knew would go back home with her, untouched, at evening's end.

She had a paste tiara on her head, her body wrapped in a blue-and-white tallis, toga-style.

"Isn't wearing that, um, like that…sacrilegious?"

"Sacrilegious, schmacrilegious," she pooh-poohed me. "I always wanted to be a princess, but who in their right mind would want to be Cinderella? All those chores to do first. So what? I'll repent next Yom Kippur." Then she looked at me, wagged her finger. "Pam's not going to like this."

Ding-dong!

And there was Delta, obviously dressed as Little Bo Peep, with a hoop skirt that barely made it through my door for all the crinolines, her hair in loose curls, a shepherd's staff in one hand, a plate of chocolate cheesecake brownies in the other.

"I lost my sheep," she said, "and damn am I glad! I got a sitter for Mush and Teenie. I'm going to leave them alone and not come home until I'm tired of wagging my tail behind me. But shit, Scarlett," she said, in the midst of her astonishment messing up and using my old name, "Pam's gonna kill you."

"I don't even know who Scarlett and Pam are," said Pat from the library, coming up right behind Delta, "but I'll bet Pam will kill you, too."

I tried to figure out what Pat was supposed to be, but she looked no different than she did every afternoon when I worked with her at the library: pleated slacks belted above a slight bulge, matching turtleneck tucked in, glasses in place, sour.

"I came as me," she said, reading my expression. "What the hell kind of adults play dress-up on a kids' holiday?" She looked at the brownies Delta was still holding. "Oh. Was I supposed to bring something?"

"Help yourself to some vodka punch," I offered.

"Oh, is there vodka in here?" my mother asked, already halfway through her first glass. "I thought it was just juice."

Ding-dong!

Saved by the bell one last time.

Pam.

Pam dressed as a giant pumpkin.

Angry Pam dressed as a giant pumpkin, staring at me with serious anger in her eyes.

There was going to be no saving me this time.

"You…*bitch!*" Pam seethed.

"You must be Pam," said Pat, vodka glass in one hand, brownie in the other, shaking her hips to "Werewolves of London."

I took Pam's green elbow—she was wearing a green turtleneck under the giant pumpkin costume—and led her through a tentative chorus of "Hey, Pam" to the kitchen.

"What seems to be the problem?" I asked, arms crossed beneath the generous helping of cleavage created by the long V in my long and, okay, tight black dress. I noticed that, unlike the others—well, except for Pat—Pam had arrived empty-handed, save for a bottle of pumpkin schnapps. I didn't even know anybody *made* pumpkin schnapps.

"You," she spat, "you're the problem. By wearing that costume, you're breaking the rules."

The costume in question involved the aforementioned dress, which had fringe on the ends of the bell sleeves and at the hemline, mile-high black heels, perfectly applied makeup, and hair, while still short, that had been gelled into a sporty, slightly spiky shape. I'd left off my glasses in favor of contacts.

"Am not," I replied. "It's Halloween. People get to dress up as whomever they want to on Halloween, even people like Lettie Shaw. It's the Halloween Rule."

"Who are you supposed to be, anyway? Vampirella?"

"I'm Morticia Adams," I huffed.

"But Morticia had long hair," she objected.

"So," I said, hands-on-hipsing her as I leaned forward, the better to get myself in her face, "Morticia cut it. She cut it because she let her best friend in Danbury talk her into some insane idea."

"But—"

"Besides," I said, feeling very testy, "is it my fault you chose to come as a pumpkin? That with all the possible costumes in the world you could pick from, you chose a *pumpkin?*"

"Can I help it," she huffed, "if I lack imagination?"

"No," I said, "but that's not my fault, either."

"But—" She tried to "but" me one last time, but I stopped her.

"Look," I said, suddenly feeling bad for her, suddenly feeling as though maybe I had done something slightly wrong, behaved deceptively, "it's not like there are any guys here to compete for," which was a slight lie, since I had invited Saul, but it was getting later—almost ten—and I was beginning to think he wouldn't be coming.

"Ex-Al's here," she said, still pouting.

"He doesn't count," I said. "He's so in love with T.B., he wouldn't notice us if we were both naked."

"He really is in love with her, isn't he?" she asked.

"No doubt."

"How do some women get that lucky?" she wondered wistfully.

"Who knows?" I said. "The point is, the only people at

this party are you, me, Delta, my mother, Pat and a couple in love, so what does it matter if you're a pumpkin and I'm Morticia?"

Ding-dong!

Just when I'd given up on my last guest arriving—it was a quarter to eleven, after all—the doorbell rang one last time. Glass of punch in hand—that cat on my glass was starting to look a little drunk—I threw the door open, only to find...

"Al Franken?"

Okay, so maybe it wasn't really Al Franken, just Saul Waters in an Al Franken disguise that involved, well, a pair of glasses. Other than that, he had on his regular black-over-black costume. I was thinking that, really, his regular outfit could have formed the springboard for something other than a political humorist—with a cape and mask, for just one example, he could have been Zorro, mmm—when he said:

"Am I too late for the party?"

"Not at all," I said, waving my arm. "Come on in."

"Lettie?" he said, sounding surprised.

"What? You didn't think I'd still let you in—" I checked my watch "—if you were an hour and forty-five minutes late?"

"No. I mean, yes, I did still think you'd let me in. But no, that's not what I was surprised about."

"What, then?"

"You just look so...incredibly different."

"Thanks, I guess. Would you like to meet everyone?"

He nodded, but I could see he was having trouble taking his eyes off me; well, my cleavage, if you want to know the truth.

I took him around the room, feeling quite the domina-trix as he trailed behind me, curiously obedient.

"This is my mother, the Jewish princess."

My mother offered her hand for him to kiss and he obliged with a little bow.

"This is the actress who played Helen and the actor who played Tom on *The Jeffersons.*"

"Hey, Roxie Roker!" Saul said to T.B.

"Who?" I said.

"The actress who played Helen," T.B. said, pleased, "Lenny Kravitz's mother. That's her name."

I turned to Saul. "Do you also remember who played Tom?"

"Sorry," he said.

"This is Little Bo Peep," I said.

"Delta," Delta cooed in his direction. "I'll hunt for your sheep anytime."

"And Pat from the library," I moved on, figuring there was really no way for him to rightly answer Delta's remark.

"And what are you supposed to be?" Saul asked Pat, somewhat gently.

"Didn't you hear what Lettie said?" she barked at him. "I'm Pat, Pat from the library."

"Ah," he said.

"And this is…" But as we arrived in front of Pam, I couldn't bring myself to introduce her as I'd done with the others, as what she was dressed up as. I didn't need to, though. She did it for me.

"I'm a giant pumpkin," she said sourly, reaching out one orange-painted hand that was attached to one green-clad arm from out of her enormous pumpkin costume. Then she tried to turn on the flirt switch, brightening. "But you can call me Pam."

★ ★ ★

Even when a crowd is evenly matched between men and women, there's a tendency for the men to converge around the alpha female, with the women around the alpha male. Until the story's finally written, until the alpha of either sex decides upon whom to bestow his or her charms, the others figure they might as well still compete since they're technically in the running. Imagine, then, how much more competition would ensue if there were only one man—gorgeous Saul—facing off against five women. I figured it as being five against one, since T.B. and Ex-Al didn't really count in this; Ex-Al, because he was taken out of the running by his obvious love for T.B.; T.B., because she had taken Frank Sinatra to heart and knew that if you come to the party with one guy, it's not nice to blow on another guy's dice.

Truthfully, though, even T.B. and Ex-Al were somewhat taken with Saul. He was that good.

"Damn," said Ex-Al, "he knew who Roxie Roker was. I didn't even know who Roxie Roker was."

"And he even makes those stupid glasses look good," said T.B. "I might get me a pair."

No one seemed to notice or mind that Saul had brought nothing but himself to contribute to the occasion, and, thankfully, T.B. and Ex-Al were at least enough into each other that they left the Saul field clear for the five of us.

And it really was quite a competition.

I saw a side of my mom that I'd never seen before as she pulled out all the flirting stops. It was a side I'd only imagined before, a side I was sure my father had known all too well. Meanwhile, Delta did that thing that Southern women do so well, swearing like a truck driver while making it sound as though she were talking about barbecues with Rhett Butler on the rolling lawn of her family's estate. Even Pat got into the act, smiling more than I'd ever seen her smile at each word out of Saul's mouth. And Pam did the best a giant pumpkin could do to look alluring, giving Saul come-hither looks from behind her orange face paint.

As for me, well, I didn't really have to do anything. Just sitting on the couch in my Morticia getup, leaning forward occasionally to pick up an hors d'oeuvre or a vodka glass, was enough to secure Saul's attention. Sure, he was polite to all the other women, but he only really had eyes for me.

As the evening wore on, the field naturally became less populated as others moved off or threw in the towel.

The first to leave were T.B. and Ex-Al. Walking them to the door, as T.B. hugged Delta good-night, I leaned tipsily into Ex-Al.

"You know," I said, "you two make a great couple. You really should give it another try."

"We are," he said with a wink, closing the door behind them.

That made me glad.

Then my mom gave up. "I might as well leave you kids to your fun," she said. And Pat followed suit with, "I've got to work the afternoon shift tomorrow. Do you think any-one will notice if I'm still drunk?"

That left Delta.

"Omigod," she said, "is it really after midnight?"

"Only by about two hours," Saul said, smiling at my breasts.

"Shoot!" Delta said. "The sitter's probably been tied to a pair of chair legs for hours. She'll never come back again. I better go."

And then there were two: me and the giant pumpkin.

The giant pumpkin looked just about as pissed as an over-size gourd could look. I could see she was determined to play the waiting game with me: whoever waited the other out the longest would win the guy.

Maybe she'd had more to drink than I had, or maybe she hadn't eaten enough to go with the drink. Whatever the case, she'd been schnapps-ed, and, before another hour passed, the giant pumpkin was out cold on my couch.

"Hi," Saul said softly, saying it as though he were greeting me for the first time.

"Hi," I said back, not sure what else to say.

"Why, Lettie?"

"Why what?"

"You must know what. Why in the world would you go out in the world looking like you did the first two times I met you, when…"

"When what?" I felt unaccountably angry. "When I can look like this?"

"Well, yeah," he admitted.

"It's kind of complicated," I answered, the anger disappearing as fast as it had come. Then, feeling bold: "You want to come upstairs?"

I couldn't believe I was being so openly…*desirous,* but I really couldn't stand it any longer. It had been so long since I'd felt that I was attractive to a man, and Saul was now so obviously attracted to me, I had this overwhelming urge to pin him down before he changed his mind.

His eyebrows rose just a bit in wonderment and then he nodded, clearly pleased as he held his hand out for me to take.

It felt so good, I thought, having in my hand the hand of

a man who wanted me, as I led him up the wooden stairs to the loft above, leaving the snoring pumpkin below.

When he kissed me for the first time, with those lips and mouth and tongue that I'd fantasized about that first night in Chalk Is Cheap, it was like the first time I'd ever been kissed by Danny Wilcox in sixth grade and feeling like a vixen, all rolled into one. I felt something overtake me, a desperate need for validation that could only be met by making love with this man in this moment.

Saul turned me around, slowly undid the zipper on my dress. I felt deliciously like a caterpillar, poised to turn into something else as I felt the dress fall away. Then he unhooked the back of my push-up bra, turned me to face him.

"Oh, Lettie," he said, looking at me in light that came only from the late moon, "why in the world would you ever hide this? You're so beautiful."

I wanted to tell him that I was Scarlett, not Lettie. Right then, though, I felt beautiful. I also felt something else, something uncomfortable that I couldn't name, but mostly I felt beautiful.

Wanting to hide from that uncomfortable feeling, wanting to revel in that feeling of beauty, I set to work divesting him of his clothes.

"Um, I don't think you'll be needing these," I said, removing his Al Franken glasses. "This can go, too," I said, pulling his black turtleneck over his head. "And this," I said, using my teeth to undo the black belt on his pants. "And this, and this, and this," I said, taking off his shoes, his socks and his black pants, in that order. "And most of all this," I said, sliding his jockey shorts over his perfect hips.

The only thing standing between us now was my panties.

"Do you mind?" he said, laying me down on my bed, ripping the panties off me in his eagerness to get to me.

Maybe if this hadn't all been my idea, him in my room making love with me, I would have minded the financial loss of the panties, the violence of his rip. But I didn't mind. In that moment, getting him inside me was all I wanted.

But he wasn't ready for that yet.

He began kissing my neck, featherlight kisses combined with insistent kisses as he worked his way down my body, stopping a long time at my breasts, trailing his tongue over my flat stomach, moving, moving, until gently, he nudged my legs open, kissing his way up the insides of my thighs.

"You are so incredibly beautiful," he murmured. "I just want to make you feel good."

So I let him.

It wasn't until I'd come several times, experiencing the first orgasms I'd had in months that hadn't been self-administered, each time thinking to myself, *Yes, this is what it feels like to be worshipped,* that he moved up again.

All of a sudden, I had an awful realization.

"I'm not prepared," I said anxiously, thinking how even when I'd been sexually active on a regular basis, I'd never been the kind of woman to keep condoms in her drawer. I'm not saying there's anything wrong with being the kind of woman who does keep condoms in her drawer, I'm just saying I'm not one of them. "I don't have any—"

"Shh," he put his finger to my lips. "It's no problem."

He gracefully got off me and the bed, and crossed the room, removing a foil-wrapped item from his pants pocket, ripping it open with his teeth.

"You came prepared?" I don't know why, but I felt surprised. "But you were coming to the party as just my friend."

"Sure," he said easily, "but who knew in advance who you were inviting? Maybe one of your other guests would turn out to suit me. Besides," he added, rolling the condom on, rejoining me on the bed, "I was a Boy Scout. I always come prepared."

I pushed back the residual unease I was feeling as he kissed me again, letting me taste myself on his lips and tongue as he moved his hips between my open thighs and I wrapped my legs around his naked back to pull him deeper into me.

"I just can't get over how beautiful you are," he kept saying, like I was some kind of eighth wonder of the world or something. "I can't get over how beautiful you are."

And, in that moment, I was.

33

I woke the next morning, just a few short hours later, feeling awful, and not just awful because of my raging hangover or the fact that Saul was gone—I could see that, as soon as I opened my eyes—but truly awful, guilty awful, like I'd done a bad thing that I couldn't take back.

Saul might have been gone, but he'd left behind a note on the pillow:

Lettie, I had a fantastic time with you last night, but I needed to leave early to meet a tennis date. I'll call you, though. I'll *definitely* call you.
Saul.

The note should have made me feel better, but somehow it didn't. *We'll see,* I thought.

I lay in bed, trying to figure out why I felt so awful. It wasn't, after all, like an adult woman sleeping with an adult man was some kind of crime or something. I hadn't killed anybody.

So why did I feel as though I *had* killed somebody?

Admittedly, feeling as though I'd killed somebody was a little bit extreme. Still, I did feel as though I'd somehow lured Saul into my bed under false pretenses. But wasn't that insane? It was the Lettie person I'd become who was the false pretense, with her Mother Hubbard dresses and her tentative speech. It had been Scarlett who had slept with Saul last night. Well, okay, a Halloween version of Scarlett, but still Scarlett, right?

But it didn't feel that way. It felt as though the woman I had been the night before, the woman who had invited Saul to sleep with her, was a woman not myself.

Who was *that woman?* I wondered.

But I knew the answer: she was a woman who just wanted and needed attention, validation and, yeah, maybe love, I guess.

I wrenched myself away from the pleasure of beating myself up, went to the bathroom, threw water on my face, brushed the grit from my teeth and threw on a navy silk robe, tied the sash around my waist and headed downstairs. I may not have been a coffee person, but I was going to need something caffeinated to help me restore my physical sense of balance. Maybe if I felt physically better, I'd feel less like someone should take me out in the yard and shoot me.

Unfortunately, when I got down to the living room, there was someone waiting there to shoot me.

"Well, at least one of us had a good time."

Apparently, the angry pumpkin had never left, because she was still on my couch, some of her orange makeup having faded overnight.

"I had an okay time," I said. "Coffee?"

"Sure. Why not?"

Even I could boil water for instant. As I put that together, along with a serving of leftovers from the night before, the phone rang.

"Scarlett!"

"Mom!" I tried to sound equally enthusiastic, but: "Um, didn't I just see you last night?"

"I just wanted to know how things went with you and Saul after I left. Did Pam succeed in waiting you out?"

Clearly, my mom was a pro at how that little game was played.

"Uh, not quite," I said, eyeing my pumpkin friend.

"So, is he Jewish?"

"I don't know," I said. "It hasn't come up."

"But Saul's a Jewish name."

"Well, sometimes it is, but I don't think we have a patent on it or anything."

"And will you be seeing him again?"

"I don't know," I said. "We'll see."

"You know, I've been thinking," she said. "I know I said I liked the new clothes you've been wearing lately and all, but maybe it's not such a good idea? Saul did seem to like you very much the way you were last night."

Saul had liked me very much the way I'd been last night. He'd liked me in a way he hadn't liked me before. It got me thinking that in a weird way, even though the Lettie part of me was supposed to be the ruse, it hadn't been *me* Saul had wanted at all.

"I don't know," I said, not wanting to talk about it anymore. "Mom? Pam's here, so—"

"She's *still* there? Oh, well. You should have said."

We hung up.

"So you're going to be seeing him again?" Pam said, drawing her own conclusions from my share of the conversation.

"I don't know," I said, maintaining my party line. I wasn't even sure if I wanted to see Saul again or who I wanted to be when I saw him.

"You do realize," she said coyly, "it's the next day. It's not Halloween anymore. You have to go back to being the Ugly Stepsister."

"Don't you mean Cinderella?"

"So? You still have to do it."

"Why?"

She chose to ignore that. "Apparently," she said, thoughtful, "making you cut your hair and frump yourself out just isn't enough to scare men off."

"Apparently."

She mulled over the problem for a long time, toying with her coffee. Then her eyes got that nasty gleam in them again. "I've got it!" she said.

"Uh-oh."

"I know what you need to scare men off. What you really need is a couple of *kids.*"

"Did I ever say that I wanted to scare this particular man off?"

"Maybe not in so many words. But think about it, Scarlett. Wouldn't you really like to know, for once, if a man really likes you for you, or if it's just something to do with the whole package you present? Don't you think you—oh, I don't know—*owe* it to yourself to make it as hard for him to fall in love with you as possible?"

Maybe it was sick for me to think this, but what she was saying was starting to make a sick kind of sense.

Her voice wheedled. "How will you ever know if it's really you that Saul loves, if he does in fact start to love you, unless you make it as hard as possible for him to love you?" Her voice became seductive. "Come on, Scarlett. You know what you need: you need to get a couple of kids. You need to really test him."

And I realized something: For once, Pam was absolutely right. Oh, maybe not about the kids. But if I was going to go any further with Saul, I was going to need to know whether he was growing attracted to something he was finally seeing *inside* of me, or was it really all just cleavage in a good dress?

I was cleaning up the debris from the night before and wondering what my stomach could tolerate in the way of input when—

Ding-dong!

It was Sarah. Behind her I could see her familiar bicycle propped up in my driveway. She had on jeans and a sweatshirt with the name of some rock band I'd never heard the music of and a sad, too-tired expression on her face. In her arms was a brown paper bag.

"What's wrong?" I asked, letting her in.

"This is what's wrong," she said, opening the bag and removing the shirt we'd so happily bought at the Bethel Underground. The shirt was no longer intact. Instead, there was now a tear, about three inches long, from the neckline downward.

"What happened?" I asked.

"Jeff Polanski happened," she said.

"How…? What…?"

"He said yes to my invitation to the Sadie Hawkins dance. I was so happy about it. He said he was glad I had finally

230 *Lauren Baratz-Logsted*

discovered what a razor was for and that my new hair made me stop looking like a dork."

Jeff Polanski didn't exactly sound like Robert Browning, but he probably meant it as a compliment. Twelve-year-olds weren't exactly known for their verbal finesse. Not to mention that boys in particular felt the need to maintain constant cool. He was probably, at this stage in his life, constitutionally incapable of a simple, "You look pretty."

"So we met at the dance," Sarah went on. "I had my new clothes on. I was so happy. For once, I looked just like all the cool girls."

"And?"

"And we danced a couple of times, mostly really fast songs. But then at the end of the night, they played one old slow song, 'Last Dance,' and we danced close and I really liked that, it was nice, even though it made me feel a little funny, and then while we were dancing he worked us over toward one of the corners and I thought that maybe he was going to kiss me, and I was real happy about that, because no one had ever kissed me before and I wanted to know what it was like, but then he put his hand on my shirt and said, 'Hey, let's see your breasts,' and when I tried to pull away, the shirt ripped."

"Oh, Sarah…"

"So then—"

"But wait a second. Where were the chaperones? Didn't anyone see this?"

"No. Two boys had started fighting and they were too busy dealing with that to notice anything else."

"What did you do?"

"I told him he was a jerk, that I never wanted to talk to him again. He said it didn't matter that I wasn't a monkey anymore, that I was still Jiggles and that was the only reason he said yes to me, but now he was sorry because he could see I was still just a big dork."

"Oh, Sarah…"

"So I got a sweatshirt from my locker and put it on over the ripped shirt so my mom wouldn't see it when she picked me up. I knew if she saw it, she'd get so mad she'd call the school and make a fuss and that would just make everything worse. But Jeff'll probably still make up stories to tell people, probably say that I was easy or that I wasn't worth the time."

I knew she was right. He probably would say that to salve his ego, to feel cool. Only he'd probably say she was easy *and* not worth the time.

"What am I going to *do,* Lettie?" she asked.

I heard my stomach make an unpleasant sound.

"Well," I said, trying a smile, "first you're going to help me figure out what there is to eat around here that won't kill us. I'll bet you haven't eaten yet today and you're starting to feel hungry right around now."

Her blush told me I was right. When in misery, young girls either overeat or starve. Sarah looked like a starver to me.

Leaving the subject of grabby Jeff Polanski to one side for one moment, we located a few leftover chocolate cheese-cake brownies, eating in silence until the sugar was running good and high in our veins.

"What's your favorite thing about yourself?" I asked.

"My favorite thing?" She made a funny face.

"Yeah, your favorite thing. Everyone's got one thing they really like about themselves." I was almost sure of it.

"Well, this is going to sound really dorky, but…"

"Yes?"

"I'm nice." She finally exhaled.

"Yes," I said quietly, "you are nice."

"I mean really nice," she said, starting to get enthusiastic about it. "When other kids make fun of the kids who are real dorks—you know, the ones who have it even worse than being Monkey or Jiggles—I never play along."

"That's a good way to be."

"I even *talk* to those kids no one else talks to."

"Not only nice," I said, "but brave, too. Good for you. What else?"

"You mean besides being nice?"

"Mmm-hmm."

"But I thought I only had to name one."

"Well, try for two."

"I'm good at reading and writing. I love to read books, and I think I'm a pretty good writer." She looked down at the table, shy. "I may even become one some day."

She looked so wistful. I knew I couldn't guarantee her future dreams would come true, but maybe I could make her feel a little better now.

"Here's what you're going to do," I said, covering her hand with mine. "Whenever the kids give you a hard time, and they probably will, or when you think they're talking about you behind your back, and they probably will, you just tell yourself, 'I'm a nice person, nicer than all of you, braver, too, and someday I'm going to use those things to go after my dreams.'"

She wrinkled her nose at me. "Um, Lettie? That's kind of lame."

I deflated. She was right.

"But that's okay," she said, smiling for the first time since she walked in the door. "I know you mean well. And really, it's going to be okay."

And somehow I knew that Sarah would be okay, that it was going to be hard for her over the next few days and that it wasn't going to be the last time in her life that things would be hard, but she'd be fine.

Still, Jeff Polanski had taken something sweet, a night that should have been a little tiny form of magical for her, and turned it into something bitter and ugly.

I would have liked to kick his butt.

34

I was at the Circulation Desk and I still felt awful. Even though three days had passed since Halloween, I still couldn't shake the bad feelings I'd had the morning after.

"You're not yourself," Jane said.

It always surprised me somehow, working with nice Jane in the mornings when I knew sour Pat would be with me in the afternoons. Her words surprised me more. After all, it wasn't like I was known around the library for my perkiness, not me, Lettie Shaw, the serious woman in the quiet clothes.

"What do you mean?" I asked.

"I don't know," she said thoughtfully. "You may not always be the biggest talker, but you seem somehow sad today."

"I guess I'm just not myself," I said, agreeing with her.

"Who are you then?"

I looked across the desk, surprised at the voice not being Jane's. It was Steve Holt.

I swear I blushed.

"I'm Madonna," I said. "Or no," I said, changing my mind, "I'm your worst nightmare—a librarian with attitude. Hey, don't you usually come in here in the afternoon?"

"So?" He put his returns in the slot under the counter, put his takeouts on top: a literary novel that both the daily and *Sunday Times* had anointed, an early Stephen King and a book on art history. "I can't change?"

"Only if it's for the better," I said, checking his books out of the system.

"How about we change this."

"Hmm?"

"I keep asking you out—" Jane's ears perked up when he said this "—but you keep saying no. How about we just go grab lunch together, like two friends. You have to eat sometime and it's close to twelve."

"Go," said Jane, deciding for me. "If Roland comes by, I'll tell him I sent you on an errand before your lunch break."

"What errand?"

"Oh, I don't know." She looked exasperated with me. "I'll tell him I asked you to make a sign."

"A sign? For what?"

"I don't know." Her exasperation was growing. "A sign for the winter discussion series."

"But the series is still two months away. Besides, I can't draw anything to save my life."

"Lettie. Just. Go."

I went.

We went to Sandwich Submarine, a new place in town, the interior of which was decorated like the yellow submarine in the Beatles song. I sat in a bright blue plastic chair, feeling like the nowhere woman, gazing blankly at the menu, waiting for the waitress to come take my order for who knew what.

Steve leaned across the table and whispered, "It's not that bad."

"What's not that bad?" I whispered back, figuring this was a whispering moment.

"Whatever's got you down," he whispered again. "I'm sure it can be fixed."

"How can you be so sure?" I whispered. "And how would you go about fixing it?"

"Because nobody died—I know this because otherwise you wouldn't be at work. As for fixing it, I'd fall back on my profession—I'd throw a little paint at the problem."

"Oh," I practically sniffed. "Well. If *nobody dying* is going to be the sole criteria for things not being that bad in a person's life…"

I went back to my menu, only to hear a startling sound: he was laughing!

"What's so—" I started. But then I couldn't help it. I heard myself, how I'd sounded, how utterly young and childish I'd sounded, and I found myself laughing at myself right along with him.

I was feeling so good in that moment that when the waitress came to take our order, interrupting us mid-laugh, I ordered a turkey, melted Swiss and red pepper grinder and a strawberry-kiwi Snapple without remembering that I wasn't supposed to be eating because I was too busy nursing my depression.

Steve ordered something called the Budapest Bulge—I didn't even want to know what was in that—and a large iced tea, despite the cold outside, handing our menus back.

"You have an amazing laugh." He smiled after the waitress had gone.

"What's so amazing about it?" I snarked, feeling a little self-conscious.

"It's loud, for starters. It's unselfconscious, like you don't care who hears you being happy. And it's, um, well, *loud*."

"Thanks," I said, feeling completely self-conscious now. "So how was your Halloween with your brother's kids?"

"Great, great," he said. "I love kids, hope to have my own some day."

"Do you have other brothers and sisters?"

"Nope, just Tim. He's two years older. You?"

"It's just me."

"There's nothing just you about you," he said.

He was making me uncomfortable again. So…

"What's your brother like?" I asked.

"Tim? He's like an older brother—born with a sense of entitlement, and there's no talking him out of it. Still, we get on."

Our sandwiches came. I picked up mine, looked at his.

"Is that a moose sticking out the side of yours?" I asked.

He looked at the thing in his hand. "I think it's a walrus." He smiled, taking a bite. "Mmm, a good walrus."

I realized how hungry I was and we ate in companionable silence for a moment.

"I guess you could say my relationship with Tim is complicated," he finally said, still stuck on his brother.

"How so?"

"It's like, on the one hand, I want to dislike him, because he's so superior about everything."

"And on the other?"

"I idolize him," he said, as though it should be simply obvious. "Because he is good at things, always manages to be the star."

"That could get annoying," I said.

"Not always. Sometimes it's fun just to watch someone else do the things you'd never do."

"For instance?"

"When he was in college, Tim and a few of his friends went to Bermuda for spring break. There was a bar there they went to every night where they did an open mike thing, inviting people to come out of the audience and tell jokes between the musical acts. Anyway, Tim was always good at jokes. He's got this unbelievable memory where if he hears a thing once, he can remember every single detail later. Tim was pretty drunk, though, and couldn't remember any of his own jokes, so one of his friends gave him a dirty limerick to recite."

Steve stopped talking, obviously embarrassed.

"And the limerick?" I prompted.

"Well," he said, reddening a little, "if you insist. There once was a girl named Alice/who used a dynamite stick for a phallus/they found her vagina in North Carolina/and the rest of her ass in Dallas."

I laughed, even though I'd heard that one before. What can I say? I like dirty jokes.

Steve took my laughter as a license to continue.

"So Tim goes up on stage, gets in line to tell his joke, but he's really drunk, see? There's a guy ahead of him who tells some stupid joke involving a doughnut and there's Tim, reciting his own limerick in his head while half listening to this other guy. Then it's Tim's turn. He gets up to the mike and says, 'There once was a girl named Alice,' but then he stares out at the crowd, all those people waiting for him to go on, and all he can remember is the guy talking about doughnuts, and all he can think to say is, 'so I ate her.'"

I laughed so hard, I felt the strawberry-kiwi drink work its way dangerously up my nose.

"See what I mean?" he said. "Tim does these bizarre things and people just laugh."

"I can see why," I said, still smiling. "Imagine a guy wanting to eat a girl just because she was named Alice."

"But that's not the end of the story," Steve said, really getting into it now that he knew he had a good audience.

"No?"

"No. The next day Tim's on the beach, recovering from his hangover with all of his hungover friends. He gets up to get a beer and walks into the middle of a limbo contest. All of a sudden, all around him, people start murmuring, 'That's the guy…' 'From last night…' 'So I ate her!' Before you know it, all these people are laughing and clapping and someone's handing Tim an award for second place in the limbo contest. He ranked that high on the applause meter without even having to slither under the bar once."

"Tim does sound like a fun character," I conceded, "but I don't know that I'd want to make a steady diet of it."

The waitress took our plates. "Dessert?"

"No, I have to—"

"Yes," Steve cut me off. "Two of whatever the best thing you have is." Then he looked at me. "You left fifteen minutes early, and nobody knows but Jane, so you still have time left."

I relaxed back into my chair, visions of something chocolate dancing in my head.

Something chocolate turned out to be homemade chocolate chip fudge brownies with blueberry ice cream and hot fudge on top.

"Yay, no nuts," I said, taking a bite.

"You're very funny," he said.

"Oh, *thanks,*" I said sourly.

"Why the sour thank-you?"

"Because *funny* is the plain girl's bone. It's what the world throws us as compensation."

"You're not plain, Lettie," he said softly, "but you're absolutely right about one thing—nuts would spoil it." He took another bite.

"So, how was your Halloween party?" he asked. "And what had you so down when I first saw you today?"

I suppose I could have told him about Sarah, since I was still upset about what had happened to her, but that was her story, not mine to tell people. So, before I had the chance to think about what I was doing, I was telling him about Saul. I didn't tell him the part about the thing I had going with Pam, about how I'd downgraded my appearance in the last few months. I just told him that I'd met a really attractive guy a while back, I really liked him, wanted him to ask me out, invited him to my Halloween party, and then, when he saw me dressed up more exotically than he was used to, his attitude toward me had changed.

Okay, I also didn't tell him the part about sleeping with Saul.

It might have been selfish of me, spilling my guts to Steve this way after he'd asked me out twice. But I still believed that the first time Steve had asked me out it had been to mock me, the second time had been out of pity, and today, well, today he'd said we were just having lunch as friends. Shouldn't I be able to tell a friend about the things that were bothering me?

He laid down his fork.

"I'm probably the wrong person for you to talk to about this," he said.

"How's that?"

"Because I *like* you. Don't you get it? I really *like* you."

I brushed him off, not believing he meant it. "Of course you like me," I said, "and I like you. We're friends now, right?"

He didn't answer me.

"How is it," he asked instead, "that a woman like you never married?"

"How do you know I never married?"

"Well, have you?"

"No. But I almost did. Twice."

"So what happened?"

"I realized it just wasn't right," I said, "both times."

I sat there, wondering how to explain my whole Greek theory about passion, how it had been a weird sort of beacon in my life, how when I'd realized that neither of the men I'd been engaged to, however nice, had fit into that theory, I'd broken things off rather than settle.

Finally, I decided to tell it just straight out.

"Weird," he said, when I'd finished. "A librarian who loves her job and who is committed to a theory of Greek passion."

"That's me—" I shrugged, tried to smile "—weird."

"I'm going to ask you one more time. Lettie, will you go out with me?"

"Maybe."

Not long after I got back to the library, Kelly stopped by the Circ Desk.

She was wearing gray wool slacks and a pale pink button-down shirt. Apparently, she'd settled down a bit from her overenthusiastic first days and had modified her wardrobe to fit in with the library crowd, which mostly wore slacks, except for me in my Empire dresses.

"I was disappointed when Jane told me you'd already left for lunch," Kelly said.

I was stunned. "Why?"

"Why?" Apparently, she was stunned, too. "Because I was hoping to have lunch with you today, that's why."

I heard Pat cough behind me. While I'd been at lunch with Steve, the shifts had changed.

"That's very nice of you, Kelly," Pat said.

I looked at Pat, this woman who'd practically invented the word *acerbic,* and I could see that she was sincere. She was looking at Kelly all doe-eyed. *What was going on with everyone here,* I thought, *had Kelly reinvented the Dewey Decimal System?*

Not to mention, I couldn't figure out for the life of me *why* Kelly would want to spend her lunch break with me. I hadn't exactly been warm to her. Worse, every time I was around her, I turned into an even klutzier version of me: dropping books, dropping due-date cards, dropping doughnuts.

Kelly must have been reading my mind, because she suddenly leaned in and whispered, keeping an eye on Pat.

"You're the only one here who's close to my age," she said. "I thought we might be friends."

What was she up to? I wondered. Was there really something malevolent about her, or was I just jealous? I wasn't sure, but there was something about her that made me think of a red M&M.

"Yeah," I said, echoing Pat, "that's very nice of you. But since I've already eaten lunch…"

I let my voice trail off, hoping that was that.

But it wasn't.

"Fine," Kelly said. "Then we can go out after work instead."

"But—"

"We can go get massages. I'll drive."

Kelly's car turned out to be a red sports car.

It figures, I thought.

And she drove like a maniac.

"Where are we going?" I asked, as she zoomed out of Bethel.

"Westport," she said.

"Westport? We're going all the way to Westport just to get massages?"

I saw her shrug within the dark confines of the car. "There's a place there I like."

Damn, I thought. Westport was thirty-five minutes away. We were going to have a lot of bonding time together. Did I really want to bond with this woman?

But it turned out to be not so bad. Mostly, on the drive down, Kelly wanted to talk about work. Well, what else did we have in common?

"Did you ever notice," she asked, "how people there seem to treat me, uh, different from everyone else?"

Uh, yeah.

"What do you mean?" I asked, figuring it was the polite thing to do.

"I don't even know," she said, "but I just feel like Roland and everybody else acts different around me." Pause. "And I don't like it."

"How come?"

"Because I'd rather just get treated the same as everybody. Who wants to be odd girl out?"

"I don't know." I shrugged. "Maybe they treat you differently because you're so, um, helpful."

"I guess."

She cranked up the radio.

The special massage place she wanted to go to turned out to be a place called No Hands, in a building overlooking the Saugatuck River.

"What's so special about this place that you come so far to get to it?" I asked, getting out of the car, relieved to have survived Kelly's driving. I mean, jeez, thirty-five minutes to get here; we could have gotten to Snips & Moans in five. "And what's with that name—aren't hands the whole point?"

"I like the view." She answered my first question. "They specialize in using hot stones." She answered my second.

"Ah."

Once inside No Hands, we were quickly led to a room. Apparently, Kelly had called ahead and made arrangements.

"Um," I said, "we're going to get massaged *together?*"

Kelly was puzzled. "Sure, why not?"

"Well," I said, feeling a bit Puritan, "I usually get my massages alone."

Not like I was getting massages a lot. In fact, the last time I'd been massaged professionally, it'd been…it'd been…it'd been…oh, hell, it'd been a long time ago.

"What's the big deal?" Kelly asked. "We'll change separately. We'll be under towels."

When I emerged from behind the changing curtain to let Kelly take her turn, a big white towel wrapped around me, I could see what she meant by the view. One wall was all windows that were darkened on the outside for privacy. But from where we were, you could see out over the river, the stars shining against the water. It was a lot nicer than the kind of dump that I'd have probably picked out if I were picking out a massage place other than Snips & Moans. I'd have probably picked out a claustrophobic little room, no windows, with a calendar on the back of the door put out by the U.S. Beef Association.

This place felt so much more sophisticated than Snips & Moans that it made me feel like I was about to have a new experience entirely, like maybe I was a novice who didn't know what to do here.

I lay down facing the view on one of the tables, draped the towel over my backside, hoping I'd got it the way I'd seen when I'd seen characters getting professionally massaged on TV programs. In another minute, Kelly was on the table beside mine, backside under a towel.

"Hey," she looked over at me, a lazy smile playing her mouth as though she were getting sleepy or on drugs, "you have a beautiful back."

What do you say to that?

"Thanks," I said.

"I never would have guessed," she said, "under those clothes."

Just then, the masseuses came in, saving me from having to talk about my peculiar wardrobe.

Kelly closed her eyes and I did the same, as the masseuse went to work on my back. It felt strange, having a stranger touching me like that, not something I was regularly used to, even if there were stones between us. And the stones themselves felt weird, too—not hot to the point of unbearable, but pretty damn warm—and I couldn't tell if I liked the sensation or not, which for me was seesawing between heavenly and awful.

"You have no idea what it's like," Kelly said, "having people treat you differently."

"Mmm," I pretended to agree, thinking it strange to be holding down a conversation with my eyes closed. It was like Kelly and I were playing a weird kind of sensual version of Blind Man's Bluff.

"It's not easy," Kelly said. "Guys all treat you like an object, like you must be impossible to get, like you must be vain, like you must be some kind of trophy."

"All at once?" I asked. "They do those things all at once?"

"No, of course not all at once! But they all treat you like an object. The rest of the things they do depends on the individual doing it."

"Ah."

"It gets lonely," she said.

Earlier, when we'd been supposed to be bonding in the car, I'd thought that maybe if things went well, I'd tell her about Saul, tell her about Steve. It would have been a relief to talk about it with someone who was a relative stranger. But I couldn't bring myself to do it, couldn't bring myself to talk to her about how I'd just slept with this incredibly gorgeous guy not too long ago and had another guy who was really nice and whom I'd said I'd maybe go out with. You can't tell that kind of stuff to someone who's just told you how lonely they are.

"If things are that tough," I suggested, "why don't you try something different?"

"Like what?"

"I don't know." I shrugged beneath my towel. "You could try doing what I do. You could dress down for a bit, let the world take you for who you are."

"Hah!" she laughed. "I'm not *that* desperate."

I would have been offended, but then I figured, no, most normal people probably weren't.

"Hey," I said, a thought suddenly occurring to me. It was something that had been bothering me ever since I'd first seen her at the library, something I'd been unable to put my finger on until just now. I couldn't believe I was going to ask another human being that question, the one that I always hated being asked, but… "How'd you ever wind up working in a library?"

"Oh, that," she said. "My parents didn't think I was smart enough to be a lawyer or anything like that. They thought I'd be safe in a library."

Forty minutes later, we were completely massaged, back in the clothes we'd come in, and on the street again. We were also one hundred dollars lighter each, which seemed kind of steep for a couple of stones.

35

"Borrow your kids?"

Delta looked surprised by my offer.

"What's wrong?" I asked. "You're always saying how you could use a break, if only you could find someone who'd take them off your hands for a while. It's what you're saying right now, what you've been saying for the past half hour. Don't you trust me with them?"

"Oh, it's not that. It's just that, well…"

"Well what?"

"It's just that, well, I never got the idea you really *wanted* kids."

"Whatever gave you that idea?"

"The fact that you never talk about them, maybe?"

"Maybe I never talk about them, because, oh, I don't know, maybe I'm just not the type to think about them unless I've found someone I'd want to have them with first?"

"Really? Maybe?"

"Really maybe."

"But—" she hesitated again "—are you sure that if you're going to try on parenthood for the first time, the two kids you really want to try it on with are Mush and Teenie?"

I regarded the Mush and Teenie of which she spoke; the former had his hand down his trousers, engaging in his favorite activity, which was making sure his pecker was still there and that it still felt good to touch it; the latter had peanut butter all over her nose, a result of her unusual preferred method for consuming her daily PBJ.

"Sure I'm sure." I took a deep breath. "Really maybe."

In fact, this conversation hadn't quite started with my request to borrow Delta's kids. It had started with her inviting me over for a visit, ready to tear her hair out or kill somebody, because she just couldn't take it anymore.

"I love my kids, Scarlett, don't get me wrong."

"I know you love them," I'd assuaged her pangs of guilt, all the while wondering *how* she could love them, since they were so, well, Mush and Teenie. "Who wouldn't?"

"Exactly." She'd been relieved. "It's just that it's impossible for me to bring a man home and have a normal evening with them here."

"Really?" I'd pretended disbelief.

"You don't know the half of it. But I've, well, I've met someone new. His name's Dave, and I really like him, I'd like to invite him over this Friday night, and if the evening goes well, I was hoping he could stay the weekend. But it's not even worth the bother of having him over here if they're going to be here when he comes."

"What choice do you have? Even if you can find a place to stow them for the weekend, what are you going to do when the weekend's up—somehow pretend forever that you don't have any kids?"

I could see that she was sorely tempted by the idea, but then she shook it off. "Of course not," she'd said. "I just wish, just for once, that a man I like could get a good, long chance to get to know *me* first, to fall just a little bit, before having to meet *them*."

I'd secretly thought the same thing I always secretly thought, what I'd been telling myself my whole life: that if someone was going to fall in love with Delta, or any woman, it was going to be not because of external things, like looks or kids, but for who she was inside. But you can't tell one of your best friends that her bad luck with men was that, for whatever reason, men didn't find enough in her to love to make it worth overcoming the obstacles.

Still, I'd felt sorry for her, could see how isolated from what she wanted having kids made her feel. Wanting to make it better for her, I'd figured: What the hell? Why not step up to the plate for one measly weekend? I'd had some kid experience with Sarah lately. How much worse could Mush and Teenie be? This was when I said:

"Borrow your kids?"

And this in turn had led to my commitment of:

"Really maybe."

Which Delta took as a most emphatic yes.

"Oh, Scarlett—" she practically knocked me over with her big-boobed hug "—you won't be sorry. I mean, you probably will be sorry, probably very sorry…but I'll be so happy! And really, however you want to do it, it's perfectly fine with me. If you want to have your mother come to stay with you to, you know, reinforce you should any difficulties too big to handle befall you, I perfectly understand. Or if you have to go out yourself at all, if you can somehow manage to get an alternate babysitter, don't even worry about it—just tell me how much it is afterward and I'll be glad to reimburse you."

Delta couldn't seem to stop herself from talking. She was suddenly like that cartoon bird on the old Cocoa Puffs commercial—"I'm cuckoo for Cocoa Puffs! Cuckoo for Cocoa Puffs"—just happy-dancing her way off into a rainbow sunset of dizzy happiness.

"Oh, I just can't believe it," she said, clapping her hands together. "Do you know the last time I had a man in this house without kids underfoot?"

I shook my head at her rhetorical question as I caught sight of Mush checking out his pecker again and I began to get a glimpse of the enormity of what I'd offered to take on.

"Well, I can't, either!" Delta barked a laugh that was downright scary in its near-hysteria.

"Borrow your kids?"

Three more insane words were never spoken.

36

An hour into my weekend with Mush and Teenie—a whole weekend?—and already I was regretting my impulsive generosity towards Delta. These kids weren't kids; they were monsters!

When Delta dropped them off Friday at six, I already had a home-cooked dinner on the dining-room table, which I'd set with my best tablecloth and serving dishes, figuring that while they were with me, I'd try to provide a nurturing environment. I was sure that under my care, however brief, Mush and Teenie would blossom into the truly great kids they must surely be under all that noise and dirt.

Okay, so maybe it wasn't home-cooked. It was Chinese takeout from Noodle Fun, but don't all kids love takeout?

"You got any peanut butter?" asked Teenie, sullenly pushing her plate away.

"Raw cookie dough?" Mush added hopefully.

"Well, yes," I said, taken aback. "But peanut butter is for

breakfast," I rationalized, remembering I'd seen Teenie eating it at that meal, "and the raw cookie dough was supposed to be for dessert." (All single women keep raw cookie dough on hand. It's one of life's few absolutes.)

"Why wait if you can have it now?" Mush wondered. "I could have a heart attack during dinner, and then where would I be?"

"You don't want us to *starve,* do you?" Teenie demanded, more sullen than ever.

"No, of course I don't want you to *starve…*"

I looked at the two creatures I'd voluntarily invited into my home: Mush with his tousled dirty-blond hair that was definitely more dirty than blond, his mushy jeans hanging low on his mushy eight-year-old hips, his oversize Chicago Bulls shirt stained with a substance I didn't even want to guess at; Teenie, with her mother's bouncy Southern looks, wearing a gauzy top, giving me an unlooked-for look at breasts that appeared to be growing bigger even as I looked at her.

I wondered, in passing, if they'd somehow be more likable if they weren't so visually unappealing, well, okay, *disturbing.*

"How old are you, anyway?" I demanded more than asked her.

"Eleven," she said, all defiance.

"Eleven?" I asked, surprised. She was almost as old as Sarah, and while there was something more…*sexually knowing* about Teenie, she also seemed less mature. "Weren't you playing with Lego when I was at your house a few months back?"

"So? I've grown up quickly," she said. Then she backed down. "Okay, I'm ten! Eleven's just what I tell my boyfriend. He's in high school."

"He is not your boyfriend," said Mush. "She's lying," Mush then said to me. "Max Wilbur don't even know she exists."

"Well, he would," said Teenie, "if you weren't always hanging around with me and my friends, staring at our breasts."

This was *so* much more than I ever wanted to know about these kids. I excused myself to the kitchen.

"Dessert, anyone?" I offered brightly, coming out with a tray on which I'd put a big new jar of Jif, a spoon, a roll of Pillsbury cookie dough and a knife.

"Cool," said Mush, ignoring the knife, then poking a hole after much effort in the plastic around the cookie dough using only his dirty thumbnail and scooping out a large mouthful's worth with his pointer and middle fingers.

"We're bored," Teenie said, about a quarter of the way through the jar of peanut butter, having, like her brother, neglected to bother with the cutlery.

"How do you know that Mush is bored, too?" I asked, oddly offended, trying to enjoy the remainder of my lo mein. Damn, that cookie dough looked good. "Maybe Mush is having a great time, only his mouth is too full for him to say so."

Teenie looked at me over the top of her jar as though I were the stupidest sow who ever lived. "I know that Mush is bored, 'cause he's started to eat slower," she said.

I looked at Mush, saw that she was right: he was down to using just one finger, his middle one, and it looked like his heart was no longer in it. I could relate. I'd noted in the past that it was really only the first half dozen or so spoonfuls of cookie dough that were satisfying; after that, it was merely rat-pressing-a-lever-for-cheese kind of behavior until the roll was done and then all that was left was an empty tube with that pathetic little metal thing still tying together the end like a twist on a sausage casing. In really desperate moments, that metal thing could be forcibly removed, the plastic tube cut open so that a person could get to the one or two millimeters of cookie dough left in the creases. Not that I would know about such a thing.

"Y'all done with dinner?" I said, lapsing into the kind of speech I found myself lapsing into whenever around T.B., Delta or Delta's kids.

"We-all are bored," Teenie reiterated, sneering a bit to let me know what she thought of my adopting their form of speech.

"We could play a game," I offered.

"Or we could go to the mall," Teenie said.

"We could watch some TV," I said. "I'm sure there must be something educational on PBS."

"Or we could go to the mall," Mush said.

"Or," I said, forcing a smile, "we could go to the mall."

Somehow, I'd always imagined my first time at the mall with kids to be different.

When I'd imagined it in the past, it had always been singular kid, not plural kids, and the kid in my mind had been a newborn baby—mine—whom I would push through the mall as it slept peacefully in its stroller, accepting the compliments of passersby. I'd stop to get a bite to eat—something warm if it was winter, cold if it was summer—and my baby would drift up to consciousness, open her eyes, and we'd cast beatific smiles on each other.

What I got instead was...

Teenie: "Can I have some money for clothes?"

Mush: "I want to go to the video arcade!"

While I could see that Teenie could indeed use a new look, I was worried that if I took her into a clothing store, she'd talk me through my own weakness into buying her something wholly inappropriate, and later I'd have to worry

I'd done something to contribute to an increase in the world's population without even getting any sex for myself out of the deal.

"The video arcade sounds great," I said.

Of course, it was something less than great, but it was a sight better than preteen pregnancy, and by the time they'd cleaned me out of forty dollars' worth of tokens, I had a headache from all the flashing lights and noise, but at least I'd learned how to kick ass on Planet Puke, a game I'd just as soon not describe.

"I'm hungry," said Teenie, when I refused to change any more bills into tokens.

"You never gave us any dinner," Mush accused, "only dessert."

So I bought them, on request, pizza at Sbarro's, cheesy fries at Nathan's, mocha-chip sundaes at Häagen Dazs and coolattas at Dunkin' Donuts on the way out to the car.

"I'm kinda full," Mush burped.

"That's because of all the cookie dough you had before," scolded Teenie.

I didn't know much about kids, but I kind of had the impression that if the older kid was ten, the parents felt reasonably safe leaving them home alone together for brief periods of time. And yet Delta always got sitters for Mush and Teenie. As soon as Teenie had told me how old she was, I'd wondered why that was. Now, with my own firsthand knowledge gleaned from a whopping four hours in their company, I could see why: if left to their own devices, like goldfish, they'd eat until they blew themselves up.

Not that I'd done anything to try to stop them.

I could see that it was tougher to be a parent than I'd

thought. Well, okay, maybe not tougher to just *be* a parent; anybody could be the bare husk of anything. But I could certainly see where it would be tough to be a good parent, a disciplined parent. After all, it was so much easier just to give in, to do anything to cut off or forestall the dreaded sound of whining.

"You said we could watch TV," Mush said sullenly when we got home.

"You said there'd be games," said Teenie.

Thinking it would be better to engage in some form of social interaction, rather than merely plunking them down in front of the TV, but realizing that I probably had no games in the house that they would recognize as such, I fell back on the old standby: a deck of cards.

It was easier than one might think, teaching those two seemingly brain-cell-challenged kids how to play poker— five-card stud to be specific. What was hard was accepting the fact that once they learned, they alternated beating me every time. I could not draw better than three of a kind to save my life.

"This is fun," said Mush, raking in a pile of leftover Halloween candy, which was what we were playing for.

"Yeah," said Teenie. "It's like being part of a real family."

I was charmed with them and charmed with myself for winning them over.

"TV, anyone?" I beamed my best June Cleaver smile. I would have liked to play a little longer, but I was out of chips, which in my case were mini Snickers bars. Tempting as it was to beg Teenie for some of her mini Three Musketeers—she somehow seemed like she'd be more amenable to sharing during a game than Mush—it felt like it would somehow lack maturity to do so.

I put their winnings in a big wooden bowl, then set them up in front of a scary movie with the remote.

When I'd originally extended the offer to Delta, somehow I'd pictured the good-night phase as being me tucking them in, even though I didn't have a spare bedroom to tuck them in to. But they'd absolutely worn me out, no doubt, and if I wanted to have energy to deal with another whole day with them the next day—and I needed that energy— then I was going to have to leave them to their own candy-eating, remote-clicking, sleeping-bag devices.

But there was one thing, despite their relative, um, *uncleanliness* that I had no intention of leaving out.

"Good night," I said, kissing Mush on the forehead.

"Good night," I said, kissing Teenie on the forehead.

Teenie looked at me, startled.

"Hey," she said, looking at me more closely, suspicious. "Didn't you used to look different?"

How long had it been since I'd started changing my looks? Hell, I'd been at their house the other day and they'd seen me then…

Mush yawned at the bad guys on the TV. "She used to have longer hair," he said, "and she didn't wear glasses. The big dresses are a new thing, too. You can't see her boobs as much in them." Then he stole his gaze from the TV long enough to settle it on me, a disturbed frown worrying his brow. "You can't see her boobs at all in them."

It made me slightly uncomfortable in a real squirming-in-my-seat kind of way to think that Mush noticed me…*as a woman*.

"Huh," said Teenie, considering. "Why'd you go and do that? If you saved your hair, I could probably do something with it."

I hadn't saved my hair, hadn't thought to do so, and didn't like to imagine now what Teenie would do with it. But somehow, she made me wish I had kept some, as a part of a memory of someone I used to be.

"Sometimes," I answered her, "I don't know why I did it."

"Weird." She shrugged. Then: "It don't matter. I like you better like this."

"You do?" I was surprised.

"Yeah," Mush answered for his sister. "We're here, aren't we?"

Saturday morning I woke to the phone ringing, feeling nearly as bad as I'd felt on the morning after Halloween. This time, I wasn't hungover from too much drink, I was just dreading the day ahead, wondering how I'd keep Mush and Teenie occupied for another whole day and night. Not to mention Sunday, too, until Delta came, hopefully early, to collect them.

"Scarlett! Phone!" I heard Teenie yell.

I scrambled for the receiver by my bed, shocked that she'd actually answered my phone. God only knew what she might have said to whoever was calling.

But I didn't have a horrified moment to spare for that, because who was calling turned out to be…

"Hey, it's Saul," he said. "I haven't been able to get you out of my mind."

He had a funny way to show it, I thought, given that more than a week had gone by since our night together, with no word from him. In another incarnation, I would have most definitely said something about this and then I probably would have made him suffer for a bit; not to be a tease, but on general principle. Still, given that I was on kiddie overload, I was grateful, pathetically grateful, to hear his voice.

"Hey," I said, feeling twelve.

"That girl answered your phone funny," he laughed softly. "She said 'Scarlett Stein's residence.' Wasn't that the name you first wrote on the napkin the night we met? What have you got, some kind of alter ego?"

"I, um…"

But he wasn't waiting for an answer. "Are you free tonight," he asked, "whoever you are?"

I scrambled around in my brain, wondering how I could make myself free tonight with Mush and Teenie on my hands. Well, Delta had said that she didn't care if I hired another babysitter, and I was sure my mother wasn't doing anything…

"I think I can be," I said, and we made arrangements before hanging up.

When I picked up the phone again to call my mother, I heard the special dial tone that meant a message had come in on voice mail while I was on the phone with Saul. I'd had voice mail ever since my mother, trying to reach me one night and failing to do so for two hours because I was on the phone with Best Girlfriend, had said, "Get voice mail, dammit. What if I died one day? How would I reach you?"

But I ignored the dial tone, calling my mother first to see if she could sit for Mush and Teenie that night.

"Did you just call?" I asked her.

"No, why? Were you on the phone?"

I didn't answer, preferring to dive right into my request.

"Of course I'll be happy to sit for Delta's kids while you go out with Saul," she said. "What a question! I'd be delighted."

"But they are rather, um, difficult."

"Difficult, schmifficult. I raised you, didn't I?"

Not wanting to know what she was getting at, I set a time and we hung up. I figured that if she arrived early enough, maybe I could just leave her in the house with the kids and go out to meet Saul in the driveway.

Having dispensed with my mother, I punched in the code for voice mail, listened to the message that had come in while I was making my date with Saul.

"Um, hi, Lettie? This is Steve. I know this is incredibly short notice, so I'll understand if you say no, but you did say that you'd be maybe willing to go out with me, and while I've been trying real hard to restrain myself, I was wondering if that maybe could be tonight. I should be in and out, so just leave a message whenever you want. If maybe not tonight, then maybe you could maybe go out with me another night soon."

He left his number and I took it down, put it aside, not knowing what to do with it since I'd just made a date with someone else.

How bizarre. After the longest drought I'd ever recorded, to be asked out by two different men on the same day for the same night. Hey, maybe having kids was working for me!

We spent the entire day pretty much how we had the night before: at the mall, with Mush and Teenie spending dollar bills like they'd been minted to be exchanged for tokens. It may have been the lazy-mother's way out, but it kept them occupied, contained in a relatively small space, and it gave me the opportunity to fantasize to my heart's content about the coming evening with Saul while mastering my skill at saving Venus from getting doused in a bucket of vomit, using only my plastic gun against the screen.

As I rushed them home at the end of the day, I realized that we'd stayed too long for me to have time to do much of anything about my appearance before it came time for my mother and then Saul to arrive. That was all right, though, I figured. After all, Saul had known me to look like this *before* our getting together on Halloween. Certainly he'd still like me like this, now that he liked me, now that he "couldn't get me out of his mind."

Okay, so maybe my not allowing myself time to change had been a subconscious decision on my part. So sue me.

As luck would have it, my mother, for the first time in her never-been-late-once life, was late.

I had just barely had time to change my dress. Well, I did need to not smell, didn't I? The dress I'd selected was the most daring of my Empire tents, dark blue with silver trim in honor of the Hanukkah season yet to come. I'd washed my face, combed my short hair that never needed combing anymore, wiped the lenses clean on my glasses.

Ding-dong!

It was Saul, arriving five minutes early to my mother's fifteen minutes late.

"Hi—" he smiled when I opened the door, continuing on to what was obviously a preplanned "—you look…" And he stopped. I'll never know how he would have gone on to finish that sentence—would he have continued on to the preplanned "great" or "fantastic" or "amazing"? or would he have dropped back to a more moderate "clean"? or worse, "as bad as you used to"? I'll never know, because it was then that Mush and Teenie made their joint entrance from the kitchen, where they'd been cleaning me out of house and cookie dough.

"Mommy!" cried Mush, hurling his big little self at my skirts.

"Mommy!" cried Teenie, coming up beside me and grabbing on to my hand. "Is this hunk of man your date?"

Saul looked unaccountably embarrassed. I supposed it could be merely Teenie's words that were doing it, but somehow I suspected it was something else.

"These aren't my—" I started to say, only to be cut off by Saul.

"You didn't tell me you had kids," he said. "Where were they the night of the Halloween party?"

"These aren't my—" I tried again, only to be cut off by Mush.

"Mommy got a sitter for us," said Mush.

"Mommy wanted a night without the kids," added Teenie.

This was all very well and true, but Delta was the mommy who'd got the sitter, who'd wanted the night out, not me.

"I understand," Saul said. "Really."

Even as I tried to come up with the best way to clear up the misunderstanding, I saw Saul backing out of the doorway.

"I really only came by," he said, "to tell you I can't make it after all tonight."

"You can't—"

"Something's come up, something unavoidable. I would have called, but your place was on the way. It just seemed easier."

He was already at the door to his car.

"Hey," I shouted. "You never finished your sentence! I look...what?"

He was confused a minute. Then: "Okay. You look okay, Lettie."

And he was gone.

When my mother arrived two minutes later, I was still standing in the doorway, still feeling that hit-by-a-bus kind of stunned. Sure, I'd agreed with Pam that Saul's feelings needed to be tested, but I'd never imagined Mush and Teenie so thoroughly taking things out of my hands and I'd certainly never imagined it going like this.

"I'm sorry I'm late." My mother bustled past me. "I stopped to pick up some videos for the kids."

I saw, as she unpacked her schlep bag, that she had three videos—all with either *scare* or *fear* in the title—as well as several two-liter bottles of soda and industrial-size bags of salty foods. Apparently, my mother knew kids a lot better than I did.

"Where's Saul?" my mother asked.

I shut the door behind her. "Been and gone," I said.

"How…?"

"I don't think that man likes kids," Mush said, looking glum.

"He left soon's he saw us," said Teenie.

"He ain't good enough for Scarlett," said Mush.

I wanted to know why they'd insisted on calling me Mommy in front of Saul, but their support somehow pushed my question aside.

"He sure ain't," said Teenie, "no how."

It was touching, really, in its own grimy way.

"Oh, Scarlett," my mother said, reaching out to touch my arm in a reassuring gesture. "I'm so sorry."

Being the object of anyone's pity is never a comfortable

thing; being the object of one's mother's pity is its own separate circle of hell.

"That's okay." I wanted to find a way to make light of it, couldn't.

The next thing I did was not a pretty thing, not by any means. But I was *supposed* to be on a date that night. I'd arranged for a babysitter for the kids, I'd cleaned myself up as best I could under the circumstances. I *wanted* to be on a date.

Excusing myself, I went upstairs, found the piece of paper on which I'd written Steve's number that morning. Before I could second-guess myself, I punched in the numbers, waited, hoping he hadn't made other plans.

"Hello?"

There was his friendly voice.

"It's, um," I paused, forgetting for a minute who I was supposed to be right now. Recently, I'd been Mommy to the kids, Scarlett to my mom, while to Saul I'd been… Oh, that's right. "It's Lettie," I said.

"Hey," he said, and I could hear his smile. "I didn't think you were going to call."

"I did get your message this morning," I said, "but at the time, I'd just made plans for tonight. And now…" God, this was lame—rude and lame. It was a lonely, crappy, small-person thing I was doing here.

"And now you find yourself suddenly free?"

"That's about the size of it." I realized that I wouldn't blame him if he hung up on me. "I know it's—"

"It's fine," he said. "What would you like to do?"

I had a sudden burst of both energy and inspiration, I felt that good. "I want to take you out," I said. "I want to show you a good time."

"Fair enough," he said, "I like that plan. But just one thing. I insist on picking you up."

I started to object, thinking of the no-neck monsters downstairs, but then I thought: *Fine. You want to pick me up? Pick me up.* If he turned tail as Saul had done, I'd be no worse off than I'd been before.

My mother kept the kids busy just long enough in my bedroom that I had a chance to show Steve around.

He'd arrived more dressed up than I'd ever seen him— khaki pants with a belt, a white button-down shirt so crisp I was tempted to ask him if he'd do my ironing, real shoes with real laces. His hair had that staticky kind of look like he'd tried too many times with the comb to get it just right and he smelled…like a man, naturally giving off that pheromone-infused scent that makes you want to celebrate the other's otherness.

When my mother did finally come downstairs, I could tell she was immediately impressed. "This one seems so *nice*," she whispered, as Mush and Teenie made their loud entrance, both those things worrying me intensely: my mother's approval and the kids just being themselves.

"Mommy!" cried Mush, hurling his big little self at my skirts.

"Mommy!" cried Teenie, coming up beside me and grabbing on to my hand. "Is this hunk of man your date?"

Steve looked at Teenie, smiled wide. "Yes," he said, "I guess I am."

He didn't ask any questions about the kids and I didn't say. Instead, I took him to Chalk Is Cheap.

I knew that Delta, if her date with Dave had extended

through the weekend as she'd hoped, would not be there. And I knew, from conversations I'd had earlier in the week with Pam and T.B., that neither of them would be there, either, so the coast was clear.

"You shoot pool?" He smiled his wonder as I put my quarters on the table, marking my coins with the chalk.

"What's so surprising about that?" I challenged.

He thought about it for a minute. "It's not surprising at all," he said. "It's wonderful."

I wondered if he'd still think it was wonderful as I proceeded to whup his butt, as well as the butts of the next four guys with quarters on the table.

"You're *good,*" he said, when I returned to the table for a sip of my Chardonnay.

"You don't mind just watching?" I said.

"Not at all. You said you wanted to show me a good time. Well, I'm having one. I like watching someone else do something they love to do."

"What would you like to do next?" I asked, when I grew tired of beating all comers.

"Your call," he said.

So I took him to the Danbury Public Library. Of course, it was closed for the night, so we sat outside on a bench in front of the fountain in the cement courtyard.

"I used to work here," I said, feeling the cold, feeling the wine, staring up at the stars.

"Why did you leave?" he asked.

"I guess I needed a change."

"So, what—you exchanged one library for another?"

"Something like that." I could smell him next to me.

"Did you ever think of doing anything else?"

"Not recently. I belong in libraries." He smelled a lot nicer than a library.

"How's that?"

"It's where the stories that get told are kept." I didn't want to talk about me anymore. "How about you?" I asked, realizing how little I knew about him. "Is painting shop windows for the holidays the extent of your ambitions?"

"Not exactly." He smiled. "I've always wanted to be an artist, capital A. I study the works of the masters. It's not very popular these days, where the emphasis is always on the new, but what I want to do is paint big things, like Tintoretto, things with lots of people and expression, realism made better. Of course, there's no guarantee that anyone will ever want to look at my work, much less buy it. Until that happens or doesn't happen, I'm content to do carpentry—which is what I do when I'm not painting windows—and paint the windows to pay the rent. Besides, I like talking to the people who come to watch me work, particularly the kids. It's not possible to get that kind of interchange when I'm working indoors on a big canvas and I need a certain kind of light." He looked at me. "I'd paint you."

I looked at him close. "I'm going to kiss you now," I said, deciding it even as the words were coming out of my mouth. "I hope that's okay with you, because that's exactly what I'm going to do."

I didn't wait for an answer, moving in closer to him, looking up at his face, placing my lips on his, taking in the soft feel of his lips for a long moment before parting them with my tongue.

I kissed him exactly the way I'd been wanting to be kissed myself for so long, no more, no less.

We stayed like that, connected only by our lips, as the night intensified around us.

"I'd like to take you home with me," he said, stopping the moment.

I debated with myself, wondering if I could do it. "No," I finally decided, "it wouldn't be fair to my mother to ask her to stay with the kids overnight."

"Well, let me at least see you safely home," he said.

At home, the kids were still up. Well, obviously; it was only twelve-thirty. They were glued to the TV so firmly that they didn't even notice that the population in the room had just increased by sixty-six percent.

"They were little angels," my mother said, putting on her coat, a parka thing that looked like maybe she thought Fairfield County was about to go tundra.

Angels? Who was she talking about?

"You sure you wouldn't like me to stay a little longer?" she offered, nodding her head at Steve. "Maybe you two could, I don't know, talk in the kitchen?"

"That's all right," he told her. "I think we've got it covered."

Then Steve walked my mother to her car, saw her safely behind the wheel and returned, turning off the TV.

"Hey!" Mush objected.

"Hey!" Teenie brightened, seeing who it was. "The hunk is back!"

"I'm going to tell you two a story," Steve said, "but first you have to get into your sleeping bags."

"We're too old for stories," said Mush.

"Shut *up*," said Teenie, punching her brother before heeding Steve's words. "We don't even have to brush our teeth, so what are you complaining about?"

With visions of periodontal work later in life for Delta's kids dancing in my head, I sat down at the dining room table where the kids couldn't see me, but where I could still hear Steve spin whatever tale he was going to spin.

"This is a story," started Steve, "about a painter and a librarian…"

"We don't know no painters," objected Mush, yawning.

"Maybe you do," said Steve, and he proceeded to spin a lovely tale, a tale that succeeded in putting Mush and Teenie, with their reliance on fear-based entertainment, to sleep; a tale that succeeded in showing me that he was seeing things in me that I certainly hoped were there, but that I'd never dared hope another human being would see in me. It was like being naked, in the best way possible.

"I think they're—" he started to whisper as I walked into view.

"Shh," I said, reaching out my hand for his, "come on."

I led him upstairs to my bedroom, feeling a disconcerting sense of déjà vu. This was so like the night with Saul on Halloween, but so different, too.

"Wait here," I said, leaving him seated on the bed as I went to the bathroom, exchanged glasses for contacts. I didn't want the feel of even the glasses between us, but I also wanted to be able to see the man I was making love to.

He didn't remark on the change, just took my face in his hands, kissed me again.

"I've loved your eyes since the day I first saw you," he said, looking deep into me, and there was that thing again: that amazing recognition of at once seeing the other person and being seen.

I let him pull my long dress up over my head, wanting

the moment to move faster, wanting to freeze the moment in time.

"Oh, Lettie," he said, "I always knew that you'd be beautiful."

And then I was being my most indelicate self, hurrying him out of his clothes because I'd always known, somewhere, that he was going to be beautiful, too.

I kissed my way down his body, hit my knees in front of him, feeling so…*grateful,* wanting to thank him for seeing me.

But he stopped me; my mouth having barely grazed his cock, he stopped me.

"No," he said, pulling me to my feet. "I want you so bad, I'll probably come in an instant. If I do, I want to feel you around me."

If I was another woman with another man, I might have been disappointed at the prospect of what I wanted so badly being over in an instant. But it wasn't like that. I loved what his words were telling me so much that I wanted it to be like he wanted it, him coming quickly inside me, waiting for the time to pass for him to become hard again, to do it much longer.

I lay down on the bed, spread my legs for him to enter me. Then:

"Shit*shit*SHIT!" I said, remembering all of a sudden who I was.

He stopped, pulling back.

"Um," he said, "that's not exactly the response I was hoping—"

"You don't know who I *am,*" I said, punching myself in the forehead with my fist.

"Who are you?" he asked.

"I'm the woman who never has condoms in her bedroom drawer," I said, cursing myself, "that's who I am."

He rolled over to the side of me on his back, striking himself in the forehead with his fist. "Shit*shit*SHIT!" he said.

"What—you, too?"

"Yes," he spoke his frustration through gritted teeth. "I'm the guy who never keeps condoms in his wallet."

I sought for a solution. "We could go out together to get some," I suggested. But then I remembered the kids downstairs. Sure, they were sleeping now. But if they woke for a minute and discovered themselves to be unchaperoned, who knew what they might do? "Or you could go by yourself and I could stay here…"

"Shh," he said, pulling my head onto his shoulder. "As much as I want to make love with you right now, I don't want to leave you right now even more."

"Well, but we could at least—"

"Shh," he said, stroking my hair. "I don't want the first time we're together to be anything but me inside of you with you around me. Shh, Lettie, we'll get another chance."

You wouldn't think that two naked people, the sexual tension crackling all around them like an exploding fireworks factory, would be able to sleep, but eventually we did.

I awoke in the morning to rain striking the windows and an empty pillow, two sheets of paper laid on it, beside me.

Was I doomed, I wondered, to be the kind of woman that men easily left in the morning?

The top sheet was a letter:

Dear Lettie, I'm sorry I had to leave without talking to you first, but I like to paint in the mornings and I didn't want to disturb you or the kids. I've left a little something for you, in appreciation for the most wonderful—and most frustrating!—night ever. I hope you like it. In a way, the part of me that's scared you won't like it is relieved that I won't be there to see your face. By the way, I think I might be falling in love with you, if I'm not already there. Steve

I turned over the second sheet of paper, wondering what it could be.

It was a picture of me in profile, sleeping, done crudely with an unsharpened pencil. My short hair stood out at all angles and there were creases around my eyes that I usually tried to avoid looking at whenever I looked in the mirror. Somehow, under Steve's hand, those creases had become marks of achievement, something I'd won in a long battle, hard fought. My smile, in the sleep he'd captured, was warm and smart, my cheekbone lonely, aching to be touched.

At first, I didn't think I knew this woman, wasn't sure I wanted to, certainly not the lonely part, but then I recognized her and wondered how he had.

I felt conflicted, looking at that drawing, a swirling mixture of fear and wanting: wanting to be seen; fearing that, once seen, truly seen, I would no longer be loved.

37

Knock-knock.

Knock-knock.

Knock-knock-KNOCK!—

The knocking, followed by abject surprise from me, who, having finally flung open the door to confront my impatient caller, was met with:

"Best Girlfriend!" I shouted as she dropped her backpack-in-place-of-a-suitcase at our feet, obviously sensing that she'd need both arms free to hug me back when I flung myself at her, which I of course did. In between my attempts to hang on to my trusty old life raft of sanity, I did my share of further exclaiming: "Oh, my God, ohmyGod, ohmy*God!* What are you *doing* here?"

"I came to save you from yourself," she replied, slowly extricating herself from my death grip of a bear hug. As she took a step back, I could see that she was just as startlingly beautiful as she'd ever been. Some things never changed, nor would they ever change, not as long as we two drew breath.

"Save me from myself?"

"Well, you never come out to see me."

"True."

"No matter where I happen to be living."

"Also true."

"No matter how great a place wherever I happen to be living might make as a travel destination for you, no matter how many weeks you get off a year, no matter how badly you need a change of place, no matter how badly you could use my help, no matter how screwed up your life—"

"Are we going to cover any new ground today, or are we just going to keep rehashing old territory?"

"Both," she conceded.

"Excuse me, but my memory is failing now that I'm nearly as old as you were eight months ago, so refresh it for me. Just what exactly are you doing here, without a phone call first, without checking to see if I was available this weekend, *without any advance notice?*" Seeing the look on her face, I hastily added, "Not that I'm not the happiest person in the world to see you here right now, of course."

"As I said before," she took a deep breath, "I came to save you from yourself."

"And, as I believe I asked before, save me from myself?"

She took my hands in hers and really looked at me, with that penetrating kind of depth that human beings rarely use on another, unless they're a Freudian analyst or they're playing parts in a movie about people falling in love and they're trying to simulate that look-deeply-into-each-other's-souls look that new lovers get at the dawning of love. This rarely happens in real life unless they're between the ages of puberty and legal drinking age, that penetrating seeing-and-being-seen that most people avoid due to—God, I hate using such a canned phrase, but it is true—intimacy issues.

I knew exactly what she was seeing with her pinning-the-bug-to-the-lepidopterist's-slide look.

She was seeing the hokey glasses, the unnecessary few pounds of weight gain that I'd only become aware of myself that morning in the shower, the unattended hair, the nonsexual clothing. But that wasn't all that she was seeing, for she was seeing past the careful packaging to the person underneath, the person whose core might still be essentially the same but who had allowed herself to change in some small ways to accommodate the package, in ways that were *wrong* somehow for the lack of conscious choice behind those changes.

I knew exactly what she was seeing, because through her eyes, for the first time, I was seeing myself.

"I came to save you from yourself," she said one last time. "And from the looks of things—" she moved to embrace me again "—I came not a moment too soon."

Which was the moment that Mush and Teenie chose to come bounding out of the kitchen, hurling themselves at our legs while shouting, "Mommy, Mommy! Who's the pretty lady you were hugging? Are you going to be a *lesbian* now?" Mush punctuated his enthusiasm by attempting to hump himself against Best Girlfriend's leg, the combination of his and his sister's behavior providing Best Girlfriend with game, set and match, as she scored the only point she really needed to make, the point she'd traveled across the entire country to make, changing planes four times.

My life had gotten too damned weird, even for me. Something had to give.

It was probably best to start with the small things. I looked at Mush and Teenie.

"What?" I said, sounding like an exasperated Borscht Belt comedian. "What's with the Mommy nonsense? First, you did it with Saul, then you did it with Steve, now you're doing it with Best Girlfriend." I looked at Best Girlfriend. "I swear they're not my kids." I turned back to Mush and Teenie. "What? Why are you doing this to me?"

I would not have believed it possible, for the no-neck monsters to blush in shame, but redden they did.

Mush studied his feet. "Mama put us up to it," he said.

"Don't blame Mama." Teenie roused herself out of the depths of embarrassment just long enough to punch her brother. "It was her friend Pam's idea."

"Wait a second," I said, not sure who to question first. "What do you mean it was Delta's idea, it was Pam's idea?"

"Well," said Mush, "it sure wasn't T.B.'s idea."

"No way," said Teenie. "T.B. said it was a sucky idea."

Even when you know that it's likely that your friends talk about you when you're not around, it's still a shocking and invasive feeling whenever you realize you were right, all your paranoid little fears coming home to roost.

But there was no time to be Woody Allen.

"What was the idea," I asked, clarifying, "the idea that was Pam's idea and Delta's idea, but definitely not T.B.'s idea, no way?"

"Mama said—" Mush started, but Teenie punched him again.

"*Pam* said," Teenie said, "that whenever anyone we never met was around you, that we was supposed to call you Mommy."

"Did they say why they wanted you to do this?" I asked.

"They said it would be a lot of fun," said Teenie, "seeing what would happen next if we did."

"Nice friends you've got," Best Girlfriend said.

"They're mostly okay," I said, thinking that at least T.B. hadn't gone along with it.

On the one hand, it was hard to defend my friends' turning my life into a kind of sideshow. On the other hand, it was hard to criticize, seeing as how I'd turned my life into a pretty big sideshow all on my own.

Still, I was glad when Delta came by a little later to collect the kids. As much fun as we'd had together, I was tired of having fun.

"Did they behave nicely for you?" she asked nervously.

"Yes, *Mommy,*" I said. "They sure did."

She looked at me funny, having caught my italics.

"I had a great time with Dave," she said, very cautiously, "in case you're wondering."

"That's great," I said, and I actually meant it. "I'm glad."

"I think I may have a chance with him," she said, "you know, having him get to know me before introducing him to my kids."

Sometimes, from the way they talked, it really was hard to believe that most of my friends were officers of the court.

"I'm really glad," I said, still trying to feel it. Then: *"Mommy."*

On the second try, she got it.

"Oh, Scarlett, I'm sorry. We didn't mean nothin' by it. We just thought it'd be fun—"

"To play with the circumstances of Scarlett's life without her consent?" Best Girlfriend interrupted before I could say anything.

It was kind of weird, having my faraway Best Girlfriend, like, clash swords with my Bethel/Danbury life.

"Like I said," said Delta, "we didn't mean nothin' by it."

"No doubt," said Best Girlfriend, arms crossed.

Instinctively, Delta seemed to sense that Best Girlfriend represented some kind of force that was bigger than her and Pam and even T.B. combined.

"You're the one from out of town, ain't you?" Delta said with a chin nod, like maybe Best Girlfriend was Gene Hackman in a saddle instead of an extraordinarily pretty woman currently living on the Oregon coast.

"Does that matter in the slightest?" Best Girlfriend asked.

Whether it mattered or not became immaterial, since Delta, deciding perhaps that Best Girlfriend was too big a force to reckon with on a Sunday morning, gathered up the kids and their sleeping bags and left.

Once Delta was gone, Best Girlfriend reached into her backpack, came out with two perfectly wrapped turkey sandwiches and two cans of Pepsi One, my favorite.

"The little place at the airport was open," she said, offering one of the sandwiches. "I thought you might be hungry."

I settled down on the couch—to hell with crumbs—suddenly realizing how hungry I was.

"What are you really doing here?" I asked, my mouth half full of food, not caring about manners in the not-caring-about-manners way that one can only be in front of a best friend.

"What the hell kind of greeting is that?"

"I didn't mean it that way. Of course I want you here. It's just that you've never visited me unannounced before."

"It's like I said," she said, also speaking around a mouthful of food. "I'm here to save you from yourself."

"And?"

"And I'm in the middle of an existential crisis. Like I've been saying on the phone, I'm confused about my relationship, confused about my work. I thought that maybe in coming here to help you, I'd help me, too. Besides, one of the nice things about being a photographer is that I can write the whole trip off as work. I'll take a few snaps while I'm here, call it 'The Bethel Series.'"

She reached into her backpack again, came out with a camera, snapped me sitting on the couch.

"I'll call it 'Best Girlfriend Changes Her Face,'" she said.

"Great," I said, wishing she'd given me some notice so I could wipe away the mustard I could feel on my cheek.

"Why don't you tell me what's been going on," she said. "Give me a chance to help myself by taking care of you."

So I told her everything, about the conversations I'd had with Pam that had led up to my making the changes, about Sarah, about Saul, about Steve, even a little bit about my conflicted feelings about my looks and how it all somehow related to my feelings for my mother and my feelings for her.

She used her tongue to work a piece of turkey loose from between her teeth.

"So," she said, "this is somehow your mother's fault, or my fault?"

"No," I said honestly, feeling the need to pull back from the hurt look on her face, but wanting to still be honest, "it just *is*. I'm just telling you what some of the antecedents and aftershocks are. I know that no one made me pull the trigger."

"You know what I think?"

"No, but I bet you'll tell me."

"I think Saul sounds like a toad and Steve sounds like a prince."

"Maybe."

"And I think something else."

"Hmm?"

"I think that what you should really do, Scarlett, what you should really-really finally do, is be yourself."

"Be yourself"—two throwaway words, like something you'd see in a high school yearbook alongside "don't ever change" and "friends 4 ever." Two simple words, which were in essence the two words I'd really been saying to Sarah with my longer-winded exhortation to focus on her positive attributes, designed to put people at their ease; in reality, two of the most fear-provoking words in the English language.

Well, they certainly struck terror in me.

"I also think you should tell Steve everything," said Best Girlfriend. "If he really is falling in love with you, if he's fallen in love with you, you should give him the chance to see who you really are."

"We'll see."

38

Over the course of the next week, Sarah came by the library less than before. And when she did come, she seemed less naive, more serious. But I thought that in time she'd be okay. What had happened to her was awful, no doubt; but the truth of the matter was that, in light of the horrible stories every day on the news and on TV, it was a blessing that the worst that had ever happened to her so far in life was nowhere near as bad as the worst life could be. Hopefully, she'd use the experience to learn how to separate shallow guys, like the detestable Jeff Polanski, from guys more worthy of her attention.

Also over the course of the next week, as Best Girlfriend talked to me during the days and slept on my couch at night, I began the slow process of returning to myself.

It was proving to be surprisingly true what people say, that it's a lot easier to gain a few pounds once you've reached a certain age than it is to lose them once again. Almost everything in life is somehow easier to lose than to gain—keys, sunglasses, high-school French, return receipts when you need them—but not those damned few pounds.

And then there was the rest of the process necessary to de-frump myself. I'd come to realize that it was a lot easier, a lot less time-consuming, never worrying if I'd run afoul of the Fashion Police. But if I was going to become myself again, then I was going to have to start paying attention to at least whether one item clashed with another; I was going to have to show at least some modicum of interest in accessorizing.

I started small, that first Monday back at work wearing my contacts instead of my glasses. I didn't really think it would be such a big deal, didn't think anyone would notice really, but I was in for a surprise. You'd have thought I'd had an Extreme Makeover or something.

"You have such pretty eyes," said Jane.

"You look like a whole different person," said Roland.

"What do you *mean* you always had the contacts but just chose not to wear them for a while?" Pat practically shrieked, coming on afternoon shift. "What kind of a crazy person does things to make themselves *less* attractive? If I could stand to put contacts in my eyes without getting the complete heebie-jeebies, I'd do it in an instant, probably find me a new husband tomorrow."

I was still too intimidated by Pat to tell her that I didn't think that exchanging her glasses for contacts would increase her appeal to anybody, man or woman.

"What can I say?" I said instead. "I was going through a dowdy stage, but now I'm coming back."

I'd added the last to kind of pave the way for the changes I'd be making in the days to come.

On Tuesday, I dug out my lipstick, pretty dried out as usual but at least it gave me some color.

On Wednesday, I put some gel in my hair, not enough to make me look like Elvis, but just a touch so that I looked kind of wild and fun.

On Thursday, I traded in my sensible shoes for a sexy pair of high-heeled boots that Best Girlfriend and I had each picked up pairs of at the mall. Underneath my oversize dress, they lost something in the translation, but they did give me some badly needed height that I'd been missing.

On Friday, figuring that some of the other women wore jeans to work so long as they were neat and not too faded, I crowbarred on a pair of ultratight dark jeans, over which I put a simple black turtleneck and a tweed jacket. Having combined them with the sexy black boots, when I looked in the mirror before heading to work, I thought that I looked like I could be a cat burglar or something, like maybe a twenty-first-century Audrey Hepburn about to pull off a heist.

"Stop," Roland finally said. "I can't take any more. If you make yourself look any better, I might have to give you a raise."

I thought that last part might be legally actionable, but then I saw by his smile that he was kidding. I also saw that he was confused.

One day, I realized, if I kept on working here, I was going to have to eventually change back my name. After all, being Lettie Shaw had been okay for a while, but I didn't want to do it for a lifetime. If I was going to go back to being me, the journey was going to have to be complete somehow. Then I'd have to legally change my name back, too.

"I just don't get you, Lettie," Roland said. "You have to

be the strangest woman I've ever hired. But I'll tell you one thing. I've never had *anyone* who could check out patrons quicker."

Feeling that while he was dwelling on my strong points, it was probably the best chance I'd ever have to fess up without getting fired, I fessed up.

"Wow," he whistled when I was done. "You're even stranger than I thought."

I waited for the ax to fall.

Roland must have seen my wincing expression. "What?" he asked. "Did you think I was going to *fire* you?"

I nodded meekly, like Lettie might.

He thought about it. "I'm not sure I legally can. After all, what did you really do wrong? So, you changed your name. But how is that so different from Pat wanting to be called Pat instead of Patricia? Or, oh, I don't know. And, so maybe you doctored your transcripts a bit, but it's not like you upgraded yourself or anything. It wasn't like you were one of those guys pretending to be a surgeon with a degree they bought off a donkey cart. You actually made *less* of your accomplishments. You doctored things in a way that you wound up getting *less* money."

I could see that from where he was sitting, I was a bargain.

"I suppose it will take some getting used to," he said, "all of us having to learn to call you Scarlett instead of Lettie. But it's a small price to pay. I mean, have you ever *seen* how slow Pat is at checking patrons out? And how *rude?* The woman could scare the balls off a tiger."

He had a point there.

"Lettie. Scarlett." He chuckled. "Damn, but you're a strange woman. If I weren't already married, I'd want to date you."

Of course the scariest part, in terms of my library life, was coming clean with Sarah. The way I shuffled my high-heeled boots in front of her, you'd think she was the mother figure and me the preteen in need of guidance.

She looked at me long: my improved hair and clothes, my lack of glasses.

"Well," she finally said, "I *did* used to see you looking like this at Danbury Library. Well," she added, "with longer hair, of course. So it's not like I didn't know…."

I had always wondered what she thought about my appearance downgrade. When I'd run into her and her mother that first time in Super Stop & Shop, she'd started to ask, but I'd cut her off. She never tried again, and I, grateful that she was probably just preoccupied with her own youthful preoccupations, never offered.

Now, for the first time, she told me what she'd thought.

"I just figured something bad had happened to you or you were confused about something," she said. "I thought maybe you were just hiding out for a while."

She was so forgiving.

But I still had to tell her the last part, that even the name she'd been calling me by, the only name she knew me as, wasn't my real name.

She chewed on that one a little longer than she did the appearance changes.

"Yeah—" she finally nodded "—I can see it. It's like when I was little and I wanted my mom to call me Andi and start getting everyone else to call me Andi, but of course she never would. Everyone wants a name change sometimes, a tomboy name for sports or a more exotic name just because. But Scarlett to Lettie? What in the world were you thinking of?"

★ ★ ★

Even though I didn't owe it to them—what were they, after all, my keepers?—I told Pam and Delta and T.B., each in phone conversations that week, that I was going back to being myself. The hair was going to take some doing. And, who knew? I was getting older. I might never grow it back, was kind of starting to like it short, so long as I felt free to de-frump it. But everything else was going back to being the way it was before; better, if I could manage it.

T.B. was relieved, Delta was relieved and hoped I'd forgive her for the part she'd played in siccing the kids on me, but Pam seethed.

I even called my mother, who wholeheartedly approved.

"You know," she said, "I was thinking the same thing. There's something wrong with the world if when I look at my daughter's clothes, my immediate thought is, Hey, that would look good on me."

In fact, the only person I didn't telegraph my changes to was Steve.

In the week since the Saturday when I'd gone out for about five minutes with Saul, not even making it past the door, Saul hadn't called once. No surprise there.

Steve, on the other hand, had called every day, but I'd been putting him off. I'd told him right away that Best Girlfriend was visiting, length of stay unspecified, and he readily understood.

"Wow," he said. "I wish I had a friend that I'd known for a quarter of a century."

"Well," I said, "you've had your brother for a lot longer than that. I'll bet he could teach you to limbo."

"I hope I still know you twenty-five years from now," he said.

I was glad we were on the phone and that he couldn't see my face, glad he couldn't see the fear and wanting that was surely there.

In order to make sure he couldn't see my face, I played with my hours at work, made sure I'd never be behind the desk at any of the times that he typically came in. I couldn't have said why. All I knew was that I was only able to talk to him over the phone. I wasn't ready to have him see my face.

Not just yet.

39

Life is unpredictable. *A* does *not* always follow *B,* no matter how much we might like it to. The ending we most dearly hope for becomes lost in the actions of others and our own folly.

"Are you *proud* of being a crazy woman?"

I sat on the edge of Steve's couch, contrite, hands dangling between my knees. "No, I wouldn't use the word *proud* exactly—"

It was another Saturday night and I'd been hoping to have somebody, but it was beginning to look like I was wrong. I'd called Steve up, inviting myself over. Then I'd arrived, dressed as Scarlett, ready to come clean.

If I'd been seeing Steve's place for the first time under better circumstances, circumstances under which he was *not* totally annoyed at me, I'm sure I would have been impressed. His house was so homey and artsy, all at once, like somewhere that van Gogh might live if he'd let Barbara Bush help him decorate. All over the wall were huge paintings, Steve's work, each one startling in how good they were, jumping out from walls that had been painted an off shade of red. The furniture in the high-ceilinged living room was off white, big and cushiony, each piece offering the comfort of an entire bed.

I could easily picture myself living there.

"So, basically, *Scarlett,* you've been lying to me, about damn near everything, since the very first moment I met you."

Sarah had been so much easier than this, so incredibly forgiving. Funny, you'd expect a twelve-year-old girl to have more trouble than a grown man at understanding human nature—granted, *my particular* human nature—but there you have it.

"Not *every*thing," I said. "Those were just some particulars that I lied to you about, but it wasn't everything."

"Oh, right. It wasn't everything. You only lied to me about what you really look like, about what your name is, about having kids—"

"I didn't lie to you about the kids. They were the ones who insisted on calling me Mommy."

"Right. And you didn't correct them."

"Right, but I didn't lie to you about everything."

"What's missing on my list? What part of 'everything' didn't you lie about?"

The word came out in a whisper. "Me."

"What?"

"I didn't lie to you about what's inside of me. For the first time in my life, I let a man see inside of me."

He laughed, a kind of bitter-sounding laugh that didn't suit him at all.

"How would I know if that was the real you or not at all, *Scarlett?*" he said.

"Because you drew me, in that picture. You couldn't have done that if you weren't really seeing me."

"I don't know," he said. "I *liked* that stuff you said about Greeks and passion, and about being a librarian. I wanted to know that woman, I wanted to be with her."

"I'm still that person," I said, "maybe more so."

A part of me was surprised in a way by the bitterness of his reaction. A part of me thought he should have been happy about it. After all, he was getting a better-looking woman than the one he'd had before. He was upgrading. Shouldn't he have been sort of pleased with that, like Roland had been when he'd learned that he'd gotten a far more experienced librarian for the price of an inexperienced one?

And there was something else weird about his reaction, something underlying it that was tough to put a name to, something that would have smacked, if I didn't know better, of guilt.

"Don't you like the way I look?" I asked, perplexed.

"Of course I do," he said. "But I liked the way you looked before, too. Not that it made any difference. I would have liked you no matter what you looked like."

"Why?" I couldn't help asking.

"Because you're you. Because you're funny and you're different and you're quirky and abrasive sometimes in a way that makes me want to draw closer rather than pulling away."

"I could still be that way," I offered, still campaigning.

"Could you?" he asked, and I saw the tide turning behind his eyes. "Could you really? Because if you could be the same person, the same person I was originally attracted to, then we might have a chance."

Okay. There I was, on the brink of having exactly what I wanted. He was going to give me another chance, I knew he was, if only I could say the right thing.

"What is it you want?" I asked.

"I just want you to be yourself," he said. "That's what I want. Just be yourself."

There that was again.

Instinctively, perversely, I drew back from it.

"I'd like to try," I said, my actions belying my words as I inched backward toward the door. "But maybe we need to wait and see. This is an awful lot for you to think about. Maybe you'll feel differently in the morning."

"I won't—"

"No. Really. You might."

Then I fled.

40

I went back to being a fucked-up person just long enough to fuck up the life I wanted, the life I would have given all my books for.

When I got back from Steve's, I picked up the mail, among which was a postcard from the owner of the house.

I hope you haven't changed too much, it read.

How bizarre!

Still, I didn't have time to spare a thought for that, since I was…

"What are you doing?" Best Girlfriend asked as I shot by her and up the stairs.

"Going out."

It's a lot easier to dress as a dowdy version of a librarian than it is to vamp it up for a night on the town. For my purposes, purposes unspecified, I wanted something that would be eye-catching.

Going through my closet, my drawers, I rejected the usual tight jeans and sweaters. Then I glimpsed something in a heap at the bottom of my closet: the Morticia costume from Halloween. I held it up. It was a little rumpled, but I knew that if I hung it on a hanger next to the shower, the steam would pull most of the wrinkles out; not to mention that the tightness when I put it on would take care of all the rest. But the hem of the dress was way too long for anything but a costume party, so I got my little gold scissors from the bathroom, the same ones I'd used to cut off my own hair all those months ago. You'd think I would have learned by now, gone out to buy a more professional pair of shears just in case, but no. So I used the little gold scissors, imitating the hem that already existed, but taking it up about two feet, from ankle length to mid-thigh.

As the steam did its work, I went through my jewelry, finally settling on a dangling pair of marcasite-and-garnet earrings, but rejecting all necklaces. What, after all, was the point in distracting from the all-important cleavage? True, there was the theory that jewelry drew the viewer's attention to certain parts of the body, but I knew that with that dress, nobody would have to be drawn anywhere. Why gild a perfect lily?

I thought about asking Best Girlfriend if I could borrow some of her makeup, but then thought: Why bother? I'd never become deft with the stuff and there was always the danger of going overboard. I didn't want to look like a slut, did I? So I just did some softer-than-usual spikes with my hair, slapped on some dark lipstick, fished out my bondage heels from the back of my closet—wouldn't you like to know—and then slid the dress over my head, shimmying it over my hips, looked in the mirror and called it a wrap.

"Where are you going?" Best Girlfriend asked as I came downstairs.

"Out," I said, "to shoot pool."

She must have seen something in my eyes. "Would you like company?" she asked.

"Thanks," I said, "but not tonight. We'll have breakfast or lunch together tomorrow."

Once in my car, driving, I did an unexpected thing; unexpected to me, at any rate. I fished my cell phone out of my purse, punched in the number for information, asked for Kelly Seaforth's number. Then I called Kelly to see if she was home, see if I could stop by for fifteen minutes.

She said sure, she wasn't doing anything, anyway.

As I pulled up to the address she'd given me, I saw that Kelly lived in a condo in Bethel, not much different than the one I'd lived in when I was still living in Danbury, except that hers had a deck but no pool.

Kelly At Home looked different from Kelly At Work, I could see immediately as she opened the door. She didn't have any makeup on, and without it, I could see uneven coloring and a few acne scars. She was also dressed a lot less formally, with loose jeans and a sauce-spattered shirt.

Weird: all of a sudden, I was back to being the best-looking woman in the room.

"I was making pasta." She indicated the shirt apologetically. "Care to join me?"

"No," I said, "but you go on and eat, if it's ready."

She led me through to a small maple dining room set,

where she'd set a place for one and had already poured herself a glass of red.

"Would you like one?" she offered, stumbling a bit before: "Scarlett?"

I shook my head on the wine. I needed to stay sober, so I could drink a lot later.

"I have to say," Kelly said as she brought over a plate of pasta and sauce for herself and I took a seat at the table, "it's going to take some doing, learning to call you something new. When Roland told us…"

"Yeah," I said, "you don't need to say anything. I really am the strangest woman who's ever lived."

"Well, I wouldn't say you're the *strangest*…"

"But close?" I suggested.

She smiled, an easy smile. "Well, maybe."

I watched her eat for a minute. I wouldn't exactly say her manners were revolting, more like nonexistent. She didn't bother with a napkin in her lap, didn't notice when she spilled a little more sauce on herself, and she didn't bother twirling the pasta neatly around the fork; she just scooped up a bunch and shoveled it in, dangling ends sticking out of her mouth be damned.

It was odd seeing her like this: the sloppy clothes, the unmade face, the deficient manners. It was like being in Oz and finding the Wizard behind the curtain.

"So," she said, washing down a mouthful of pasta with a mouthful of red, "what can I do for you?"

Well, now, that was the big question, wasn't it?

I'd made the snap decision to go talk to Kelly because it seemed like there was no one else to turn to. I certainly wasn't going to Pam; Delta had helped Pam set me up with that whole Mommy thing, so she was out; T.B. was undoubtedly occupied with Ex-Al; and I really didn't want to talk anymore about it to Best Girlfriend, who seemed to be hurt by some of my self-revelations. Who did that leave—my mom? *Pat?* Definitely not Steve, since my feelings for him lay at the heart of my problems.

So, instead, I'd chosen to come to the Good-Looking Woman for advice. After all, people used to ask me for man advice, so I figured she could perform the same function for me. Surely, despite my vague recollection of what she'd said about being lonely that night we'd gone together to the massage parlor, looking the way she did—at least in daylight hours—she had a lot of experience with men.

But when I asked her point-blank, having told her about Steve, what I should do about fixing things, if that's what I ultimately decided to do, she practically spewed wine across the maple table.

"Oh, hell, Scarlett, I don't know!" she laughed.

"But surely you've had tons of dating experience," I suggested.

"What in the world makes you say that?"

I thought about it. It wasn't like, when people gossiped at work, I'd ever heard anyone say anything about her having a boyfriend, or even about her going out on any dates.

"Don't you remember the things I told you," she said, "when we went for the massages?"

"What things?"

"The things about me and men and how men always act all screwy where I'm concerned."

I didn't want to confess that it's kind of hard keeping track of other people's social dilemmas when you're already obsessed with your own, so I just nodded, hoping there wasn't going to be a quiz later.

"Well, then, you must realize, with men always treating me like some kind of object, I haven't let myself get close to too many. And other women are even worse. That's why I thought we could be close. You seem so nonthreatening and nonthreatened."

I thought that if she let herself wear that sauce-spattered shirt in public she probably wouldn't have to worry so much about being objectified, but I kept mum.

I looked at this woman who had actually thought of becoming my friend, as if I was a desirable thing, and it occurred to me that she wasn't who I had taken her for; she wasn't the Good-Looking Woman, she was merely a woman. I'd made assumptions about her, wrong assumptions, just like others had so often made them about me. But she was just like anyone else. She wasn't a red M&M at all. She was just like anyone else, trying to make sense out of a nonsensical world, sometimes failing miserably, but still trying all the same.

"Well," I said, "if you can't tell me how to fix things with Steve, can you tell me why I'm screwed up about all of this 'be yourself' stuff?"

"'Cause you're screwy?" she offered.

That was helpful.

I figured I'd try one more time. I told her about Pam, Pam's plan, and how I'd gone from Scarlett to Lettie and back again.

"Why?" I asked her. "Why do you think Pam put me through that? And why do you think I let her?"

Kelly squinched up her pretty nose. "Because women are screwy?" she repeated. "Because you're kind of screwy, too?"

It was good enough for me.

★ ★ ★

Chalk Is Cheap was already pretty crowded for what was considered to be still early on a Saturday night. All the usual suspects were there: the French Canadian contingent of working-class stiffs, holding the bar up and waiting for yuppies to come in, from whom they would later take money off at eight ball; the young guys just trying out their recent legitimate IDs to see how it felt to be both legal and drinking; the little clusters of girlfriends, wondering if they'd get lucky, never wondering if they'd still feel lucky in the morning.

Plus Pam and Delta and T.B.

They all looked at me as I sat down, no one commenting on my appearance.

"I was supposed to go out with Ex-Al tonight," said T.B., "and Delta was supposed to go out with Dave, but Pam said it'd been too long since we'd done something just-us-girls. Ex-Al understood."

"Dave actually seemed to like the idea," said Delta, "said he'd appreciate it more, having to wait to see me until tomorrow."

I didn't ask why no one had called me. Instead: "Has he met Mush and Teenie yet?" I asked.

"Yes."

"And?"

"And he didn't hate them."

"Hey!" I said, putting my hand up for a high five.

"I'm very happy," she said shyly, slapping my hand.

"I'm glad," I said, meaning it.

"You look great, Scarlett," said Pam, addressing me for the first time.

I looked at my Default Best Friend closely, trying to figure out what it was I was hearing beneath her words. I couldn't figure it out, but I did see that the transformation Pam had craved for herself was now complete: she'd lost all the weight she'd wanted to, her tasteful clothes fit nicely, she had good hair. Hell, she looked like the kind of woman that anyone would be happy to date, until she opened her mouth and the bitterness flew out.

"But you didn't discuss this with me," she said angrily.

I shrugged. "I made a unilateral decision for once. So sue me."

I excused myself from the table, bellied up to the bar, watched, waited, not knowing what exactly I was watching and waiting for, but knowing I'd recognize it when I saw it.

I was almost ready to give up, half my mind wondering if I could shoot pool in this dress, at least salvage some fun out of the evening, when Saul came in. As he stood at the bar next to me, I don't think he even knew who I was.

"Hey," I said.

He looked down the height that still separated us, even with the bondage shoes.

"Hey!" he said, enthusiastic, source unspecified. "You look—"

"Come on," I cut him off, making another unilateral decision, grabbed my bag off the bar, headed for the door, "let's go."

"Where are we going?" he asked, but he followed.

"Your place," I said. "You do have a place, don't you?"

I realized that I was very angry, source unspecified.

"Of course I have a place," he said. "But what about your kids?"

"Those weren't my kids," I said.

"You don't have to—"

"What? Do you think I'd disown my own kids, if they were my own kids, for social expedience?"

"Okay, Lettie," he spoke steadily, softly, perhaps in an effort to calm down the crazy lady.

"Scarlett," I said as he fired up the ignition, "not Lettie. My name is Scarlett."

He looked at me in the dark of the car.

"Sure," he said, "whatever you say."

Saul's place was so different from Steve's that the only thing you could say that they shared in common was that both were occupied by men. Where Steve's place had been all an expression of self, Saul's place was a pantheon of want: the electronic toys, the magazine selections, the *right* furniture all serving as a means to impress rather than express.

I accepted a glass of wine, figuring I needed at least one more for nerve.

"What is it you look for in a woman?" I asked, spinning the stem of the wineglass back and forth between my fingers.

"Look for?" he asked, sitting close to me.

"Yes, look for, want. I'm curious," I said. "I really would like to know."

"Honestly?" he asked, and, thinking that he no longer impressed me as being particularly bright or witty, I nodded. He ticked them off on his fingers. "Intelligence, a sense of humor, good looks and—" here he blushed just a bit "—she has to like sex."

"Let's go," I said, getting up.

He was surprised, but he followed my lead.

"Where?" he asked.

I half wondered what he was thinking: that I'd had enough? That I was ready to leave now? That I wanted to go bowling?

"Your bedroom, of course," I said. "You still have those condoms, don't you?"

I was good at getting Saul's clothes off. I'd already proved that, hadn't I, on Halloween? And he was good at getting mine off, too.

But when he tried to touch me, I wasn't having any.

"Uh-uh," I said, flipping him over onto his back.

"Um…no foreplay?" he asked.

"Uh-uh," I said, rolling the condom onto his hard penis and inserting him into my body.

I sat upright on him, not even letting him touch my breasts, as I looked down at him, at that incredibly handsome face. My hips rocked back and forth gently, taking him in a little deeper, letting him go for a while, sometimes pulling so far back that we almost separated.

"You really are an incredibly beautiful woman," he said.

I didn't say anything, didn't thank him, just kept rocking, a little bit harder.

"Oh, Lettie," he said.

"Not. Lettie." I took him all the way in, tightening my insides around him until I felt him shudder inside of me. "Scarlett."

Afterward, as I got my clothes together, he wanted to know when he could see me again.

"Um, never," I said, distracted as I looked for my other shoe.

"Never?"

"Well, okay, maybe not *never* in the purest sense, since I have no intention of leaving town and you probably don't, either. And, no, if I run into you somewhere, it's not like I'm going to spit in your face and walk away. But as far as seeing each other again goes? Romantically? Or *as friends?* Never."

"I don't get it," he said.

Well, of course he didn't. The Sauls of this world are not used to women not wanting to see them again.

"Do you remember your list from before, about the things you look for in a woman?"

He nodded cautiously, on his back, looking vulnerable as a flipped beetle.

"Well," I said, "when I first met you, I was intelligent, I had a sense of humor. But you didn't want me. It wasn't enough."

He didn't say anything.

"Tonight, though, I wasn't intelligent, I wasn't funny at all. What have I done here that was smart or funny? But still you wanted me."

"I still do," he said, and from the accompanying rise in the sheet, I could see he wasn't kidding.

I thought of Jeff Polanski, only being interested in Sarah once she started to look a certain way. I thought of how he'd hurt her, been thinking about it in the back of my mind all night long.

"No," I said, "you don't want *me.* You want someone who looks a certain way or performs a certain way, but you don't want me."

"What can I do?" he asked, abject.

I knew he was asking me something else entirely, but I answered, "You can help me with my zipper." I turned my back. "That's what you can do.

Who knows what I'd really been looking for in going to Chalk Is Cheap that night? Surely, I'd come to realize, if only on some subconscious level, that the kind of attention that accrues from good physical appearance was satisfying in some way. And, not so much that, but it was also so much easier to deal with than putting your real self on the line, letting the world see inside.

Who had I been kidding? I'd wanted the validation, again, because it was easier, because it was less scary, because it had absolutely nothing to do with being myself.

I was scared shitless of the kind of future Steve represented, a future in which we were always our truest selves, and in anger at Saul, in fear of Steve, I'd had one last fling.

41

When I got home from Saul's, I saw right away that Best Girlfriend was no longer there. Had she decided to return home? I wondered. But her things were still there, her backpack still in one corner of the couch. Oh, well, I thought. She wasn't chained to me. She could go out and do something on her own.

I changed out of my clothes, tossed the shoes back into the bottom of the closet, threw some water on my face, tied the robe around my waist. Then I went downstairs and grabbed some caffeinated soda out of the fridge, hoping to stave off the next day's hangover, and settled down in front of the TV, not even noticing what program was on.

Once upon a time, I'd been a little girl. I'd been the kind of little girl that gets told, at an early age, how pretty she is. I'd been the kind of little girl who, every couple of years, finds her picture on the front page of the local newspaper—snapped in a fire engine on a class trip to the fire department or in a pumpkin patch on top of a giant pumpkin—because some photographer had decided that she was the cutest-looking kid around.

I looked good, people liked that I looked good, I liked that it gave them pleasure.

But somewhere along the way, it had grown confusing.

I grew a bit older and I realized that lots of people didn't have the advantages that I did and this bothered me. I became the kind of person that's known for being nice to everybody, until given reason to behave otherwise; the kind of person that has their cooler friends rolling their eyes in high school whenever she stops to talk to some dork that no one else will stop for unless it's to make fun of. I had been kind of like Sarah. But it wasn't enough. I couldn't level the playing field for everybody else. Hell, I couldn't even make the playing field be what I wanted it to be just for myself.

And then it had really grown confusing. I'd wanted to separate the person from the looks and hadn't been able to—maybe a little bit, but not entirely.

And, okay, maybe I wasn't as virtuous as I'd thought, maybe Saul wasn't as awful as I'd thought.

Not that I'd ever go out with him again.

Had I sometimes been dismissive of guys, of men, because they just weren't good enough on some external scale?

There had been Tom in high school, the French horn in the band. I'd liked him. He was smart, made me laugh. But when he asked me out, hopefully, tentatively, fearfully, I'd said no. He'd been my friend, right? Why would we want to louse that up? But what, I wondered, if Tom had looked like Saul?

And then there was the whole way that, when I thought about it, I realized that T.B., Delta, Kelly, all of us were judged by externals. T.B. could no more change the fact that the first salient feature people saw about her was that she was black; despite the desirability of ultimately judging people on the content of their character, skin color and sex are the two most salient features we take in when we meet new people, and we make snap judgments based on those features—racist, sexist and liberal alike. Delta could not change what people thought of her based on her kids, except for when she'd hidden them away with me. And as for Kelly, well, even I had prejudged Kelly. I'd assumed that because she was the Good-Looking Woman that she must somehow be snooty or malevolent. I'd assumed, wrongly, that she was a red M&M. So, I figured, if we were all going to be judged by externals, anyway, the only way we could affect things was by how we chose to react to the world's reactions to us; it was how we all felt about those externals themselves that would make the difference.

It was too confusing. I wasn't going to find any answers. The essential truth I had been searching so hard for had turned out, quite simply, to be confusion.

It was more than I wanted to think about.

All I knew was that every time I'd made it hard for Steve, I hadn't been saying *Don't hate me because I'm beautiful* and I hadn't been saying *Don't hate me because I'm ugly.* What I'd really been saying was *Just love me. Love me, anyway. Love me.*

42

Oh, the things that happen off camera while your mind is occupied elsewhere.

Apparently, Pam, in her eagerness to finally best me with a man, had attempted to seduce Steve.

Apparently, he, in his eagerness to dull the pain of what he saw as my deception, let her.

It was Best Girlfriend who sussed it out.

"It was at that bar you always want to take me to when I come to visit. You know the one. What's the name of that place again?" She snapped her fingers. "Texas? Wyoming?"

"It's called Minnesota's. Actually, it used to be called Minnesota's, but now it's called Chalk Is Cheap."

"No wonder I could never remember it before."

"I don't see why it should be so difficult. They do have pool tables there."

"And?"

"And what?"

"And that's why they called it that? Because they play lots of pool in Minnesota?"

"How many times do I need to tell you? You don't play pool, you shoot it."

"The NRA must be loving you."

"And I don't really know if they play lots of pool in Minnesota or not. You're the one who keeps moving all the hell over the country. It was just the guy's name, that's all."

"Whose name?"

"Minnesota Fats."

"What?"

"Look," I sighed, "are you going to tell me whatever it is that you saw that you don't really want to tell me, or are we going to play stupid all night?"

"Stupid could be good."

I just looked at her, staring her brave again. "Come on," I said. "You can trust me to handle whatever it is you have to tell me. And if I can't handle it, you'll pick me up afterward, I know you will. Now," I said again, voice soft, "spill."

"Fine. I was worried about you."

"Go on."

"You looked strange when you left here earlier."

"Go *on*."

"So I figured, why not pop into that Minnesota place? Sure, it's not the cleanest place in the world, and everyone there's always already drunk, no matter how early in the day it is, but so what? For such a dirty, alcoholic place, it—I don't know—always seems so *safe* there."

"True...*go on*."

It was as though that last *"go on"* was the final brake release on the train, because all of a sudden, her words came speeding down the tracks at me, with no pauses, no more station stops in between. By the time I realized where what she was telling me was headed, I felt like Penelope Pitstop lying facedown on the tracks, all trussed up and with no Canadian Mountie in sight to untie me.

"By the time I got there, you'd already left with Saul. Delta—the one I met here last week?—she told me. She also introduced me to T.B. and Pam. Well, of course I'd met Pam a few times before, even though Delta and T.B. didn't seem to know it. I liked T.B. She's nice."

I didn't bother asking what she thought about Pam.

"Anyway, they told me you'd been and left with Saul. T.B. was very worried about you and I told her how I'd been worried about you, too, that I knew you were confused about how things were going with Steve and that I was worried about what you might do."

"They didn't know about Steve before," I told her.

"No," she said. "I realized that as soon as I saw their reactions. I was still worried about you, though, more worried than before, so I drove around for a bit, hoping I could find you."

"I'm a big girl," I said. "I can take care of myself."

"I know you are," she said, "and you're responsible for your own actions, too. It doesn't mean I can't try to stop you, though, from doing something stupid."

"Thanks," I said.

"Not that it did any good," she said. "Anyway, I quickly realized that it wasn't doing any good, that I wasn't going to find you. So I went back to Minnesota's."

"Chalk Is Cheap."

"Right. I felt like having a beer, didn't want to spend the whole night here waiting and worrying about you, and I had liked T.B. And Delta, a bit. By the time I got back there, apparently someone else had come looking for you—Steve. Your friends had figured out who he was when they heard him ask the bartender if he'd seen you. He must've figured that since you'd taken him there on a date, it might be a place where he could find you when he couldn't reach you at home."

"What did he want to see me about?" I asked.

"Who knows?" she said. "You'd have to ask him. Maybe he didn't want to see you about anything. Maybe he just wanted to see you."

I let that sink in.

"T.B. told me that Pam had already told him that you'd been and left with Saul. And there was Steve and Pam at the bar together, looking like they'd just got there, but looking like they'd been together for at least a few hours already, if you know what I mean. When he saw me, when T.B. introduced me as the friend from out of town who'd been staying with you, he got one of those guilty looks on his face, except I got the weird impression that he'd already been wearing some version of that look before he saw me, but that seeing me somehow advanced the feeling for him somehow, exponentialing remorse into all-out regret."

"*Exponentialing* is not a word," I automatically corrected.

"I know, but it should be, shouldn't it? Anyway, Pam didn't look like she was feeling remorse or regret at all, neither one. Instead, she looked positively happi*er* when she saw me, like making sure you'd find out was the whole point of the exercise."

"I'm not sure that the English language allows for positively happi*er,* either."

"Probably not, Scarlett. But, God! Don't you want to hear what I'm trying to tell you?"

"Actually, no," I said, because I'd realized that it was the truth. "I don't want to hear this at all. Can we stop now, please?"

She grabbed my hand. "Oh, shit, Scarlett. You don't want to hear it, and I sure as shit don't want to be telling you about it. But I have to, you know? If it'd been anyone else, if he'd been with anyone else, I'd never say a word."

"You wouldn't?"

"Of course not. Why would I? I mean, come on. It's not like him deciding to deal with his feelings of betrayal by you by possibly sleeping with another woman is exactly what we'd choose for him to do, not in a perfect world, but people do have a tendency to deal with things that way. Sure, we'd like it if, while hurt, he recognized somewhere deep down inside that you're the one, that you're the only one, and even though he was angry he still managed to remain true to you. But come on, we've all seen *Friends.* When people are confused, and wounded by love, they have a tendency to react, sometimes in ways that are self-destructive and counter to their own interests. Men have a tendency to find someone to fuck, preferably while very intoxicated, and—"

"And women eat tons of ice cream. I know, I know." And I did know, even if I didn't want to, not then, not when it was me. And of course I also knew that I'd behaved self-destructively myself earlier that night, more like a man than like a woman.

I knew it was unreasonable, for me to be upset at what Steve might or might not have done with Pam, in light of what I'd done with Saul. But what can I say? I'm not always reasonable. I'm a woman.

And. It. Was. Pam.

"I know it's weird for me to be telling you that it doesn't matter that he did this," she said, "but it doesn't matter."

"Tell me," I said, feeling the knife twist in my heart. "Tell me how this doesn't matter."

"Because it wasn't about wanting another woman, or loving another woman. It was because of wanting and loving you too much, and then feeling let down, maybe not forever but for now. He wasn't going to sleep with her because he stopped loving you—he was going to sleep with her because he loved you so much."

"Is that supposed to make me feel better?"

"No, not at all. It's just supposed to make you think."

"And you wouldn't have told me this, not if it'd been some other woman he was with?"

"No, I honestly wouldn't have. I would have left it up to him whether to tell you or not, and I'd have found a way to make it clear to him that I wasn't going to decide his future for him. After all, it is his story to tell. Or not."

"But it being Pam makes everything different?"

"Well, *yeah*. I mean, the way I figure it, he didn't betray you at all. But her? Shit, yeah."

I mirrored her words back at her in a whisper of dawning realization: "Shit, yeah."

Best Girlfriend got it: it wasn't the What of the thing; it was the Who With.

"And you have to know, Scarlett, I just plain couldn't stand it, seeing her sidling up next to him, having co-opted your clothes, your style with just about everything, your look—some of the best surface parts of you—not to mention the man you so much love, even if you're too stupid to know it. It was like I could see the whole thing right there, how everything had played out to that point, her always being jealous of you and wanting to have everything you have—"

"Well, except for my job," I put in, getting into the spirit of things, trying to think about Pam objectively as opposed to thinking about her as a vampire that I had willingly, mistakenly invited into my life. "I don't think she ever wanted my job."

"True enough. But everything else? Your look, your sense of style, the way you are in the world and the way that the world feels about you—oh, yeah, baby, she wanted all of that."

"How long have you known this?"

"Like, hmm—" and here she consulted the ceiling "—like since you met her? Like since that time you introduced me to her for the first time when I came home to visit right after you originally met her? Like when I could tell right away that she hated who I was in the history of your life and that she would have done anything to erase me?"

Infuriation speaking here: "And why didn't you tell me?"

Soft whisper: "Oh, no. I could never tell you that."

"How come?" I was offended. "I thought we tell each other everything. Well, except of course for the fact that the man I'm in love with might have slept with someone else because you think I'd be better off not knowing, but that's a whole new situation we never encountered before, so I'll accept the precedent you've set for now."

"Actually, I did tell you. I only said that I wouldn't have told you if it'd been anyone else but Pam."

"Right. Pam. The snake in the grass. The snake you always knew was there. I believe you were about to tell me why you couldn't tell me that, even though you knew it all along?"

"Because I can't tell you who to be friends with."

"Not even if you're fairly certain they're going to hurt me?"

"Nope. Not even then."

"Why the hell not?"

"Because it wouldn't be right."

"How could protecting your best friend ever not be right?"

"Because what if my radar started going all phlooey on me? What if I started seeing shadows? What if I was wrong about somebody and only saw the bad in them because I was jealous of your other friendships and wanted to keep you for myself? Huh? What kind of friend would I be then?"

"You'd be Pam," I said.

"Damn straight. And that's a risk I can't afford to take. Not for me. Not for you. If I really love you, then I need to trust you to choose your own path with people…well, for the most part."

"And Pam? What happened at Minnesota's?"

"You mean Chalk Is Cheap?" she said.

I made an impatient gesture.

"Well, like I started to say, I could see just looking at her doing her spider-on-a-stool act there—"

"Spiders sit on stools?"

"When I'm telling this story, yeah, they do."

"Go on."

"And I could see what she was trying to be—you—and I could see how she'd gotten herself to that moment in time, how she'd been the one to first oh-so-innocently spill the beans to him about your oh-so-slight indiscretion—"

"Well, I did leave with the intention of screwing another man's brains out, an intention I fulfilled, I might add."

"True. But those are just details compared to Pam."

"Go on."

"And I could see how she'd made sure to position herself to be the one to offer him consolation over his hurt. And I could see that even though he wanted to be as far away from her as possible, she'd appealed to the chivalrous part of his nature and had guilted him into buying her a drink preparatory to sex."

"*Guilted* doesn't spell-check, either."

"Sure it does. Fuck spell-check."

"Go on."

"And I could see one thing for damned certain."

"Which was?"

"That even if it was acceptable for him to sleep with her, and even if it was on some teeny-tiny level acceptable for her to sleep with him under the guise of 'my life has been one huge long disappointment, I'm bitter, and I just want to have a little closeness and this guy, even if he is my ostensible best friend's guy, looks like he could use a little human closeness, too,' even if all that could be made to fly, there was one small thing that just couldn't."

"Which was?"

"Her coming on to him right there in Wyoming's."

"Minnesota's."

"Whatever. The point is that while Danbury might be a relatively small city, it's got its fair share of places to grab a drink. So why did she insist on having a drink with him, him who was surely not in his right mind, in your favorite place to drink? Because she wanted to hurt you. Because that was the whole point all along."

"Which made you have to tell me this now. Because even though it would be wrong for you to advance-warn me that someone might hurt me, now Pam is a definite bad commodity. He, on the other hand, you wouldn't have told me about if you didn't have to."

"Bingo."

"And you were able to see all this in—what—about the space of a minute?"

"Pretty much."

"And then you came back here."

"Well, no, not right away."

"Oh? What'd you do first?"

"Well, first I had to hit Pam, didn't I?"

"You *hit* her?"

"Yeah."

"But you've never hit another human being in your life. You're the fucking biggest humanitarian I've ever met in my life, for chrissakes. You stop your car for hurt animals."

"Doesn't matter, does it? I still had to hit her."

"Why?"

"'Cause she dishonored you. 'Cause she dishonored the friendship you'd shown her. 'Cause someone had to hit her for you, and he's too nice to do it."

How had I ever thought that Pam could be a stand-in for Best Girlfriend? How had I ever imagined that Kelly, nice and screwy as she'd turned out to be, would be better at giving me insight than this woman whom I'd known, who'd known me, nearly my whole life?

That was when I finally drooped. That was when I finally just put my arms around her and held on tight to Best Girlfriend, speaking the words aloud that one of us had said off and on at times over the years. "It sure does suck, our not being gay. Damn, but I'd marry you."

43

"Pam, you bitch!"

"Wha—?"

"How dare you pretend to be my friend all this time!"

"I—"

"Friends want what's best for the other person. Friends want what's best for the other person in spite of what's best for themselves. But that was never you."

"I—"

"All you ever wanted was to see me fall." I reflected on how I'd once asked her if she was *trying* to instill free-floating feelings of worthlessness in me and how true that had turned out to be. "You're just a small-minded person with petty wants. You figured that if you could somehow make me less, you'd be more."

"That wasn't—"

"We're through, Pam. You're not my friend anymore. You never were. You don't even know the meaning of the word."

Of course, that conversation never took place, except in my head. Even though Pam deserved to be yelled at, and I wasn't sorry in the slightest that Best Girlfriend had hit her, it would have made me feel too small to do the yelling she deserved. She knew what she had done. She knew what it had cost her. It was enough to play the scene through in my mind.

44

I called my mother.

"Hello?" I heard her voice, the dawning of alarm preparing to do battle with sleepiness.

"Hey, Mom."

"Scarlett?" Now she was wide-awake, really scared. "What's wrong? Has something happened?"

"Nothing bad," I said, sort of lying, "I just wanted to talk."

"Oh. Talk." I could almost see her settle back on to the pillows. "It's kind of late." I would have bet anything she looked at the clock. "Couldn't it wait until morning?"

I took a deep breath.

"Those men—" I finally was saying something I'd never said before "—when Dad was alive… What was that all about?"

Her answer was a long time in coming. Perhaps she was wondering how I knew and if she should ask me about that. Perhaps she was debating if complete denial might not be the safest route.

"Your father loved me very much," she said softly. "He loved me for myself. I knew that. But I just wanted... I also wanted..."

"What, Mom?"

Big breath on the other end of the line. "I also wanted to be still found beautiful."

Were those two things contradictory? I wondered, the desire to be loved for who you are and the desire to be found physically beautiful in a purely objective sense? Could I get both things from one person?

"It's okay, Mom," I said. "Go back to sleep. I'm sure Dad knew how much you loved him."

45

There was one thing, as a lifelong reader, that I knew about writers, and it came to me now.

As a writer, you're always confronted with a choice: tell the people what they want to hear, or tell them the truth? Choose the first, and you might still get your happy ending; choose the other, and, well, you'd get the truth. One ending, hopeful; the other, in my case, cynical. But, if you looked at the better writers—and I don't necessarily mean the more successful ones, just the better ones—it wasn't even so much about making a clear-cut choice, one path over the other, so much as it was about striking a balance, something neither wholly comic or wholly tragic, the kind of balance seen in the best of nature, the kind of natural balance that slams you in the face every time you remember that children's poetry and art still managed to grow at Auschwitz, every time you remember that every comedian who has ever lived to make you laugh must one day die.

The sun rises, the sun sets, sometimes the fiddler manages to stay off the roof, sometimes he just fucking falls off. And right there, right fucking there, was my entire story in a nutshell; for, if the choice of the writer was to be a crowd-pleaser or a truth-teller, then my own personal choice came down to this:

Did I really want to be a tragic heroine, or did I want to have a happy life?

Hmm, rubbing my chin here, *be a tragic heroine, or live a happy life? A tragic heroine, or…? A tra…?*

Nah.

Why?

Because it's not in me, not in me to choose expedience over truth, not when I already know the truth that lies in the tale. And I was still hoping I could be cynical *and* hopeful; that maybe truth could still be truth and contain a part of happy.

46

"But how can you say that?" I asked.

"Which part?" Steve asked.

We were in the Sandwich Submarine, having decided to talk about us on neutral ground, the talking-about-us part turning out to be talking about us by way of talking about me. We were studiously *not* discussing what I had done with Saul or what he had done with Pam, if he had done anything with Pam at all after Best Girlfriend hit her and left. If he had done something with Pam, I didn't want to know it, not because I would blame him but because I would never be able to get the images out of my mind. I was guessing he felt the same way about Saul.

"All of it," I said. "But, really, how can you say that you know you'll love me all the time? Never mind the whole frump/not-really-a-frump issue, etc., etc. Do we really need to get into that again? Sometimes I'm difficult. Sometimes I'm a complete bitch. I'm *changeable*. Sometimes, the me you get in the morning isn't even the same as the me you get in the afternoon."

He shrugged. "But you're still you."

"And that's enough?"

"No, it's not enough."

Aha, I thought. I finally had him.

But that masochistic victory didn't hang on the board very long, because that was when he chose to floor me for all time with:

"No, it's not *enough,* Scarlett. It's everything."

epilogue

In spite of his words, his wonderful words, I still do not know how our story will end.

Will I forgive him his betrayal of me?

I don't know.

During our little talk at Sandwich Submarine, it came out that Steve had his own confession to make, which finally explained the unaccountable expression of guilt I'd seen on his face when I first told him of my deception.

"I need to tell you something," he'd umm-ed at me.

"Hmm…?" I'd still been looking at him dreamy-eyed, lost in his unconditional acceptance of the person I was.

"I'm rich," he'd said with a guilty grin.

"What?" That snapped me out of it.

"My brother and I made a small fortune building property developments. Remember how surprised you were to hear he lived on Deer Hill Avenue?" He blushed. "Well, I'd decided to live incognito for a while since I was tired of feeling like the only reason women liked me was for my money."

"But," I butted, "what about all of your 'be yourself' stuff?"

"Look," he'd sighed, "we all hide parts of ourselves, wanting to be liked for ourselves but fearing we won't be liked for ourselves, fearing that who we are is ultimately unlikable."

"So, what, you were *masquerading* as a relatively poor person?"

It turned out that while I was busy being not quite who I was, he was busy being not quite who he was as well.

And, somehow, we were getting past that, too.

Will he forgive me my betrayal of him?

I don't know.

Whether we ever finally decide to discuss it or not, I just don't know if either of us will ever forget.

I do know that I will never forgive Pam.

Is it because I believe it to be Pam's fault, everything bad that happened to me? *Was* it really Pam's fault?

No, I know whose fault it was. It was mine. I choose, we choose, we all choose, we make the rules, we choose the game, even if we think that the only reason we're choosing a path is because it's been so well-trodden before us that it appears irresistible, we still choose; even if we think we're choosing something just to be different, to set us apart. That said, I'm still not going to ever forgive Pam, simply because I *choose* not to.

There are a few other things I know now as well.

Remember my list of things that were important to me? Books, friendship and that one true love?

Books, sad to say, can sometimes let you down. Not only

that, but a day may come, hopefully not for a long time, but it still may come, when I am no longer able to read in the way that I am used to; age will get me, either in the form of decreasing eyesight, or decreasing mental capacity, or simply in decreasing patience.

Is Steve that one true love for me?

Oh, I think he is. I truly believe that. If not him, I cannot imagine another man ever even coming close.

But, even if our mutual betrayals can be overcome, lust has a tendency to fade over time; that in-love feeling mutating into something else.

So I am left with knowing two things.

For as long as I live, I will have Best Girlfriend. Friendship, real friendship: it is the one relationship that endures. It is the one thing that should never depend upon appearances, but rather upon what lies at the core.

And now, for the final thing I know:

No matter what happens, you should never lose your sense of humor.

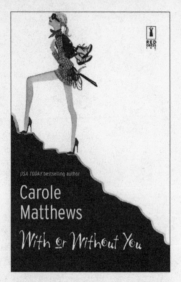